RAVENS' ROOST FARM

LACYNDA MATHES

World Castle Publishing, LLC
Pensacola, Florida
Copyright © 2025 Lacynda Mathes
Hardback ISBN: 9798280662780
Paperback ISBN: 9798891263758
eBook ISBN: 9798891263765
First Edition World Castle Publishing, LLC, May 19, 2025
http://www.worldcastlepublishing.com

Cover: Cover Designs by Karen
Editor: Karen Fuller

I dedicate this novel to the communities of Oak Grove and Colonial Beach, Virginia, to the memories of my Grandma Nettie Hinton, Aunt Ella Mae, and cousins Jackie and Joe Joe, to my father and stepmother, to all the kids I grew up with, and to my sister, Tammy. As always, a special thank you to my ever-supportive husband, David, and my tirelessly helpful partner in crime and proofreading, Liz Welker. Much love to you all.

PROLOGUE

Oak Grove, Virginia
November 1964

Alec's brown hair was thick with grease, but that had been intentional. The grease on his hands and smudged under his green eyes were the result of his working on the engine and were not intentional, however, unavoidable. He reached in through the open driver's side window and turned the ignition. The '49 Ford F1 roared to life. He wiped his hands on the rag he pulled from his overalls back pocket. The engine sputtered and coughed but did not cut out.

Melanie, who was dancing with the chickens, stopped prancing to applaud his achievement. "Ya fixed it! Ya fixed it!" she exclaimed, jumping up and down, curls bouncing, looking like a little Shirley Temple.

Her Mary Janes were scuffed and dusty, her socks uneven. Her knees were dirty. Her school dress's lace ruffle was tearing away from the bottom hem and dragged on the ground like a train. One puff sleeve hung off her shoulder.

He laughed, folding one arm behind his back and flourishing the rag, bowing at the waist to the five-year-old. "Thank ya, ma lady," he replied with a lopsided grin.

He knelt on one knee. Melanie ran and jumped into his arms and hugged his neck. He kissed her cheek and smudged it with grease.

"You been fightin' again, Melanie?" he asked, giving

her tummy a tickle.

She giggled. Then her countenance adopted a serious expression. She furrowed her brow and screwed her mouth tightly to one side. "That mean ole Sally Rose. She said ya ain't my brother, Maggie ain't my sister, and Mama ain't my mama. So, I popped her a good 'un. Unfortunately, she popped me back."

"Don't mind nuthin' Sally Rose says," Alec told her, setting her off his knee and back on her own two feet as he stood. He took out a cigarette and lit it, doing his best James Dean. He looked the part well enough, just a little more threadbare.

Mama was going to be upset about that dress. Melanie's spunk made him laugh, though. Sally Rose deserved what she got. He figured Melanie would know the truth soon enough. No need to rush it.

A cloud passed over, blocking the sun momentarily. He shivered in the autumn chill of the afternoon. A flash of Maggie's bruised face and swollen lip, her torn petticoat and buttonless blouse crossed his mind like the cloud. No. Melanie never needed to learn that truth. Never. He wished to God he didn't know.

They didn't have much money, but they managed. He was only seventeen himself, but he'd been working full-time for two years for Deacon Willis at the hardware store in town, he helped his granddaddy with the farm, and he worked part-time with Uncle Elmer at the quarry. He earned a say in how the money got spent. He'd get the girl a new dress tomorrow. He took a deep drag on the cigarette.

"Unfortunately, huh?" he laughed, exhaling a cloud of smoke. Melanie sure talked like an adult sometimes, especially when she was full of it. There was nothing "unfortunate" about it. She relished the fighting. He hoped she whooped Sally Rose.

"Well..." She drew out the word and let the thought hang in the air.

"Yeah, that's what I thought," Alec said, nodding and taking another drag.

The door to the farmhouse swung open. Mama stuck her head out. "Alec, grab one of them chickens for supper. Any one of 'em except Henrietta. She's my best layin' hen," she called.

Melanie moved to hide behind the old blue pickup, but she wasn't fast enough. Mama saw the torn lace and sleeve. "Melanie Gardner! Get in here this minute!" she yelled, stepping out onto the porch holding the door open.

Melanie kicked the dirt in front of her and hung her head, golden locks falling over her blue eyes. She pointed at a fat chicken she'd been dancing around with moments before. "Get that one there, Alec. She's fat and greedy. I named her Sally Rose," she said as she shuffled past him and disappeared into the house.

CHAPTER 1

Oak Grove, Virginia
November 2024

Bethany Benson pulled into the driveway of the old farmhouse. The wooden sign by the ditch hanging on a crooked post gently swayed in the breeze. The faded black paint on a peeling white background read "Ravens' Roost Farm." The sound of the rusted chain groaning as it swung was mournful, somehow. Her heart sank. Was this house even inhabitable? The foundation looked good, but a large limb off the massive oak tree in front of it had fallen, completely collapsing the roof of the front covered porch. The upstairs windows were boarded up, but remnants of their jagged broken panes were still in the sills. The front entrance was completely blocked by the falling porch roof and massive tree limb. She could only imagine the windows were also broken behind the tangle of branches and twisted metal from the tin roof. Bare wood siding covered more of the house than painted. What paint remained was cracked and peeling.

She looked up at the structure in pure horror. "Oh, God," she sobbed. What was she going to do? She looked into the rearview mirror at the two sleeping children in the backseat. This had been her last hope. She had exactly $12.86 left to her name. She couldn't even afford a hotel room.

Melanie Horton, a cousin of Greg's mother, had left the property to Greg when she had unexpectedly passed away 2 years ago from a massive stroke. She had been widowed at 25 and never remarried. She had no children of her own and had taken a liking to Greg. She had only been 63 when she passed away, and Bethany had only met her once, at Greg's sister's wedding five years ago, but her memory of her had been of a kind, plump woman who was boisterous and good-natured. She had laughed easily and loudly. Was she laughing at Bethany now? No. She couldn't have known the state of the place when she had bequeathed it to Greg.

"Oh, God, what do I do?" she asked the air, laying her head on the steering wheel.

She must have cried herself to sleep because the knock on the car window startled her awake. "Bethy?" the man asked. He was tall, at least 6'3", and handsome, with wavy dark brown hair, cut short, but not too short, emerald-green eyes, a straight Greek nose, and a rakish smile. There was something about him that made her heart flutter. He was good-looking, but it was more than that. She just didn't know what.

"Bethany. Bethany Benson. That's me," she responded, lowering the window.

"You're early. We weren't expectin' you until the evening. It's barely dawn." He sounded dejected.

"Oh. I drove all night," she responded. "Sorry. Who are you?" She might as well have slapped him by the expression on his face, though she had no idea how she had offended him. Still, the look on his face, the hurt in his eyes, it broke her heart a little.

"Um...Joe Gardner. Melanie was my 2nd cousin... twice removed...somethin' like that. And your husband would be maybe...three or four times removed," he said, laughing cordially, recovering from whatever had upset him. "I rent the farmland from you. Mr. Morgan just told me yesterday evening you were coming. I planned to get that tree out of your way, at least before you got here. But I guess that plan's moot," he explained, winking.

"Is the house even inhabitable?" she inquired, afraid of the answer.

"Oh, sure. It's a fixer-upper, to be sure, but the foundation and roof…at least on the house itself…are good. I boarded up all the broken windows, and it's clean and dry inside. That branch just fell last week in a big storm. Took out your porch roof, I'm afraid, but the house is good."

"Is there any way inside?" Bethany asked.

"There's the side door. But there aren't any steps, and it's 5 feet up. I'm happy to give you a boost," he chuckled.

"Huh?" Bethany asked, horrified at the prospect of the handsome man helping her into the house like that.

He laughed. "I'm just jokin' with you. I have a ramp I use to load my tractor onto the trailer. I can move it to the door for you."

"Oh," she giggled. "Thank you. That would be a big help. As would getting rid of that tree limb. I'll pay you, but I have to wait until Mr. Morgan gets me the check. I've got like twelve bucks on me now."

"Nah. You don't need to worry about that, Bethy… Bethany. I was goin' to get rid of it anyway. I'll even chop it up for firewood for you if you like. You're goin' to need it. The wood stove works fine, but your furnace is shot." When he called her "Bethy," it felt like a warm ocean breeze on her face, something she'd only ever experienced once in her life, but still natural, easy. It was strange.

"Really?" she asked, crestfallen again. "How's the plumbing?"

"Old, but in workin' order," he answered honestly. "I wouldn't drink the water, but it's good for bathin' and flushin'. The well was replaced with an artesian well in the early eighties. It can smell a little like eggs, and you get some black sand every once in a while."

Bethany sighed heavily. "Thanks for the honesty. Ug. What am I going to do?"

His brow furrowed. "Well, you're going to get out of the car and go inside and start a fire first. Then you're goin' to clean up a bit and start unloadin' that U-Haul trailer… because it may not be Biltmore Castle, but Ravens' Roost ain't all that bad. It just needs a little work."

"A little?" she sobbed.

"In the scheme of things…yeah. Me and my son'll help you. It'll be alright. You'll see."

She forced a smile. "I need your optimism, Mr. Gardner."

"Joe. We're family…by marriage…three or four times removed," he joked, smiling that rakish grin again. "Let me start a fire in your wood stove. Then I'll get that ramp for you and get started on that tree limb."

Joe sauntered away. He was only about her age, she decided, late twenties, early thirties, certainly not as old as thirty-five. Something about him was familiar, a family resemblance to Greg, she supposed. She found herself watching his butt as he walked around the side of the house. "Oh, God!" she exclaimed, realizing the impure thoughts that suddenly flooded her brain. Greg had been killed in a car accident a year and a half ago. No matter how unhappy her marriage had been, that was nowhere near long enough for her to be lusting after his cousin…three or four times removed.

At 29, she felt really old and also incredibly young. It didn't help that she'd had Ryan when she was still only 17. She shouldn't have a twelve-year-old son already. But she did. Meghan, her 4-year-old daughter, was too mature as well. It felt like her kids were raising her at this point.

"Mom?" Ryan said from the backseat.

"Yeah," she answered.

"What the hell?" he asked, looking at the house.

"Watch your mouth," she demanded. "It's going to be fine. The guy who rents the farm is going to get rid of the tree limb."

"What's he goin' to do about the ghosts?" Ryan quipped.

She couldn't help herself. She laughed. "We may be on our own there," she conceded.

Within minutes, Joe had come back around the side of the house. He stooped to look in the car window. "Why don't you pull around to that side, so you don't have so far to carry your stuff inside," he suggested. "I started a fire in the wood stove for you. It'll warm up soon enough…on the first floor, anyway." He winked again, this time at Ryan.

Joe rounded the side of the house before he collapsed against the old structure, clasping his chest. He'd held the tears as long as he could. It was bad enough that Bethy didn't know him, but the proof of his memories lay sleeping in the back seat. How did he not know? Why hadn't Melanie told him?

He took a couple of deep, cleansing breaths and regained his composure. Fine. He'd find a way to stay close. He had to.

With renewed resolve, he headed back to the barn and

pulled the ramp out, dragging it back to the side of the house and the side door.

Bethany had pulled her car around, as he had suggested, and was leaning against the car door. She turned and smiled as he approached with the ramp. Even if she didn't know him for some strange reason, she was still her, still Bethy... or Bethany. He still loved her, and his heart raced when she smiled.

The little girl was awake now. As expected, her eyes were a bright emerald green. He opened the door and put the ramp in place. "Voila!" he said, standing and walking halfway up and bouncing to show it was secured and safe to move on.

The child's eyes lit up. She bounded over and reached up, pulling on his pant leg. He squatted to be closer to her level. "Can I go down your slide, Mister?" she asked excitedly.

He laughed. She was the cutest thing he'd ever seen, and he loved her in an instant. "Sure, but only when an adult is around and not while your mom and brother are using it to get into the house," he replied with a grin. He picked her up, stood, and carried her to the top of the ramp. He sat her at the doorway, legs pointed outside. "Ready?" he asked. She nodded and hugged her doll. He gave a gentle push, and she slid on her bottom down the incline to the ground below.

"Wee!" she squealed on her way down.

Bethany laughed. "Okay, now we have to start unloading the U-Haul, and Mr. Gardner has work to do. Grab your blanket and pillow out of the car, Meghan," she told the little girl.

Joe's heart was pounding so hard. He hoped Bethany couldn't see it. "Your name is Meghan? That's a good name," he said to the girl.

"Yes, Meghan Alice Benson. Thank you for letting me

go down your slide."

"Anytime, Meghan Alice Benson. I'm Joe...Joseph Alexander Gardner. Nice to meet you." He smiled at the child. She grinned back at him. It was a good moment.

CHAPTER 2

Other than a little dust, Joe was right about the house being clean and dry inside. The furniture, though old, had been covered and was in fair condition. The kitchen appliances dated back to the seventies but were in working order. The floors, at least on the first floor, were worn and needed refinishing, but they were level and firm. Bethany was pleasantly surprised to find that the front window, hidden under the collapsed porch roof and the massive tree limb, wasn't broken. And while the furnace was indeed inoperable, the wood stove was effective at warming the dining room and kitchen. The foyer, where the stairs and bathroom were located, was a little chilly, and the downstairs bedroom and formal living room, where the side door was, were definitely cold.

Still, as she and the kids worked to clean the house, sweep the floors, wipe the surfaces, remove the covers from the furniture, and then unload their meager belongings out of the U-Haul, they didn't really feel the cold.

Having finished cleaning downstairs, Bethany tenuously headed up the stairs. There was a bathroom and three bedrooms, and despite the broken windows that Joe had boarded up, she realized he was right about the condition of the house, as even the second floor appeared sound. The kids each chose a bedroom, and she took the largest.

She started cleaning the upstairs bathroom. The clawfoot tub was amazing. She was looking forward to a good soak in it tonight. The pedestal sink was large and cleaned up easily. The pipes groaned, but the water ran clear and hot. Her mood improved steadily, and she even started to feel hopeful.

The feeling was buoyed by the sound of the chainsaw running as Joe worked to remove the tree limb. Something about Joe's presence was comforting and familiar, even though he was a complete stranger. Bethany felt things she hadn't in a very long time around him, but beyond the initial attraction, he was a bastion of optimism. Plus, he was hard-working, and he seemed to know what he was doing. She wouldn't mind his hanging around more.

The day warmed up quickly, and as she cleaned her bedroom window, the only intact window on the second floor, Bethany saw Joe remove his shirt to continue working in the sleeveless undershirt through which his well-developed torso muscles rippled. She noted the cuff tattoo around his upper bicep. She bit her lip. She fantasized about showing him her tattoo and then blushed at the thought. It was in a very private area, and that wasn't normally how she thought. She wondered what had gotten into her today. This lustful spying was out of character.

Once he had finished cutting the limb, he proceeded to pull large sections of it off the porch, clearing the way to the front door, one branch at a time. As she watched dreamily, the tee shirt came off as well.

The strong attraction was odd, though. She had never met someone and immediately wanted to throw herself into his arms before. She imagined his saying "Bethy" softly against her neck as she ran her hands down his bare back. She could practically feel the brush of stubble on her skin. His scent was a mixture of fresh-cut grass and sandalwood, and she could almost smell it enveloping her as she imagined his soft lips moving ever so slowly down her neck to her clavicle.

"Mommy," Meghan called from her bedroom across the hall, breaking the spell. Bethany blinked back to reality and ran to help her child.

By early afternoon, Bethany and the kids were ready to start unpacking boxes. She started in the kitchen. They didn't have any food, but they had a well-organized kitchen with all the proper cooking gear and tableware, most of which she had bought at thrift stores and hidden in the trunk of the old junker car she'd got at an auction in preparation for her escape. She filled the ice trays and put them into the empty freezer. She sighed and pulled her cell phone out of her back jeans pocket. 1:32. Her stomach grumbled. The kids had to be hungry, too. She'd given them the last of the fruit and crackers for breakfast. She needed to get something for them to eat.

"Kids!" she called. "I'm going to go get us something for lunch! I'll be right back. Ryan is in charge until I get back."

"Ugggg!" Meghan groaned. "Why is he always in charge?"

"Because he's 8 years older than you," Bethany called back in response to the complaint.

She made her way to the side door and down the ramp. She looked at her car, with the U-Haul trailer still attached. "Oh, crap," she mumbled.

She went over and tried to unlatch the trailer, not noticing Joe coming around the corner of the house.

"Don't do that!" he exclaimed suddenly. "You have to put down the prop first. Or it'll tip."

"What?" Bethany said, startled. "Oh. How? I need to go get us some lunch."

He held out his keys and pointed to his old F250. "Take my truck instead," he offered. "I'll get the trailer unhitched for you while you're gone."

She breathed in relief. "God, what would I do without you? I think you must be heaven-sent, Joe."

He smiled, and her heart did a little flip-flop. "Nah. Just bein' neighborly. You'd have figured it out." He took out his wallet and handed her two twenties. "My son gets out of school at 1 today and will be here to help soon. Go ahead and get a couple of chicken boxes and sides...and enough sodas for the five of us...at the Stop In. Go left out the driveway. Straight to the end. Left again on Route 205 all the way to the light. The Stop In is the Shell through the light on the left."

"You don't have to pay," she said, feeling embarrassed.

He smiled again. "Don't be silly. You said you were waiting for Mr. Morgan to deliver a check, and you have like $12. Pay me back when you get your money if it's that important to you." God, he really was heaven-sent. She didn't know people could be this nice. They certainly weren't this friendly in Connecticut. And if they were, they had an ulterior motive. Did Joe have an ulterior motive? Greg always seemed to. For the first time since meeting him, she felt wary. Then he smiled. His eyes were genuinely kind. And he had been working so hard all morning without asking for anything in return.

She remembered suddenly his saying he and his son would help, and not wanting the conversation to end, she broached the subject of the child. "How old is your son?" she asked, realizing for the first time that he was probably married. Of course, he was. How could a great guy like this not be?

"He's 12," Joe said, running his fingers through his hair. "I was 20 when he was born. Young and stupid. But at least he's something good to come out of my stupidity." He smiled again.

"I look forward to meeting him. I'll be right back, then," Bethany said, taking his keys and the cash. "Thanks. Should I get a soda for your wife as well?" she asked over her shoulder as she walked toward his truck, hoping to slide in the query about his relationship status subtly.

"I'm not married," he answered, grinning, as he started to work on the trailer hitch. "Jess's mom died when he was born, and we were never married, anyway."

She stopped in her tracks. "Oh. I'm sorry. I..."

He laughed. "Don't worry about it. It's been 12 years."

She nodded and continued to the truck.

She found the Stop In easily enough. The fried chicken smelled wonderful. She ordered two 8-piece boxes, a family-size potato wedges, and a family-size coleslaw. She decided to get three two-liter Cokes instead of individual bottles. She still had some cash left, so she also got some baloney, bread, mustard, and a gallon of milk. She was sure Joe wouldn't mind, and at least she could give the kids sandwiches for dinner this way.

She loaded the items onto the counter, and the cashier quickly rang her up. "$43.28," the cashier said. She was in her late 20s or early 30s with short brown hair, about twenty earrings, and as many tattoos showing on her arms, 2 angel wings just below her clavicles being the most prominent. "Why you drivin' Joe's truck?"

"Hmmm? Oh. He lent it to me because my car has a U-Haul trailer attached at the moment," Bethany answered with a smile. "You know Joe?"

"Everybody knows everybody," the woman laughed. "For example...you must be Bethany Benson. Hi. I'm Jillian Fox. I'm your neighbor...sort of. I live in the house across the street from the veterinarian on your street...about a quarter a mile from you. My great-grandparents owned the farm next to yours."

"Oh. Wow! Nice to meet you, Jillian."

Jillian looked tough, but she seemed nice. Again, so unlike New Englanders. "Joe gettin' that tree off your porch?" she asked, good-naturedly.

"Yeah. That was quite the surprise," Bethany chuckled.

"I bet," the woman responded.

"Whatever, it's gotta be better than what I left behind," Bethany said, inexplicably overwhelmed by emotion. The house in Connecticut had been large and well-maintained, but the horrors she had endured inside made the broken windows and peeling paint of Ravens' Roost seem a mere nuisance. Her eyes briefly teared up.

Jillian bagged up Bethany's purchases. She smiled and handed her the bags. "You're goin' to be fine, Honey. I don't know what hard times you've been through, but this is a good place, even for weirdos like me. A pretty girl like you…you'll thrive."

"You're not a weirdo," Bethany laughed. "I think we're going to be great friends."

"Yeah. Me too. Isn't that funny? I've never had such a prim and proper friend before. You might be a good influence on me," Jillian laughed.

Bethany blushed. "Oh, I'm not as prim and proper as you might think. I'm the black sheep in my family."

"Screw them, Honey," the woman laughed. "Here. Here's my contact info. Call me anytime. I'll show you what a black sheep really is."

Bethany laughed and put the information into her phone before leaving.

Back at Ravens' Roost, she parked. Joe had unhitched

the trailer and secured it. The tree limb was mostly removed. He'd even removed the dilapidated roof, having pulled it free of the house with his tractor. He'd started a debris pile behind the house, back by the old barn. She wondered briefly where he was but was so happy to be able to use the front door she decided to go inside first and then find him.

Just inside the door, she suddenly felt cold and shivered, but as she moved inside, the cold dissipated, replaced by a homey warmth. "One of the ghosts," she joked to the empty room.

A laugh sounded, seemingly responding to her quip, but then she realized it came from the dining room to her left. It was a boy sitting at the table with Ryan and Meghan. He was probably around Ryan's age, of mixed race, with shoulder-length brown curly hair, a tawny complexion, and striking emerald-green eyes.

"Jess?" she asked, entering the room.

"Yes, Ma'am," the boy responded, standing politely. "Actually, it's Jessup, but my daddy calls me Jess."

"Do you prefer Jess or Jessup?" she asked, smiling, placing the bags on the table.

"Jessup," he said, looking down.

"Alright. It's nice to meet you, Jessup," she said cordially, holding out her hand for him to shake. He beamed. His green eyes lit up like Christmas. "I'm Bethany. You've already met Ryan and Meghan."

"Yes, Ma'am...Bethany. It's nice to meet you, too."

"I've got us some lunch. Ryan, Meghan, go wash up and set the table. There are 5 of us. Where's your dad, Jessup?"

"He's out in the barn. You want me to go get him?"

"No. You go wash up. I'll get him," she said, winking.

"Bethany...Ma'am?" Jessup said, stopping her. "Daddy

ain't goin' to say anything, but our landlady is kickin' us out of our trailer. She sold it. We gotta be out by the end of the week…and it's already Wednesday. Do you think…could we stay here until Daddy finds us a new house?"

"Jess!" Joe's voice boomed from the doorway. The boy looked down. "I'm so sorry. He shouldn't have done that!" Joe said, clearly embarrassed.

"No. It's okay. Why have you spent all day helping me when you have so much going on in your own life?"

"It's not that bad," Joe retorted. "I can get us a room at the hotel in Colonial Beach. And then I'll find a place. You needed the help. Besides, I had to do some maintenance on my combine out in the barn. Please, pay it no mind."

Bethany looked back and forth between the two of them, Jessup and his dad. "Absolutely not!" she insisted. "I will pay it as much mind as I like. There is that empty bedroom. I need help. You're right. You need a place to stay. You help me, and I'll give you a place to stay. Deal?" She stuck her hand out to Joe.

He looked at his son, who grinned. He closed his eyes and sighed heavily. "Deal," he said, shaking her hand.

"I don't have to return that U-Haul trailer until Friday. Why don't you use it to move your stuff over? Whatever doesn't fit in the house can be stored out in the barn until you find a place. We're nearly unpacked here. Need our boxes?" she offered. Imagine kicking someone out over Thanksgiving. What a bitch that landlady must be. "The kids and I will help you pack up, too. We're old hats at it now."

"It's not much. We rented furnished," he said sheepishly. "Just some clothes and personal items…and Duke."

"Duke?" she asked.

"Our dog," he answered. "Is that okay?"

"Of course. I love dogs," she assured him. It was a lie. She was terrified of dogs, but she was determined to help him. He'd been so kind to her, and he had done a ton of work for her already without even asking for anything in return. And she couldn't shake that feeling of familiarity. She shivered again as a draft blew through her. Then she warmed up again and smiled.

"Let's get washed up and eat already," she laughed.

He smiled and nodded.

———

Ryan sat there with his mouth wide open. They'd just gone from a family of three to a family of five, and he seemed to be more aware of the implications than his mother or the man she'd just agreed to let move in. The boy who had suggested cohabitation had scored a mom and was grinning mischievously. Meghan had been asking for a new daddy, being young enough that she didn't remember their father. She was clapping and giggling. Ryan shook his head in disbelief.

"It's alright," a voice seemed to whisper in his ear.

He looked around, but nobody was there. It was just in his head. But he wasn't sure he agreed with the voice. How was this alright? This guy was a complete stranger. And the kid seemed nice, but how weird was it to ask somebody if you could live with them five seconds after you met them? How weird was it to say yes? Had his mother said yes because of the weird way she'd been looking at that guy all day? That wasn't okay! None of this was okay! This weird ass haunted house was not okay. Leaving Connecticut like thieves in the night was not okay. All these damned trees and no houses within half a mile were not okay.

"It really is alright," the voice whispered again.

"Are you insane?" he bellowed at his mother. "You don't even know these people!"

His mother's eyes clouded in anger. She turned and scowled at him. "Mind your manners, young man. You don't know how much work Joe has done for us and how much work this house needs, and I have no idea how to do it. We can help each other. And that's what people should do!" Was she under some kind of spell? So, this guy had been nice to her. So what? Dad had never been nice to her, that was true, but that didn't mean she should let the first guy who smiled and was polite move in with her!

"Oh, so you plan on replacing Dad with some hillbilly from the sticks, and I got no say in the matter! I see," he yelled.

"Woah!" Bethany yelled back at him, her hands on her hips. "First of all, I'm the mother. You don't talk to me like that. Second, nobody is replacing your father."

"Really, because you've sure been throwing yourself at him like a whore all day!" he screamed. She smacked him across the face. And he deserved it. But he ran from the room and up the stairs, slamming his door behind him. He flung himself face down on the bed.

"That's your mama, boy. What's wrong with ya?" the voice said. It was clearly a young man's voice, and it was no longer a whisper. "Joe ain't that kind, either."

Ryan jumped up. The room was empty. What the hell?

CHAPTER 3

Joe emptied his refrigerator and put it into one of the boxes
Bethany had given to him. He double-bagged the turkey in
two trash bags before placing it inside the box. He had plenty
of food, having bought groceries just a few days ago before
Mrs. Mason had delivered the eviction notice. It was an illegal
eviction, he knew, but he didn't want to stay anywhere he
wasn't welcome. He didn't like owing people or intruding on
them.

He wasn't sure how this was going to work. Bethany's
son was understandably upset. But he knew it really was the
best option. Bethy clearly needed his help. He farmed her
land anyway. He had a crop of winter wheat planted in her
fields, and it would be convenient to be on the property. His
equipment was all in her barn, too. It was why he'd rented this
trailer out behind Ravens' Roost to begin with. And it would
be nice to be close to her. She'd been through hell. He knew
that even if she hadn't said it. The blank way she'd looked at
him when he knocked on her window…

He told himself that it was a pragmatic solution to his
dilemma. And then an image of Bethany Benson filled his
brain: big blue eyes, long brown hair, jeans that hugged her
hips like liquid, fastened just below her navel that peaked out
from under that crop sweater, the stud in her belly button.
The thought of her unhooking that brass button, of her slowly
pulling down that zipper, was torturous.

"Oh, crap," he said out loud, dumping the bag of

potatoes on the floor. He shook his head to clear his mind and erase the image, quickly gathering up the potatoes and putting them back into the bag. He swallowed hard. "God, Bethy," he whispered to himself. He stood and turned on the kitchen faucet, splashing cold water on his face. "Get it together, Joe," he told himself. He returned to the fridge, determined to make quick work of packing. He cleaned the fridge and freezer after he packed all their contents in the box and carried them out to his old truck.

Jess followed him out with the last of the boxes. They really didn't own a lot, he noted. It's not like he didn't have any money. He worked hard, and he had more than enough for them to live on. They just didn't stay in a house long enough to accumulate a bunch of stuff. They'd been in this trailer for 6 months, longer than any other place since Joe had left the Marines 6 years ago…and before that…well, he'd been a Marine. He'd brought Jess back to Oak Grove with him, thinking coming home would give the boy some kind of sense of what a home was, but so far, he'd moved the kid 8 times, including this time, since they'd gotten here. He was failing his son.

Joe climbed behind the wheel of his truck. Jess climbed into the passenger seat. He looked over at Joe and smiled. Joe whistled, and Duke came running and jumped over Jess to sit in the middle. Jess closed the truck door and said, "Good boy," petting the German Shepherd behind the ears.

Joe started the ignition and pulled away. It was getting dark. He'd bring the groceries in tonight, but other than some clean clothes, the rest could wait until morning. He pulled into the driveway, and Jess and Duke were out of the truck almost before he put it in park. He watched his son run toward the house, Duke running and jumping happily with him. "He's a good kid, Jemma," he said to his late girlfriend's spirit. She had died of a postpartum hemorrhage. She could surely hear him, he thought. She could surely see their son. He believed that.

The image of Bethany filled his brain again. He shook his head. Stop it, he thought to himself. But he could almost hear Jemma telling him, "She cute, Boo."

He and Jemma hadn't been a serious thing. Jessup had been an accident. He had been on the rebound from…well, his unreasonable, intense emotional bond with a girl he only knew for a few hours. Jemma knew he was head over heels for Bethy, even though he'd only met her the one time. He loved Jemma, but he hadn't ever been in love with her. Still, he missed her deeply sometimes. She had been one of his best friends.

His heart raced as Bethany appeared in the doorway. She froze momentarily as Duke bounded toward her, fear in her eyes, but while he watched, that fear dissipated. Duke jumped up on her, his front paws on her abdomen, his tail wagging in a blur. The fear in her eyes was replaced by love, and she reached out and scratched his jowls. "Oh, this sweet baby. You're just a sweet baby, aren't you?" she cooed. Joe smiled. This would work. It had to.

He grabbed the box of groceries as he got out and headed into the house. Jess put Duke in the downstairs bedroom that the two of them would share and closed the door.

He headed into the kitchen, where Bethany was standing against the stove. She put the tea kettle on and stared at it expectantly.

"That will never boil if you watch it," he teased, setting the box on the floor and opening the near-empty fridge; a few leftover pieces of chicken, baloney, milk, and 1 and ½ bottles of Coke. Thank God he'd shopped on Monday. She'd at least have something for Thanksgiving now. Lord knew when Mr. Morgan would get here. It was already close to seven.

She smiled and moved to help him unpack the box. "Oh, you have a turkey...and all the stuff for tomorrow!" she exclaimed, peering into the box. "I was beginning to be afraid we'd be having baloney sandwiches if Mr. Morgan doesn't get here soon," she laughed. "I love Thanksgiving."

He laughed at her enthusiasm. "Yeah, I can even cook it," he offered. "I have mad skills."

"I know that already," she said kindly. "You've shown me that all day long."

He started unloading the box into the fridge, and after a few minutes, the tea kettle whistled.

"I have this really good tea I bought from a tearoom in Manhattan. Would you like some?" she asked, standing and taking the tea kettle off the burner.

"Ah, no thanks. I'm not really a hot tea guy. I like iced tea, like any other good southern boy, but I prefer coffee to hot tea," he answered as he worked. "Your accent isn't really Connecticut," he hinted, just wanting to keep her talking, even if it was about things he already knew. "You sound more midwestern."

"Oh, yeah. I'm originally from Sterling, Illinois. It's about ninety miles due west of Chicago. I moved to Connecticut when I married Greg."

She fixed her tea and took a sip.

"You were pretty young, I take it," he noted. Again, he knew that she had been. Ryan was already 12. She was only 29. She would have married Greg shortly after he'd met her. He would have to be careful not to reveal that he knew her age. It might freak her out.

"Yeah. I was 16. My parents were old-fashioned and wanted us to get married because of...Ryan. Greg was a *few* years older than me. He was 26 at the time. I lied about my age when we met. I said I was 21 to get into the bar. Anyway, it was either marry me or face statutory rape charges. He was a lawyer, so he really didn't want that. And he was a good man. He never would have...if he'd known how old I really was. We told everybody I was 18, but...I wasn't. Still, he was a good husband," she said. She sounded so incredibly sad when she lied.

He stared at her for a minute. He shook his head. "Sorry. Spaced out there," he said, hoping he covered his shock. He didn't care about her being a teen mom. Hell, he'd only been 19, just a few months after he'd first met Bethy, when Jemma got pregnant, and Jemma had only been 18. That wasn't a big deal, but lying about how old you were for a man who had to know she wasn't really 21 at the time *was a big deal*. Hell, she looked barely older than 16 now. He remembered very clearly what she had looked like back then. That was bullshit.

"Greg was related to Melanie through her father...so yeah...you're right," a voice whispered in his ear. He jumped and looked over his shoulder. Nobody was there.

"You okay?" Bethany asked, taking another sip of her tea.

"Oh, yeah. Just a draft. Kinda gave me goosebumps," he said, completely flummoxed.

"Somebody walked on your grave," she said, smiling wickedly.

He chuckled. "Yeah. I guess." He returned to emptying the box.

The doorbell rang, and she put down her teacup to

answer the door.

"What the hell?" he asked, looking around the room again. But the kitchen was empty and quiet now that Bethany had left.

Moments later, he could hear Duke barking from inside his room and Bethany's talking, along with a man's voice, from the foyer.

"Jess!" he called, "get Duke quiet!"

"Yes, Daddy!" Jess called from upstairs, where he was playing with Meghan. Ryan was still shut up in his room and not talking to anybody.

"Oh. Hello, Jess," Mr. Morgan's voice said, sounding shocked. Joe could almost see his face. He laughed. Served that nosy old man right.

The dog quieted, and Joe took some ground beef out of his groceries and dug around for a pan. His mama's goulash was quick and easy. And his stomach was rumbling. Surely, Bethany and the kids would be hungry now, too. He chopped an onion.

His mind drifted back to Bethany. What kind of personal hell had she been living through? Why did Greg's wife and kids show up in Oak Grove with only $12.86 left to her name and her driving an old beater like that '89 Olds when everybody knew they were loaded? He sighed and shook his head, throwing the onion into a skillet with the hamburger.

Half an hour later, the goulash was ready. He grabbed an oven mitt, picked up the skillet, and walked into the dining room, where Bethany and Mr. Morgan were sitting going over Melanie's estate.

"Wait. I thought Mrs. Horton left her estate to Greg, and Greg left it to me." Bethany was saying.

"Um. No, Ma'am. Melanie named you her sole heir.

Your late husband had nothing to do with it. He did contact me after Melanie passed away to claim the property, but I told him you were the one who needed to make the claim. That's why I was surprised when you called last week and didn't know anything about the inheritance. I sent you all the information by registered letter," he said.

"I don't remember ever seeing it," she professed. "But Greg handled all of that stuff."

"Of course," Mr. Morgan said, patting her hand. He was a nosy old man, true, but he had a good heart, Joe recalled. He'd always been generous. And he had taken care of everything when Joe's mother had lost her mind. He'd helped Joe through a terrible time. Joe needed to remind himself of that. Filmore Morgan was a good man. So, what if he wanted to know what his neighbors were doing at all hours?

Mr. Morgan was born at the end of World War II, just a few miles down the road near Ingleside Winery. He had been the first in his family to go to college, graduating summa cum laude from the University of Virginia, staying to earn his law degree, and then returning home to the great benefit of the farming community. His office was in his home, the same house where he had been born and where his mother had also been born, a structure not unlike this house architecturally, though in better condition. He had been in practice since 1970, and he never profited greatly. But the farmers sure were lucky to have him.

He was a trim man, bespectacled, nearly bald, with kind eyes and rosy cheeks. He smiled as Joe entered, setting the skillet on a trivet on the table.

"Dinner is ready," Joe announced. "Would you like some, Mr. Morgan?"

Mr. Morgan leaned forward, peering over his wire-rimmed glasses. "Well, I wouldn't want to impose…"

"Don't be silly," Bethany said, touching his hand. "It's no imposition, though I do need to get some cash to pay Joe back." She smiled. Joe caught his breath. Damn. She really was cute.

"Ah, yes. Well, I don't have cash for you, but I do have a cashier's check for…" He looked down at the papers in front of him. "$47,987.92. That's the balance of Melanie's checking and savings accounts after taxes and fees. Oh, and here's a check from the estate for $1600 from Joe's lease of the land last year and this." He handed Bethany the checks. Here's the deed to Ravens' Roost. Um…This is the title to Melanie's Caddy. I stored it for you in my garage to keep it out of the weather. I drove it here, so I will need a ride home…after dinner," he said.

"Of course, Mr. Morgan. I'll take you home," Joe offered. "Y'all ready to eat, or you got more business to discuss?"

"No…no, that's the gist of it. If you have any questions, Mrs. Benson, just give me a call."

Joe smiled and then yelled, "Jess, Ryan, and Meghan! Come eat!"

Mr. Morgan jumped.

Joe walked back into the kitchen, getting 6 bowls and spoons, as well as the open bottle of Coke from the fridge. He set them down on the table and then returned to the kitchen for glasses and the full ice trays.

Meghan bounded down the steps with a doll tucked under her arm, her curly dark brown hair bouncing. She blinked her green eyes. "Ryan said to go to hell," she announced innocently.

Poor Bethany buried her head in her hand, blushing

adorably.

"Fair enough," Joe chuckled.

"It's really not funny," Bethany said, trying not to laugh and failing.

"He'll eat when he's hungry," Joe assured her, taking a seat and doling out the goulash into a bowl, which he handed to her.

Jess came in silently and sat next to Joe. "Goulash again?" he asked.

"It's cheap and makes a lot," his father explained. "And it's good." He finished serving everybody and folded his hands in front of him, bowing his head. Bethany smacked her daughter's hand to keep her from eating. Joe smiled. So damned cute.

"Bless us, oh Lord, for these thy gifts which we are about to receive from thy bounty, through Christ our Lord. Amen," he said, making the sign of the cross as he finished. "Eat."

"Amen," Mr. Morgan said, taking up his spoon and digging into the dish comprised of hamburger, tomatoes, onions, elbow macaroni, and Joe's mama's secret ingredient, garbanzo beans.

"What are your plans for tomorrow, Mr. Morgan?" Bethany asked, taking a bite.

"Me? Oh, I'll probably just go to the Moose," he replied sadly.

"Nonsense!" Bethany exclaimed. "Joe brought a 20-pound turkey over. Come eat with us!"

"Are Joe and Jessup staying here?" Mr. Morgan asked, curiosity finally getting the better of him.

"Yes, for the time being. As you know, Mrs. Mason sold the trailer and asked us to be out by Friday. Bethany kindly offered us a room in exchange for help with the house repairs," Joe explained.

"I told you that wasn't a legal eviction, Joe. She can't do that," Mr. Morgan said, taking another bite.

"I know. But I don't want to be...I'd rather just leave on good terms. Besides, Bethany could really use the help. That furnace needs to be replaced soon, for instance, before winter. And if I'm here, I can keep an eye on my crops and such," Joe answered. "I'd be happy to sign a lease if you'd like to draw one up for her."

"That's not a bad idea," Mr. Morgan said brightly. "It would protect both of your rights. I'll draw something up tonight and bring it over tomorrow. What time do you think?"

Joe chuckled again. "Anytime ya like. Ya can help cook if ya want."

All in all, despite Ryan's not coming down, it was a pleasant dinner. Joe had more fun than he'd had in a long time. Bethany laughed a lot, too. She had a great laugh.

CHAPTER 4

Bethany filled the clawfoot tub with hot water and bubbles. She lowered herself down into the tub and sighed in deep satisfaction as the foam pushed up around her neck to her chin. She let her arms float just beneath the surface of the water. The room was thick with steam. She stuck in her earbuds and hit play on her Spotify playlist on her phone, which was just outside the splash zone on a folded towel on the black and white tiled floor.

She closed her eyes and relaxed to the music. She must have fallen asleep because she was back at Greg's younger sister's wedding 5 years ago when she'd first met Melanie Horton. Melanie was sitting at a table with her plus one…a young man. Bethany couldn't quite picture him. No matter how much she tried in the dream, she couldn't see his face...

There was a knock on the bathroom door. "Occupied! Go to the bathroom downstairs," she called without opening her eyes.

There was no answer. She grabbed her bath puff and started to lather it up.

There was another knock. "I said to go downstairs!" she called again.

"It's the first time I knocked," her son huffed from the other side of the door. "Whatever!" She heard him stomp away.

A few minutes later, she heard him stomp back up the stairs and then slam his bedroom door.

"Lord, help me," she sighed. She soaked for about half an hour before draining the tub and stepping out onto the cool tile. She wrapped a clean towel around herself and looked in the mirror. She leaned in closely. A word was written in the fogged mirror's corner. "Alec," it said.

"Alec?" she asked, looking at it. One of the kids must have written it after she'd cleaned the mirror earlier, and the steam had revealed it. But who was Alec? And why had they written it on her clean mirror? She grabbed a towel and wiped it away. She looked at herself, letting her hair out of its tie so that it fell to her shoulders. She ran her fingers through it at the scalp, shaking it loose. She didn't look too bad, considering she'd packed all day yesterday, driven all night last night, and worked all day today. Still, she was going to sleep like a log.

She dried herself off, slipped into her underwear and nightgown, hung the towels on the rack, picked up her phone, and headed to her bedroom.

———

Joe snuggled down into the pillow. Jess was already asleep. That kid could sleep anywhere, he thought. Of course, they were in a comfortable bed, and the wood stove was keeping the downstairs warm and cozy, so he really shouldn't have problems sleeping. It was just Joe.

He couldn't seem to get Bethany's belly button stud out of his brain. Every time he closed his eyes, there it was, peeking out from under the crop sweater just above the Levi's 501 stamp on the brass button clasping her jeans shut. He groaned and buried his face in the pillow, punching it several times.

"What's the matter, Daddy?" his son's sleep-laden tones inquired.

"Nuthin', Honey. Just havin' trouble fallin' asleep," he

answered.

"It's alright, Daddy. Just close your eyes and breathe," his son said, giving the advice he had given to him any number of nights when Jess had lain awake worried about one thing or another...mostly deployment...when he'd been young.

"Thank you, Sweetheart. I'll do that. Sorry, I disturbed you," he said, kissing his son's forehead. Jess was quickly back to sleep.

He closed his eyes. Belly button stud. Flat waist, curved hips, long legs, 501. So easily unhooked. Oh, God. He sat up. A walk. He needed a walk. He quickly dressed and slipped on his boots.

"Come on, Duke!" he called. The dog jumped up. He slipped the leash onto the dog's collar and headed out the front door.

It was dark out here. It was something he had noticed while he was in the Marines. Other places weren't as dark as Westmoreland County at night. The sky was black, not charcoal like it was in other parts of the world. The stars seemed brighter, too. And you could really see the Milky Way.

He and Duke walked around the house. He stopped in his tracks. There was a light on in the barn.

He knew there hadn't been a light on when he'd gotten back from taking Mr. Morgan home. He'd made sure to check.

Duke barked. "Hush, Boy," he said, moving to his truck and grabbing his shotgun from behind the seat. He loaded both barrels and headed toward the barn.

"Somebody in here?" he called, opening the door.

"Just me," said a voice from a dark corner.

"Who are you?" Joe asked, aiming the shotgun in the direction of the voice.

"Nobody now. I used to be Alec Gardner," the voice said.

Joe lowered the weapon, not believing his eyes, as a young man of 18 or 19 materialized in the corner, still in his Army uniform, circa 1965.

"Who?" Joe asked.

"Melanie's brother…no…uncle. She found out the truth just before…"

Joe sat up. He was still in bed. "Weird ass dream," he said, looking at his still-sleeping son. Duke slowly wagged his tail from the dog bed in the corner.

He lay back down, folded his hands on his chest, and closed his eyes. "Weird ass dream," he repeated as he fell back to sleep.

———

Jillian smoked her cigarette on her front porch. Tears ran down her face. Lyle was drunk again. He was an angry drunk. She wanted to call…*him*. Michael Gabriel Poole was the inspiration behind the angel wing tattoos and a major source of contention between her and Lyle. She wouldn't call him. She couldn't. He'd come, she knew, and then Lyle would accuse them again…She wondered briefly if that new girl, Bethany, might still be awake. She heard the crash from inside her house and decided it didn't matter. She needed to leave before Lyle started taking it out on her. She didn't even bother to go inside to get her purse. She just started walking down the road in the direction of Bethany Benson's house. It was dark, but she could see the road.

Minutes later, she was in front of the old farmhouse. It was as dark and spooky looking as ever, but anything was better than going home to get beaten up by Lyle or thinking about the man she had always really loved, whom she knew loved her, too. That was pure torture.

She walked up to the front door, which had finally been cleared of that tree limb. She hesitated. Then she knocked.

A dog barked from inside. The foyer light came on, and the door swung cautiously open.

Instead of Bethany Benson, Joe Gardner stood there with a puzzled look on his face.

"Jillian?" he asked.

"Who is it?" Bethany's frightened voice came from behind him at the top of the stairs.

"Jillian Fox from down the road," he answered. He put emphasis on "Fox." Like she needed reminding, she thought.

"Oh yes, Jillian. I met her today at the Stop In. Is she alright?" the woman asked from the top of the stairs.

He leaned toward Jillian to get a closer look. "I don't think so," he said. "Come in, Jillian." He moved aside. He sounded kinder as he spoke this time.

Jillian didn't know what to think. Why was he here? Were he and the new girl...? He hadn't so much as looked at a woman since moving back home 6 years ago with his kid. It had taken Bethany Benson all of 1 day...She laughed and stepped inside.

"You have a black eye!" Bethany exclaimed, coming down the stairs in her bare feet. She wrapped her robe around her tighter as she came.

"I'll get her some ice," Joe offered, disappearing through the darkened dining room to Jillian's left into what she presumed must be the kitchen.

Bethany was beside her then. "Come on in," the girl said kindly. Putting her arm around Jillian's shoulder. "The wood stove is in the dining room, so that's the most comfortable room to sit in until we get the furnace replaced." She directed

Jillian into the room Joe had just disappeared through and flipped on the light. She pulled out a chair for Jillian. "Would you like some tea? I have some good tea I bought from a tearoom in Manhattan," she offered.

Jillian laughed again. "Have you got anything stronger?" she asked.

"Oh, of course," Bethany replied. "I have some Jim Beam and Coke."

"Now you're talkin'," Jillian said, unable to control the nervous laughter.

"Sure," Bethany said, moving to a console table under the window. "Joe, put some of that ice into a glass and bring the Coke," she called, taking the bottle of whiskey from the cabinet.

Joe reappeared with a tea towel filled with ice, a glass, also filled with ice, and a 2-liter bottle of Coke. Bethany sat across from Jillian, and Joe sat beside her. God, they were a good-looking couple. They just looked right together. No wonder...

"Did I interrupt, y'all?" Jillian asked.

"No. Of course not," Bethany answered, pouring the whiskey over the ice.

"Lyle drinking again?" Joe asked, adding the Coke to the whiskey in the glass. He definitely had a kinder tone when he spoke this time.

"Yeah. Missy went with my Mama tonight because she wanted to help with the turkey tomorrow. Lyle took that as an invitation to get shit-faced," she responded, looking at the glass before taking a long swig. "I'm sorry to wake y'all."

Joe nodded. He was just glad Jillian had come here instead of calling *him*...She could read the relief in his eyes. He was a good friend to her true love. She'd hurt him enough.

Bethany nodded in understanding. Jillian knew she had come to the right person. The girl understood…completely.

"It's okay, Jillian. You can always come here," Bethany said, touching her hand.

"Here, put this on your eye, Jill," Joe said, thrusting the tea towel at her. She took it and covered her eye.

"Thanks. Would you mind my sleepin' on your couch? I just want to give him the time to pass out. But I don't want to keep y'all up."

"Sure. I'll get you a pillow and a blanket," Bethany offered, starting to stand.

"I got it," Joe said, stopping her. "Stay here and talk to her for a minute." Jillian felt that Joe had sensed it, too, that Bethany understood more than she appeared to on the surface. He stood and headed up the stairs.

Bethany sat back down. "Does he drink a lot…your husband?"

"Not often, but a lot when he does," she answered.

Bethany nodded. "That's worse in some ways. Because you never see it coming until it's too late."

Jillian adjusted the ice on her face. "The voice of experience?" she noted.

"It wasn't often…like you said," Bethany affirmed. "Otherwise, he was a good husband."

"Yeah, exactly," Jillian agreed. They sat there quietly for several seconds.

"Who are we kidding?" Bethany said finally. "No, he wasn't. And no, he's not."

"Exactly," Jillian sniffed, taking another swig of the whiskey and Coke.

They sat together for several minutes. Joe came back. "I put down a sheet, and there's a pillow and blanket for ya on the sofa," he said from the doorway. "I'm going back to bed now if ya don't need anything else."

"Hmmm. No, we're fine. Goodnight, Hon...Joe...I mean Joe," Bethany said, her eyes growing big as saucers as her face flushed a bright scarlet.

Jillian smiled. "He will be a good one," she said quietly. Bethany blushed a deeper shade of red.

"Oh God, I'm doomed!" she whispered. "Every time I close my eyes, I see that tattoo on his chest...He took his shirt off when he was removing the tree limb...and I didn't mean to..."

Jillian patted her hand. "Honey, who wouldn't look? What tattoo?"

"It's the Sacred Heart," Bethany groaned, burying her face in her hands. "And there's a cuff around his bicep that looks kind of Nordic...and baby feet on his back shoulder, with Jessup Leroy Gardner, April 19, 2012, in script under them." She pointed over her left shoulder.

"You could read the writing?" Jillian chuckled. "Muscles?"

"So many muscles," Bethany whispered.

"How long did you watch him?"

"Not long...five minutes...ten, tops...God...maybe half an hour."

Jillian laughed.

"I can't get involved with him, Jillian. Greg only died a year and a half ago."

"I hear you sayin' you've been single for a year and a half now. I also hear you sayin' you're hot to trot for Joe Gardner. And lucky you, he's in your house." Jillian giggled. "Ow!" She readjusted the ice again.

CHAPTER 5

Morning came, and Bethany stretched and pulled herself out of bed. She dug through her clothes, looking for her raw silk wide-leg pants. They were a dark forest green and looked pretty with her citron shell and lace blouse. She told herself that she wasn't really sure why she was dressing up, but that wasn't true. She was dressing up because Joe Gardner was downstairs. She brushed out her hair and put on a headband that matched the shell. She meticulously applied her make-up.

"Mommy! You look pretty!" Meghan exclaimed from her door.

"Thanks, Baby Girl," Bethany said, smiling. "I think so, too." Would Joe think so? She'd never been able to tell if Greg thought she was pretty or not, nor had she ever cared. She rarely dressed up. And when she did, her goal had been more to blend into the background than to stand out.

She had struggled in social situations. She had nothing in common with Greg's colleagues and their spouses. They all were highly educated, affluent people. She hadn't even graduated high school. He had preferred her not to stand out.

When she got the belly button stud and butterfly tattoo, he had berated her mercilessly. She had assured him she'd never show either at any social gathering. But she loved both little acts of rebellion.

She smoothed down her pants and stuck her chin in the air. She was pretty. If Joe didn't see that, that was his issue.

She took Meghan's hand and headed downstairs. Jillian had folded the blanket and sheet and was already gone.

Joe had made pancakes and was in the process of setting the table for breakfast when she walked into the dining room. He looked up as she entered and stared at her for a moment. Then he shook his head and said, "Wow. You're beautiful."

She smiled. Maybe it mattered a little what he thought. "Thank you," she said. "I wanted to look nice for my first-ever Thanksgiving in my new hometown."

"What town?" Ryan grumbled from behind her.

Jessup giggled from his seat at the table. Ryan took a seat.

"Pancakes?" Joe asked.

"Whatever," Ryan scowled, taking the plate Joe offered. "Do we have syrup?"

"Warm syrup in the carafe on the table in front of you," Joe responded, ignoring the snarkiness.

Bethany smiled and sat down. Things were looking up.

They ate, and once again, they all enjoyed the meal. There was conversation and laughter. Meals had never been like this in Connecticut. At breakfast, Greg had read his briefs for the morning. He had expected and had been given silence.

"Have you always been a farmer?" Bethany asked Joe, stuffing her mouth with pancakes.

"Hmmm? No. I mean, my dad was, but he sold off the farm when I was little to pay for my mother's cancer treatments. Unfortunately, she didn't make it. She passed away when I was just 2. He went to work at Dahlgren as a boat carpenter after the farm was sold. He married my mama when I was 4. My dad passed away when I was 17. I joined the Marines out of high school. Mama sort of followed me around to my posts. She took care of Jess while I was deployed. She developed early-onset dementia about 7 years ago. I was honorably discharged, and I moved us back here 6 years ago…hoping to…I don't know…make it easier for her, give her something familiar. And I wanted to give Jess a real home like I had. Even though the farm was no longer ours, my dad had made sure we kept the house. Mama sold it when I went into the Marines…so I miscalculated a little," he laughed. "I was a mechanic in the Marines, so I got a job at a garage in Colonial Beach. I saved up and started farming your land last year. I did okay. But I still have to work at the garage a few days a week," he explained. "How about you? What do you do?"

Bethany blushed. "Me? Nothing. I mean…I stayed home with the kids."

"Well, that's not nothing, Bethany," he said, smiling and taking a bite.

"Um, yeah. I know. I guess. I'm not very interesting, though. I never finished high school, and I haven't traveled very much. I'm not much of a conversationalist."

"Says who?" he asked.

"Everybody," she replied, blushing.

"Well, we've been talking for half an hour now, and I haven't been bored once. Not even a little bit. You're bright and funny and fun to be around. I enjoy talking to you. So, I don't know who 'everybody' is, but I'm not included in their number," he assured her.

"You don't talk like a farmer or a mechanic," she noted, laughing.

"What do I talk like, then?" he asked.

"I don't know. I think you're smarter than Greg was. Your…vocabulary and the way you communicate your thoughts…you're eloquent. That's all."

"So, farmers and mechanics can't be eloquent?" he teased.

She blushed adorably again. "That's not what I meant. I just meant that isn't what they're known for. Greg was a lawyer. He was supposed to be eloquent. But he wasn't."

"No offense, Bethany, but Greg was a jerk," Joe countered. "He always was. And so is his mama."

Ryan slammed down his fork.

Joe held up his hand. "You're right, Ryan. That was out of line. My apologies."

Ryan grimaced, stood, and left the table, running back upstairs and slamming his bedroom door again.

"Sorry. I shouldn't have said that," Joe said.

"Oh, it's alright. Greg was a jerk. Ryan is having a hard time with his father's death and the move. I hope he'll come around, but I get it."

"Yeah. I forgot for a minute it wasn't just you and me sitting here. I'm really sorry," Joe apologized, looking down.

"So…what's the plan for Thanksgiving? What do we do now?" she asked, smiling.

Joe looked positively dejected.

She sighed. "Really, Joe. It's okay. Ryan is going through something right now, but he'll be fine. His father has said way worse to him and never apologized."

He forced a smile. "Well, we clean the turkey, get rid of all the nasty stuff in that little packet inside. Mama used to boil it and eat it, but…blech."

She grinned. "Alright then. Let's get started."

He grinned back.

———————

Ryan, once again alone in his room, paced frantically back and forth. He wasn't mad about what Joe had said. His dad had been a jerk, worse than a jerk, monstrous, even. He was glad he was gone. But his mother was vulnerable. And Joe was taking advantage of her. He smacked the wall next to the closet. The force stung his fingers. He shook his hand and grabbed his fingers with his other hand.

The closet door popped open, and a photo album fell from the top shelf. Ryan reached down to pick it up. A photograph fell out onto the floor. It looked like a picture from Aunt Renee's wedding. He'd seen some of them before and recognized the venue and decorations. He remembered his mother telling him she had met the lady who left them this house at Aunt Renee's wedding. The picture was of his mother. And she was smiling at the camera or at whoever was taking the picture. He'd never seen his mother look so happy. Then he noticed the dark window behind her that reflected the image of the man holding the camera. What the actual hell? That was…Joe…he was certain.

Ryan shoved the picture back into the album and shoved the album under his bed. The man in the picture was certainly not his father. The image was distorted, but it was him. Ryan recognized him even with his face hidden behind the camera. He was tall and muscular, and his mother looked at him like…like she'd been looking at him all day yesterday.

"I'm such a brat," he said to the spirit.

"Nah, kiddo. You're just worried about your mama. But I'm tellin' you, it's all good," the spirit answered.

Jessup sat quietly, watching his father's smile. It was the strangest thing. His father smiled, but it had always somehow seemed sad. But this smile wasn't sad. It looked real. It looked happy. Jessup wasn't stupid. He knew what sex was, but his father had never shown any interest in anyone in his memory. This smile. This easy laughter. It felt like a different person…no, the same person, just better. It was like the attraction was healing his father's bruised spirit. Yes, he understood perfectly well what attracted his father to her. He had to foster that at all costs. Ryan needed to get over it. There was more at stake here than Ryan's hurt feelings.

As his father and Bethany disappeared into the kitchen, he looked over at Meghan, who grinned at him. "Wanna help me make your dad marry my mommy?"

He grinned mischievously. "You read minds?" he giggled.

She leaned forward. "Alec told me you're on my side," she whispered.

"Who's Alec?" he asked, leaning forward, too.

"He's the ghost," she whispered.

"Oh. I was wondering who haunted this place," he said, humoring her. "What's he like? Is he a mean ghost?"

"No," she giggled. "He looks a lot like your daddy, only younger, and he's really nice."

"Cool. At least it's a nice ghost."

"I think he keeps the bad ghosts away," she said earnestly.

"Excellent. Every haunted house should have that kind of ghost!" he giggled.

"Right?" she agreed.

"So, what's your plan, soon-to-be-little-sister?"

"Alec says we need to leave them at home alone all night, but I don't know how to do that," Meghan suggested.

Jessup thought for a minute. "Hmmm. Yeah, that's a tough one. I know that the Fire Department is hosting a youth lock-in in two weeks, but that's for kids 10 and older. That might get me and Ryan out of the house, but that leaves you."

Ryan appeared suddenly and sat beside Meghan. "I have an idea," he said quietly.

"What is it?" Jessup asked suspiciously.

"Well, Mom really likes Mr. Morgan. If we could get him to help…"

"I thought you didn't like Daddy…" Jessup accused.

There was a burst of laughter from the kitchen.

"Nah. He's alright. Mom really likes him. He makes her laugh. Dad never made her laugh. Dad never apologized when he was wrong, either. Your dad has that goin' for him." Ryan sighed. "I want her to be happy. She's never been happy," he added, wistfully.

Soon, the house smelled like Thanksgiving.

———————

Filmore Morgan stood at the front door. The smell of a turkey roasting permeated the air. He shoved his glasses up on his nose and pressed the doorbell.

The little girl answered. "He's here!" she yelled. He thought she actually seemed excited to see him. How nice! He almost wanted to cry. She swung the door open, and once more, he was struck by those familiar green eyes. Was it his imagination, or did the child look exactly like Joe? How was that possible? What had Melanie neglected to tell him about Bethany Benson?

"Hello, young lady. Your mother invited me for Thanksgiving. I've brought a pie," he said, thrusting the pie forward somewhat awkwardly. The child giggled.

Suddenly, both boys were there. Jessup, Joe's son, took the pie. "Thank you, Mr. Morgan. I'll give it to Daddy and Bethany. They're in the kitchen. Why don't you come in and watch the parade with us?" Then he was gone.

Ryan, Bethany's son, took his arm and pulled him

inside. "Yeah, come on in, Mr. Morgan. I'm Ryan. I was in my room when you came last night. I'm sorry for being so rude. Let me take your coat," he said.

Filmore was overwhelmed. The boy took his coat, and the little girl grabbed his hand, leading him into the living room. Then Jessup was back.

"Sit down, Mr. Morgan," he offered.

"Would you like a drink, Mr. Morgan?" asked Ryan.

"We're so happy to see you, Mr. Morgan," the little girl giggled, sitting on the floor in front of him.

He sat down on the sofa and laughed. "Well, this is quite the welcome," he winked. "What, pray tell, do you children want?"

"Nothing. We're just glad you're here," Jessup assured him.

"Jessup, my good lad, I'm old. I know perfectly well that the three of you aren't excited by my company," he laughed, feeling flattered nonetheless.

Ryan looked over his shoulder and sat beside him. He whispered, "Here's the thing: We want to get Mr. Gardner and Mom together."

"Ahhh!" Filmore said, conspiratorially. "And you wish to enlist my assistance?"

"Yes, sir!" Jessup added, sitting on his other side. "We want to get them alone here together…overnight. Me and Ryan can go to that lock-in, but we don't know what to do about Meghan."

Filmore chuckled. "It seems clear to me, dear girl, that you need a friend with whom to have a sleepover."

"But I don't have a friend," she replied sweetly.

"Yes, well, you've come to the right man. I know everybody!" he announced. "Hmmm. How old are you, young lady?"

"I'm 4 and a 1/2," she answered plainly, her pigtails bouncing with emphasis.

"I see. Yes. And you like your dolly there…Do you sing and dance?" He did some quick math. Five years ago, Melanie had taken Joe to a wedding…Could it really be?

She giggled. "Yes! I do!" Her pigtails bounced again. Had to be. She was the picture of Joe.

"I have just the friend. Kelly Madison. She's 4 and ½, too, and she happens to be my neighbor. Leave it to me, young ones." he said, nodding.

"Leave what to you?" Bethany asked, coming into the room with a glass of Coke that she offered to Filmore.

He took the glass and chuckled at the crestfallen look on the children's faces. "Oh, Jessup and Ryan pleaded for my assistance in gaining permission to attend the Youth Lock-in at the Fire House on the 13th," he offered.

"Really?" Bethany asked, looking at Ryan. "You want to go? You're…giving it a chance?"

"Yeah, Mom. It sounds like fun, and I'm done being mad," Ryan assured her.

"Well, it's okay with me. Jessup will have to ask Joe, though."

"I will!" Jessup exclaimed, jumping up and running to the kitchen.

Bethany shook her head.

"Oh…my dear. I wanted to ask if you might be seeking employment?" Filmore inquired as she started to turn to walk away.

She stopped and turned back to him. "Um, yes. I'm not very qualified for anything, but I need to start looking."

"Well, I happen to need a new secretary. Mrs. Smith

retired last month," he offered hastily.

"I...I don't know anything about being a legal secretary," she protested.

"What's to know? You answer the phone, you type, you file. Please, my dear. I'd rather have you than someone I don't like." He smiled and peered at her over his glasses.

"I...wow...Thank you so much, Mr. Morgan. I'll give it a try if you really think I can do it," she replied.

"Wonderful! You'll start Monday morning!" he exclaimed, clapping his hands together. "Now, do you need my help, or shall I watch the parade with this young lady?"

"Um, just enjoy the parade, Mr. Morgan. You're our guest," she chuckled happily. "We'll be in the kitchen if you need anything..." She looked back over her shoulder and smiled before walking away.

———

Joe shivered, suddenly feeling cold. "Brrrrr. I better check the fire in the wood stove," he said to himself, putting down the knife he was using to chop the mirepoix.

He turned as Jess ran into the room. "Daddy, me and Ryan want to go to the lock-in at the firehouse. Bethany said okay for Ryan, but I have to ask you."

"Uh...sure, if you want. Ryan wants to go with you?"

"Yeah. Ryan's okay, Daddy. He was just in a bad mood. He really wants to go."

Joe nodded. Jess jumped in excitement and turned to run back to the living room.

"Hey! Let Duke out!" he called to his son's retreating back. Joe laughed.

The fire was a little low, so he added a couple of pieces of wood. Bethany came back. She smiled at him.

"I got a job!" she whispered excitedly. "Mr. Morgan

asked me to come be his secretary. I don't know if I know what I'm doing, but he's willing to give me a chance...and I sure need it."

He beamed at her. "That's great, Bethy...I mean Bethany. You'll be great."

She shrugged. "I think things are going to be okay," she agreed. "It's okay to call me Bethy. I like it when you do it. I'm not sure why."

———

Bethy. He'd called her Bethy. It was an oddly familiar feeling, even though no one had ever shortened her name... ever. Her own parents had only ever called her Bethany. It made her heart sing. Bethy.

He had started sautéing what he called mirepoix, but it seemed to just be a mixture of carrots, celery, and onion. "Can ya get me that sausage out of the fridge, Bethy?" he asked.

"Sure," she answered, fascinated by Joe. He had said he had mad skills as a joke, but he really did know how to cook. He wasn't just a good cook for a bachelor. He was a good cook for a cook.

"Did you learn to cook in the Marines?" she asked, handing him the sausage log.

"Nah. Mama taught me mostly. Some things I picked up from cooking shows," he said, laughing.

She couldn't help it. His laugh just made her want to laugh, too. She giggled.

"Didn't your mama teach you to cook?" he asked.

"My mother never taught me anything," she scoffed.

"Nothing?"

"Well, nothing good," she admitted.

He shook his head. "Well, you get it from somewhere."

"Get what?" she asked, tasting the cranberry sauce he

had on the stove.

He smiled again. "The good."

She smiled back at him. She took a step closer and quickly kissed him. She smiled again. "Sorry," she said, blushing.

"You don't look sorry," he chuckled.

That's when the bottom dropped out. Bethany's phone rang. "Happy Thanksgiving!" she answered cheerfully. She felt the smile disappear. "Mrs. Benson. Hello. Yes. We're perfectly fine. I don't need your money. I can take care of my own kids, thank you. No. No. Please don't." But her mother-in-law had disconnected. "Shit," she screamed.

Joe put everything down and hugged her.

CHAPTER 6

She pulled out of his embrace. "Screw it. Let her come. Are we about ready to set the table?" she asked. Bethany opened the cabinet. "I wish I had some pretty china. Wouldn't that just get her goat? But I didn't take anything that belonged to them. I bought these at a thrift store when I knew I was… leaving."

"I have my mama's china," Joe offered. "It's Lenox. I think that's pretty good."

Her face brightened. "You do? Can we use it?"

"Of course. It's under my bed. I didn't want it gettin' broken out in the barn." He walked out of the kitchen, returning moments later with a large box. Together, they washed the china. Bethany took it and set the table. She smiled at the table. She looked around at the pleasant house that needed work, but it looked clean and homey. It was prettier by far than that house in Connecticut. And the meal smelled better than anything the cook had ever prepared.

"Do you need any help, Joe? I think I should go check on Mr. Morgan. He is a guest…and my boss…after all," she called back to the kitchen.

"I got everything under control!" he answered.

Bethany made her way to the living room. Mr. Morgan was sitting on the couch playing Barbies with Meghan. "I'm not certain this dress is appropriate for babysitting your doll's baby," he said, staring at the evening gown the Barbie he was holding had on.

"It's okay. Your Barbie is a pop star. That's how she dresses," Meghan explained.

"Ah. I see. But if she's famous, why is she babysitting?" he asked.

"Cause she is my Barbie's best friend."

"Oh. Yes. Well, that makes sense, then," he said, nodding.

Bethany chuckled and sat beside him. "Meghan, Honey. Why don't you go play with Ryan and Jessup?" she suggested.

"I'd rather play with Alec," she replied, standing.

"Alec?" Bethany asked.

"Oh my. That's a name from the past," Mr. Morgan said.

"Yeah, he's our ghost," Meghan said, pointedly.

"Is he?" Mr. Morgan looked around. "Did you make it home after all, Alec?"

"Who's Alec?" Bethany asked.

"Who was Alec?" Mr. Morgan corrected her, holding up his index finger. "Alec Gardner. He was Melanie's…well, uncle, really…though she was raised believing he was her brother. He was two years behind me, but we were close friends as boys."

"What happened to him?" Bethany asked politely, amused.

"Vietnam happened to him," Mr. Morgan said sadly. "He was killed in 1965."

"Oh. And he lived here?" Bethany asked.

"Oh, yes. He was born right here. In that room there, I believe." Mr. Morgan pointed to Joe's room. "He was a nice boy. Hard-working. Honest." He sighed, remembering his friend. "When he shipped out, I was at the University of

Virginia. I told him I didn't think it was fair. He shouldn't have to go. But he said it was right for him to serve, and it was right for me to go to college...that we had different paths." He took off his glasses and wiped away a tear.

Meghan kissed his cheek. "He says it turned out just how it was supposed to, and he's proud of you," she said.

Mr. Morgan looked...grateful. "Thank you, Child," he said sweetly. He turned to Bethany. "Might I have a moment, Dear?" he asked. Meghan smiled and skipped away.

"Of course," Bethany said, slightly taken aback. Was a ghost talking to her daughter? Had a ghost been in the bathroom with her? An 18-year-old male ghost? No. She didn't really believe in ghosts. Did she?

She stepped out of the room and heard Mr. Morgan speak to the empty room, "Alec? My friend. I have missed you all these years. I did my best to take care of your mama and Maggie and sweet little Melanie. I married Maggie when I came home. And I raised Melanie as my own. Did you know? Maggie couldn't have children after...what Vince did to her and the botched birth. But I never minded. I had my Mellie. Your mama joined you in 1980...and Maggie passed about 10 years ago. I lost Mellie 2 years ago now. I'm alone again. But Melanie picked Bethany. And I don't feel so alone all of a sudden. So, if you're here, watch over my new family."

Bethany felt a warm sensation come over her. "Alec? Are you giving me a hug?" she asked. If that was the case, what were the cold spots? If Alec was warm, what the heck was cold?

"Meghan?" she called. The child appeared at the top of the stairs.

"Yes, Mommy," she said.

"Is there anyone else besides Alec here?"

"Yes," she smiled. "We're here, too."

Bethany smiled and nodded. She was being ridiculous. There weren't really ghosts. She let out her breath and returned to Mr. Morgan.

———

Just before 1 pm, Joe pulled the turkey out of the oven. Bethany came into the kitchen as he closed the oven door. "Hey," he greeted her.

"Hey," she replied. "Did you know that Mrs. Horton had an uncle named Alec?" she asked, her brow furrowed.

"Alec? Sure. But it's funny you ask; I dreamt about him last night."

Bethany's mouth dropped open. "He died in Vietnam… he was like 18. He was Mr. Morgan's good friend…and Mr. Morgan married his sister sometime after he died."

"Hmmm. Spooky."

"Yeah, spooky. He was born in your bedroom."

"Do you believe in ghosts, Bethy?" he teased. "I've heard about Alec Gardner all my life, Bethy. I'm even named after him. I just moved into his house. It's normal I should dream about him."

"Yeah. You're right. Of course, you're right."

He smiled. She seemed to relax a little.

"But Meggy knows things about him that she shouldn't. She's never heard of him before," she protested.

"You're just nervous about your monster-in-law's call. Come on. Let's get this food on the table."

She nodded. "Thanks," she said. "I am nervous. I needed the voice of reason."

"Sure," he said. "Anytime."

They put the food into the fine china serving bowls and transferred it all to the dining room while the turkey rested on a serving platter.

Bethany called everyone to the table. Joe said grace, and they ate until they couldn't eat any more.

"Alec says that Joe went to war, too. Did you, Joe?" Meghan asked as they sat there, letting their food digest.

Joe looked at Jess. His son had immediately teared up. He grabbed his hand. "I'm never going back again, Honey. That's all over," he assured his son. He looked at Meghan. "Yes, I went to war. Twice. In 2015 and 2016."

"You did?" Bethany gasped. "I never even thought to ask."

He smiled. "No worries. I made it back in one piece."

She sighed. "I'm sorry. I'm just worried about what Mrs. Benson may try to do. It's been preoccupying my thoughts since...before we left Connecticut."

"What do you mean, Mom? What does Grandma want to do?" Ryan asked. "She wants to take me and Meg, doesn't she?" he exclaimed, suddenly realizing the truth of why they had moved here.

"That's not for you to worry about," Bethany assured him, patting his hand.

Mr. Morgan leaned forward. "Well...it's very difficult to take children from the biological mother. It's harder still if there is a strong family unit."

"What do you mean?" Bethany asked, her interest piqued.

"A married couple living together under a single roof," Mr. Morgan suggested.

"Oh...Oh," Bethany exclaimed. "Are you suggesting...? No. We can't do that."

"Why not? You're both single, and you're already living under one roof," Mr. Morgan added.

Joe looked around the table. His heart was in his throat. But he squeaked out, "I'll do it…I mean, I'll do it if you will… if you want to…"

"Oh… we really can't…Can we?" she asked. "Can that really help?"

"It can't hurt," Mr. Morgan chuckled. Did he just wink at Jessup? Joe wondered. No.

"If she tries anything, you will have a home, a husband, a job…so two incomes, a good car…Mellie's Caddy…money in the bank. She won't have a leg to stand on," Mr. Morgan extrapolated. "Plus, you have the best lawyer around."

"Can we get married tomorrow?" she asked.

"Of course. I happen to be a justice of the court, and I can perform a civil ceremony. You just need to go get the license in the morning. You can get married the same day."

Joe swallowed hard. "Yeah. Okay. Tomorrow." He felt like he might pass out. He started to hyperventilate a little.

"Joe, you don't have to…" Bethany exclaimed, jumping up, seeing him in distress.

"No. I want to. I just…I've never been married before."

They sat there quietly for a minute. Joe suddenly jumped up and walked hurriedly into the other room. He returned after a few minutes.

"You need an engagement ring," he said. "I have my mama's rings. It's not much, but…" He opened a ring box he held in his hand. A pretty quarter-carat round solitaire diamond ring sat snuggly in the velvet case, along with a man's and a woman's wedding bands.

"Is that your daddy's?" Bethany asked, pointing.

"Yes," he replied, feeling like he might throw up from the nerves.

"Are you sure?"

"Yes." He took the diamond out of the box and slipped it onto Bethany's ring finger.

"You should seal it with a kiss," Mr. Morgan whispered.

"What?" they both asked, both exhibiting clear symptoms of shellshock.

"Kiss," Ryan said. "Geez."

"Oh. Right. Kiss," Joe stammered. Then he quickly leaned down and kissed Bethany.

After dinner, they moved to the living room and put on some music from Joe's playlist. As *I Can't Help Falling in Love* by Elvis Presley started to play, Joe reached out his hand to Bethany. She smiled and took it, moving to sway with him in his arms. He was a good dancer. Of course, he was. He was good at everything. In his arms, she found it easy to lose herself in that moment. She pressed in closer. His arm tightened around her waist. It was as if there were only the two of them and Elvis's low tones. She draped her arms around his neck and pressed her cheek to his. His other arm encircled her waist, and his hand rested on her back. She let out a breath and closed her eyes, her mouth close to his ear. She pursed her lips as her breath escaped, blowing in his ear. His heart was pounding in his chest. His hand slid up her back, coming to a stop between her shoulder blades.

The song ended, and Bethany opened her eyes. She leaned her head back to look Joe in the eyes. She bit her bottom lip and then partially opened her mouth as his mouth covered hers. She closed her eyes again. She lost herself in the kiss. Her body...no, her entire being...longed for this man, longed for him to draw her to him.

As they headed out to take a walk, Bethany leaned her head against his shoulder as they stepped off the porch. "I didn't know you liked Elvis," she offered.

"Hmmm? I don't, especially. That was a nice song, though."

She paused and looked up at him. "Well, you put it on!" she chuckled.

"Not me," he said, shaking his head.

"It was your playlist," she insisted.

"I don't know how it got there," he said. Then he grinned coyly. "Maybe Alec added it."

She smacked his arm playfully. "Stop it," she said as they started to walk again.

"I really didn't add it, though," he said.

CHAPTER 7

Rosalea Benson never showed her face. But the threat of her imminent arrival hung heavily in the air. As evening fell, it became clear Rosalea had been unable to get out of the city because of the holiday. There was a reprieve. If they could get married before that bitch showed up, Bethany felt like she'd have a fighting chance.

Once she gave Meghan her bath and got her into bed, she went into her room. She had a white dress. It had been the one "fancy" dress she had taken. She didn't know why she had even wanted it until this moment. It was going to be her wedding dress. It was a tea-length white satin dress with a halter top. There was a white lace shawl to wear over her shoulders and white satin pumps. She pulled the dress out of the closet and hung it on the back of her bedroom door. She sat on the edge of her bed. She looked down at the diamond on her finger. However small it was, it was twenty times more beautiful than the 2-carat emerald cut ring she'd left on the kitchen counter with her note two days ago. Still, there was something not quite right about it. "Why would it feel like it's the wrong ring?" she sighed.

She took out her phone and made a call. "Jillian, hi. It's Bethany Benson. Yes. We had a good Thanksgiving. You? Good. I'm glad he stayed away. I was wondering if you have plans tomorrow…and if you have a nice dress. Yes. I need a maid of honor…"

There was silence on the other end of the call…then a

squeal.

Bethany smiled, almost laughing. She bit her thumbnail.

"Good. Thank you. We have to stop at the bank before getting the license. But if you're free, I'd like to make a day of it. Of course, I want to include you. You're my best friend. I know we've only known each other 2 days, but trust me. You're my best friend. Okay. We'll see you in the morning. Good night."

She disconnected and lay back on the bed, her feet still on the floor. "Well…things sure change fast when you go looking for a change," she said to the room. "Hey, Alec! I'm going to take a bath. Stay out of the bathroom…okay?" She said it out loud…just in case.

Bethany didn't think she'd sleep at all, but she did and found herself walking on a beach in her dream, as she often did. The sun was warm. There was an ocean breeze blowing her hair. She heard a man laugh as her hair flew in her eyes. A gentle hand reached out and brushed it away, and she looked lovingly into his eyes…but she couldn't see his face. It was blurred and hazy. No matter how hard she tried to bring his face into focus, she couldn't. Even so, she knew that he loved her, and she loved him…this faceless man. Somewhere in the recesses of her mind, he was real. He was solid. But now, and for several years, he was just a dream. It was time to let the dream man go. She was marrying the real-life man downstairs. She might even love him. She certainly wanted to be with him. The dream faded away, and she slept peacefully.

———

Joe took out his suit and plugged in the iron. He ironed it neatly and rehung it. He unplugged the iron and put everything away.

He was getting married. It was such an impulsive

move. He loved that girl. Did she love him? Or was she just doing this to help buoy her case against her mother-in-law? He was shaking, but he was doing this. Shaking, or not. Ready to vomit any second, or not. He was going to marry her. And if she didn't love him now, she would eventually because she had to, because she once had. He couldn't possibly fall for someone who wouldn't love him. Could he?

He took out his phone and made a call. "Hey, Dex," he said into it. "What you doin' tomorrow? Um...sure. Do you think you could maybe not do that? Oh, well...I'm getting married. I was hoping you could get Mama out for the day... and maybe bring her...and maybe be my best man. Okay. Yeah, I'm sure. Yeah. I'll see you tomorrow. Hmmm? Oh. At Mr. Morgan's office. Yeah. I'll text you the address. Yeah...it would be okay to bring Jessup. Jess will be happy to see him... Dex? Do you think Jemma would be...okay with my...never mind. I just hope she'd understand. Thanks. I still miss her. But...this girl...She's right. Know what I mean?" He smiled. "Yeah. See you tomorrow. G'night."

"Hey, Jess," he called.

"Yeah, Daddy?" Jess said, coming in from the living room.

"Uncle Dex is coming tomorrow, and he's bringing Grandma and your Great grandpa Jessup."

"Cool," the boy beamed.

"Jess?"

"Yeah?"

"Does she like me?" he asked, fear flooding his entire body.

"Yeah, Daddy. She likes you just as much as you like her," he laughed.

"Really?"

"Really."

———

At 6:15 am, after having lain awake for the last two hours, Joe got up and showered. He shined his shoes and donned his suit. He took several deep breaths. Then he walked out of the house and climbed into his truck.

He drove to Colonial Beach. The Food Lion was opening at 7 am, and Bethy needed flowers.

He parked in a bit of a daze. He found himself standing at the still-locked door at 6:52 am. At 6:59, the manager unlocked the door, and he ran inside.

"Well, aren't you dapper, Joe?" the manager, a lifelong friend of his mama's, said. "Are you going to see Esther today?"

"Um. Dex said he'd bring her, Bev. I need flowers…" God, why was he so damned nervous?

"For your Mama? She loves daisies," Bev Howard replied, pointing toward the floral department. "We have some pretty Gerber ones in bright colors."

"Should I get Mama some, too? Oh, damn. I'm a wreck."

"Oh, they're not for your mama? Who are you buyin' them for then? I'll try to help you pick the right ones?"

"My…fiancée. I'm getting married today," he said. He started to hyperventilate again.

"Oh. Well…You alright, Honey?"

"Yeah," he said, leaning his hands on his knees. "I'm just really nervous."

"Who is she?" Bev asked, rubbing his back.

"Nobody you know. Her name is Bethany. And she's near perfect. Hah. She's so pretty, Bev. And she's kind, and honest, and funny…and I think I'm losing my mind because

every time I close my eyes, I see her, and I dream about her…
and we're getting married today, and she needs flowers. How
can she not have flowers? But I don't know what to get…"

"Roses, Honey. You get her roses," Bev laughed,
interrupting his panic attack.

"Roses. Roses are good," he nodded.

Bev picked out a dozen red roses and added some
baby's breath.

"I'll take the daisies for Mama, too, Bev," he said as she
handed him the bundle.

She nodded and pinned a rosebud to his lapel.
"Congratulations, Honey. It's about time." Then she handed
him the daisies. She kissed his cheek.

"Thanks, Bev. I…I needed your help. I'm okay now.
I… I have to pay," he said.

Bev laughed heartily. "Sure. I'll check you out."

———

Jillian rang the doorbell. Her mother had dropped
Missy back off at the house this morning, and Lyle was a bear,
so she'd grabbed her prettiest dress, her makeup case, and
Missy and had driven to Bethany's.

A boy with freckles answered the door. Hello?" he
said, looking at her like she was crazy.

"Um. I'm your mama's friend. She asked me to be her
maid of honor."

"Oh. Okay," the boy said, opening the door and
moving aside. "Mom! Your friend is here!" he yelled.

"Is Joe back yet?" Bethany called down, appearing at
the top of the stairs.

"No, but he was wearing his suit, so he's not making a
run for it," the boy said haughtily.

"Oh, geez. Thanks for planting that thought in my

brain now!" Bethany exclaimed, stomping her foot.

At that moment, Joe's truck pulled into the driveway.

"He's back. Happy?" the boy called.

"Yes. Oh, God. I'm not dressed." And she disappeared. Her voice trailed behind her, though. "Come up, Jillian. I'm so glad you're here. I need help!"

"Is she alright?" Jillian asked the boy.

"No. She's bat shit crazy," he replied.

Jillian laughed despite herself. "You really shouldn't say things like that," she chuckled. She moved past him, dragging Missy by the hand. "This is Missy, my kid," she said.

"Hey," Missy said. At 12, Missy looked much older, with gorgeous golden blonde hair and big blue eyes, not anything like her mother. The boy's mouth dropped open.

"H…hey," he stammered.

Jillian headed upstairs and found Bethany in her room with curlers in her hair and a dazed look on her face.

"Help me," the woman pleaded.

———

Joe paced the foyer and looked at the stairs repeatedly. Finally, Jillian appeared, wearing a purple sequined strapless dress and a black suede blazer. Behind her, Bethany was a vision. His mouth dropped open.

Her hair was pulled up, except for wispy little ringlets that framed her face. She was wearing a white satin dress that fell just above her ankles. It was backless, and the top tied behind her neck. She had a white lace shawl slung over her bare shoulders and back. She was the prettiest thing he'd ever seen, and in that moment, he knew he couldn't do it, not like this.

She had to remember him first.

Dumbly, he held out the flowers he'd bought her.

"Do I look okay?" she whispered to him, taking the flowers and smelling them.

He nodded vigorously and choked back the tears.

Jillian butted him with her hip. "Use your words," she said.

"Uh-huh...yes. Ye...You're beautiful, Bethy," he said, finding his voice.

She smiled, and he didn't think it was possible, but she was even more breathtaking.

"Do you have your documentation?" she asked.

"I...um...I'm sorry. I can't. Not...like this. I..." He didn't know what to say or how to say it.

Meghan grabbed him around his leg, and he stooped and picked her up, hugging her tightly as the tears fell.

"I'm sorry, my Meggy. I'm sorry," he sobbed, holding her close to his chest.

————

Just like that, in a flash, it all flooded back to Bethany. This man was her Joe, the only man she'd ever loved.

It started 5 and a half years ago. Renee Benson was marrying Geoffrey Phillip Wexton, III, on July 6, 2019, at Winnetu Oceanside Resort on Martha's Vineyard. Bethany was excited. Bethany had never seen the ocean. She had been born and raised in Illinois and never ventured too far out of her Connecticut New York City suburb since marrying Greg Benson in 2011 at the ripe old age of 16. She rarely visited Manhattan, even. Greg had preferred her to stay home.

Greg had planned to make a vacation of it, and they would be staying at the resort for two full weeks and over the 4th of July, while the rest of the family wouldn't arrive until July 5.

At the last minute, Rosalea had offered to keep Ryan

and bring him to the resort with the rest of them. Greg had accepted the offer. That had made Bethany very nervous. Nothing good had ever come from her being alone with Greg. But it had been too late. Greg had accepted, and he was driving. He had dropped Ryan, aged 7, off at his mother's and had headed toward Martha's Vineyard.

They had checked into their room, a beautiful room in soft gray tones with bright, warm, colored throw pillows that looked out over the pool. Greg had brought Bethany's bags up to the room and had deposited them just inside the door. "I've got a business meeting on the other side of the island," he had announced. "It may go late, and I'll probably stay the night. I'll keep my stuff in the car just in case." And with that, Greg had disappeared.

In any normal marriage, it might have been devastating for the wife to find herself abandoned, even in a 4-star resort, but Bethany had been relieved...at first.

She had unpacked. She had sat out on the balcony, enjoying the sea air. She had dressed for dinner. She had dined alone in the restaurant. It had been at dinner that she first laid eyes on Joe Gardner.

He had been hard to miss. At 6'3", he had towered over everybody in the room. His natural good looks had helped him stand out as well. He had agreed to be Melanie Horton's plus-one at the Benson/Wexton wedding. His son had been with his great-grandparents for a few weeks, and Melanie had decided she wanted to spend two weeks in Martha's Vineyard, as she hadn't had a vacation in years. Over 30 years his senior, she had insisted on paying for him to accompany her and had provided a separate room for him. As they had been led to their table, next to where Bethany had sat alone, Joe had smiled at her.

Seeing that they were seated beside her, she had struck up a conversation, at first with both of them, but as the evening wore on, Melanie had excused herself and had returned to her room. Joe and Bethany had stayed and continued their conversation.

When they had stayed as long as they could at the restaurant, they had moved to the bar. They had sat at the bar and talked until closing.

The next day, Greg did not return as he had said he would. Bethany had called him all morning, but he never picked up. She left several voicemails. She texted. She even emailed him. No answer. Finally, at 3pm, he had called her back. He wouldn't be back until the 5th. His business had required him to go to Boston. He told her to go to the beach and into town herself. She had reminded him she had no transportation. He told her to figure it out. He'd see her on the 5th before the rest of his family arrived, reminding her to keep his business private, even from his family.

Joe had found her crying, alone on the beach at the resort that afternoon. Melanie had made appearances throughout their time at the resort, but she had mostly done her own thing. Joe and Bethany had spent every waking moment together. By the 4th of July, they were madly in love. They hadn't acted on it, but it was a fact, inevitable from the moment they had first laid eyes on one another.

They had planned to leave together, but they had to wait for Rosalea to come with Ryan because there was no way Bethany was leaving her son behind.

They had found a tattoo parlor in town. Joe got a cuff on his bicep, a Celtic love knot pattern, and Bethany a butterfly alighting on a lollipop, signifying her metamorphosis and the first sweet taste of freedom. She had also pierced her belly button in a moment of wild abandon. They had picked out and bought her engagement ring and wedding band at an artisan jeweler in town. They had spent the night together, wrapped up in each other's arms on the beach.

Before dawn, she had returned to her room to find Greg waiting for her.

She had played it off that she had fallen asleep on the beach.

And then Rosalea had not shown up until the 6th, the day of the wedding, and without Ryan. She proclaimed that it would have been too hard to watch Ryan and attend the wedding and that she had hired her housekeeper to babysit him at her home until the next day.

She had found it hard to shake her husband. But at the reception, Greg had returned to his philandering ways and had disappeared with a bridesmaid for several hours.

Joe had told her it was fine. He'd come and get her and Ryan in Connecticut on Monday when Greg returned to work.

Come Monday, Greg was waiting for Joe. Bethany didn't know how he'd found out, but he had waited. Joe had flown home and had driven back in his old pickup truck. When he had gotten out of the truck at a service station down the street at 3 am, Greg had appeared out of nowhere and stabbed Joe in the back. He had videoed it on his phone. He had shown it to Bethany before gleefully telling her he'd spent the two weeks with his secretary and her 15-year-old daughter in Boston. Then he had committed her to a private mental hospital in upstate New York, where she had given birth to Meghan while being psychologically tortured and hypnotized to erase Joe from her memory.

———

"Joe," Bethany whispered. She took a step toward him. A strand of hair fell across her eyes. He reached out to brush it away. She grabbed his hand. "My Joe," she repeated louder, more urgently. "You're alive? You're real?" Her eyes filled with tears, too. Then she kissed him, a soft kiss full of longing, love, and regret.

He swallowed hard. "You remember? You know me?" he asked, hopefully.

Her lip quivered as tears fell down her cheeks, her mascara running in dark streaks.

"Hmmm, you're my Joe. How did I not know you?" she whispered, nodding. "Did I hit my head or something? Oh God, I hurt you by not knowing you, Joe. Do you still want me? Can you still love me?"

He put Meghan down as his cries turned to laughter. He pulled her to him and kissed her again. She melted into his kiss, her arms falling around his neck. "I don't know what happened, Sweetheart, but of course, I still love you. I'll love you until the day I die," he replied, covering her face with kisses while she clung to him.

"What's going on?" Jillian interrupted.

Ryan shrugged and looked at Jessup. Jessup shook his head.

Bethany stepped back. "Joseph Alexander Gardner. You'd better marry me. But I want my ring."

He laughed again and pulled a keychain from his pocket. On it was a claddagh wedding set. He pulled the rings off the chain, took her hand, removed his mama's diamond, and slipped on the ring he'd carried for five years and almost 5 months.

He sat Meghan back down. "Jess, get your sister's coat, please," he said, his voice shaking.

"Stepsister," Ryan corrected him.

"No. Sister," Bethany said. "Joe's Meghan's father. Got everything?" she asked, taking Joe's hand. Jillian's mouth dropped open.

He felt his pockets. "Um…yes. Documents. Wallet. Rings. Got 'em. You?"

"Yes," she nodded.

He shivered.

"Cold spot again?" she asked.

"Nerves," he chuckled.

She handed him the keys to the Caddy and took his arm.

"Um…okay…I'll get the kids and meet you at Mr. Morgan's," Jillian called after them as they walked away. She turned to look at Ryan. "I think they forgot we existed."

He nodded. "I told you. Bat shit crazy."

––––––––

Time passed like in a dream. She fixed her makeup as he drove. They went first to the bank in Colonial Beach, where they deposited Bethany's checks and moved Joe's money into a joint savings account. His savings were just more than her check at $48,976, giving them a good solid nest egg. That would help keep Rosalea at bay, Bethany noted. Then they opened a joint checking account, closing Joe's existing and depositing his $2,894.72 and her check for $1800. Joe kept $500 in cash, since his debit card would no longer work, having closed that account.

Having taken care of that business, they headed to Montross and the court clerk's office to obtain their marriage license.

By 10 am, they were back at Mr. Morgan's house and office.

Dex Lawson was sitting on the front porch in the swing. Joe waved as he pulled the Caddy in behind Dex's SUV. "Who is he?" Bethany whispered.

"He's Jess's uncle. My best friend. We were in basic training together," he explained.

"Oh," she said. She sounded dejected. "So, he's your… late girlfriend's brother…" she reasoned.

He grabbed her hand. "Jemma… Jemma was a special woman. I loved her. But it's been 12 years. I promise…there are no unresolved feelings. Dex and I served together. We're family. He'll be your family, too," he reassured her.

She smiled and nodded. They exited the car and walked toward the house.

Dex was shorter than Joe, at 5' 11", but he was trim and muscular. His hair was cut close to the skull, his eyes a soulful brown, his complexion a medium brown. There was a jagged white scar across the back of his right hand below his knuckles. He was a good-looking man, and his smile was bright and friendly. He stood as they approached.

"Hi, Dex," Joe said, shoving his hands into the pockets of his overcoat.

"Hi, Joe," Dex said back, smiling. "Good to see you." He turned his gaze from Joe to Bethany. "And this is…?"

"Dex, this is Bethany. Bethy, this is Master Sergeant Dexter Lawson," Joe said quietly.

"Nice to meet you…Dex," she said sweetly. God, she was beautiful. He took his hand out of his pocket and clasped hers.

"You, too, Bethany," Dex nodded to her. Then he turned back to Joe. "You're lucky. Your mama is having a good day. She might not remember it tomorrow, but today, she's here to see her boy get married," Dex confided.

He turned to lead the way inside.

"Oh, the daisies!" Joe exclaimed, dropping Bethany's hand and running back to the car to grab the flowers he'd bought for his mama.

———————

Bethany chuckled and grinned, watching him run. Dex watched her. Her face lit up watching Joe. He smiled and opened the door. "Ladies first," he said, motioning for her to enter.

"Oh, thank you," she said, stepping inside.

"I won't ask how you met," he said, coming in behind her. "He'll tell me when he's ready. But...I can tell you've put something right that was wrong. He's like his old self."

"Is he different?" she pondered. "He seems the same since I met him."

Dex grinned. "Then it was the meeting that fixed it."

Inside the front door of Mr. Morgan's house, they stood in a foyer, much like in Ravens' Roost, though Mr. Morgan's foyer was a bit larger. To the left was the formal living room behind a set of glass-paned French doors. To the right was an archway that opened into the dining room. A grand staircase was directly in front of the door. Another set of French doors opened down a short passageway by the stairs. Dex pointed to those doors. "That's Mr. Morgan's office."

The door opened behind them, and Joe came in, holding the flowers.

"Ready?" he asked, holding his hand out to Bethany.

She nodded. Again, she smiled. And Joe let out a breath. He looked happy. Thank God. Dex felt a wave of relief. He'd worried half the night, but seeing them together...whatever the story was...he approved.

She placed her hand in Joe's, and they walked together

toward that second set of French doors, Dex walking behind them.

———————

Bethany reached out to open the French doors and was greeted by a small crowd comprised of their children, Jillian and her daughter, an older white-haired, portly man of color she presumed was Jessup Lawson, Dex's grandfather, Jess's namesake, and a pretty woman, probably in her late fifties. She had shoulder-length fiery red hair pulled back in a loose ponytail, big violet-blue eyes, and a creamy complexion.

Joe held out the daisies, a bouquet of bright pink and deep purple Gerber daisies. "Hi, Mama," he said. She smiled and took the flowers.

"How lovely! Is it my birthday? No. That's not right," she said, her smile turning to a frown.

"No. It's my wedding, Mama," he said. "This is your daughter-in-law, Bethany." He motioned toward Bethany.

Bethany stepped forward. "Hello, Mrs. Gardner. I'm so pleased to meet you."

His stepmother looked Bethany up and down, struggling to comprehend, but as she looked at the white dress and roses, something clicked. "Oh, aren't you such a pretty bride? Don't call me that. You call me Mama, ya hear?"

"Um. Yes...Mama," Bethany replied.

Mr. Morgan stood from his seat behind his large oak desk. "Shall we?"

And minutes later, Bethany was married, 18 months, 2 days, and 3 hours after becoming a widow at 27.

As the room burst into applause, Bethany blushed. "Um, would you all like to come back to Ravens' Roost for Thanksgiving leftovers? God knows, Joe made enough food to last a month!"

CHAPTER 8

Back at Ravens' Roost, Joe heated up the leftovers, and Mr. Morgan opened a bottle of champagne he had brought from his collection. They ate and toasted. Joe put on some music.

Bethany and Joe danced again. As he held her in his arms and they swayed to the music, he closed his eyes and thanked God he'd broken through to her. He noticed she was crying. He pulled her quietly into the bedroom.

"What's wrong?" he asked, sitting beside her on the side of the bed. She looked down and picked at the quilt that covered the bed.

"I'm just confused. How come I only remembered you in dreams? How come I remember two different realities?" She buried her head in her hand. "Why didn't you come back for me? After you healed, I mean," she cried softly.

"After I healed?" he asked, lifting her chin so she looked him in the eyes.

"Greg showed me a video where he stabbed you," she said nervously. "I… I saw you die."

Joe heaved a heavy sigh and shook his head. "I've never been stabbed, Bethy. I showed up at your house like we planned. You told me to leave. You told me it was a mistake and that you wanted to stay. You said you talked to Greg, and he forgave you for cheating. I should leave. So, I did. I tried to call you a few times. You…took a restraining order out against me."

"I did?" she asked. She grabbed her head. "Oh, I'm

sorry, Joe. I think…What you say sounds true to me, but it's not what I remember. Greg…he messed with my sanity and my memory. How about Meghan? Why didn't you fight for Meghan?"

"I swear to God, Baby. I didn't know she existed until I saw her sleeping in the backseat of that Olds," he assured. "I would have fought for her if I'd known. I thought…you didn't love me."

"I remember us…now…but I also remember what I thought was real…Greg and I spending those two weeks together, his not leaving me. My fighting with him. My getting the tattoo and belly button stud when I got drunk…And there was a drunken affair with a man I can't picture… that resulted in Meghan…and the guilt I've felt…that still all feels real, too. But then I don't remember what you say happened, and I do remember the video of you dying…and I think, I'm losing my mind." Bethany wiped her eyes. "But I swear. In every version of my memory, I've never loved anyone but you. In the version I thought was real, I dreamed of you. I'll love you…for forever."

He smiled gently, squeezing her hand. "What did Greg do to you, Bethy?"

She shook her head and shivered. "Not today. Okay? Today, I just want to be happy that I remembered what I've been trying to remember for 5 years and that I have you again. Can we do that?" she whispered.

Joe nodded and kissed her on the lips ever so softly.

Duke barked at them.

Bethany looked hard at the dog and gasped. "My sweet baby!" she exclaimed. "I remember you, too. The kid, giving away puppies…in the town."

Joe nodded. "Yeah, you picked him out. I went back

to get him, even though you turned me away." Duke turned around in a circle and barked again, facing the bedroom door. Joe laughed. "And I think he needs to go out. I'm just going to take Duke for a quick walk."

She refused to let go of his hand. "I'll come with you."

He nodded. "It's a little chilly outside. Put on a sweater."

"Is it? I don't think I have anything…"

"Hold on," he said, standing. He gently pulled his hand free and walked over to the closet, pulling out a wool cardigan. "Here, put this on." He held the sweater out to her, and she slipped it on, pushing the sleeves up so her hands were able to break free. "Come on, Duke," he whistled. The dog came running to him. He reached down, scratched behind Duke's ears, and slipped the leash on. He offered his arm, and Bethany took it, lacing her arm through his as they walked out.

As the door closed behind them, she heard Jillian's laughter. "I don't think they'd notice if we left."

Dex's laughter followed. "You're right."

They walked down the driveway and down the street toward another old farmhouse, smaller, abandoned. "That was Elmer Pruce's property. There's an old gravel pit out back and down that lane," he said, pointing before they turned around and headed back.

Duke pulled hard on the leash as a car pulled into the driveway. Bethany frowned as Rosalea Benson climbed out of the car. Duke barked ferociously. And her late husband's mother jumped back, leaning against the rental car.

"Good boy," Bethany whispered, grabbing his collar and petting his head. He sat and thumped his tail on the ground, his tongue lolling out over his canines.

"Put that monster in a cage!" Rosalea yelled.

"If only I could," Bethany mumbled. "Duke's on a leash," she said, louder so Rosalea could hear. "What do you want?"

Rosalea huffed and took a tentative step forward. "I've come to take you all home."

"We are home," Bethany countered. "You wasted a trip."

Rosalea glared at Joe. "You," she said, wrinkling her nose in disgust.

Joe smiled at Bethany encouragingly.

"He's my husband. This is our property. Please get off it," Bethany said bravely. Joe winked at her. Her heart soared.

"Of course, you'd run right to him, you skanky little bitch," Rosalea hissed.

"I was forced to marry Greg. I was forced to stay with Greg. This is my life, and I get to choose with whom I spend it. You don't get to choose. I don't belong to you. I never have. My kids don't belong to you. And this house belongs to me. I get to say who can come in. You are not welcome," Bethany declared nervously, but with her chin held high. A gust of wind howled through the trees, shaking the remaining brown leaves that cascaded to the ground around them.

"This property belongs to me!" Rosalea screamed. "Greg's will left everything to me."

"This property didn't belong to Greg!" Bethany countered. "I was listed as Melanie Horton's sole heir. Not Greg. This is my property. Get off."

A sheriff's car pulled in. Rosalea smiled wickedly. "We'll see about that. I thought you'd be stubborn, so I called the Sheriff before I arrived. I have Greg's will with me," she said, pulling a document out of her Louboutin tote, hanging on her arm.

The deputy got out of the car and said, "Can you put Duke inside, Joe?" Rosalea Benson's face fell a little.

"Sure, Mike," Joe said. "Come on, Duke." He took Duke back to the door, took off the leash, and sent him back inside the house. Dex appeared on the porch, followed by Mr. Morgan.

Mike, the deputy, tipped his hat to the old man. "Hello, Mr. Morgan," he said respectfully. "Dex."

"What's going on, Mike?" Mr. Morgan inquired, removing his glasses and cleaning the lenses with his handkerchief.

"This lady claims Mrs. Benson here is trespassing on her property."

"Mrs. Benson is trespassing," Bethany said firmly, nodding at Rosalea. "I'm Mrs. Gardner."

Mike looked at Joe questioningly. Joe nodded, holding up his ring finger, revealing the wedding band.

"Um. I don't know what this lady is thinking," Mr. Morgan said, "but my Mellie left this property to Bethany Benson, now Gardner. I have all the documentation in my briefcase if you'd like to come in."

Mike walked to the front door. Rosalea moved to follow.

"Not you," Joe said, stopping her.

"Duke?" Mike asked.

"Shut up in the other room," Dex answered.

Mike walked inside. Bethany stood confidently on Joe's arm. Rosalea tapped her foot impatiently while they waited.

———

Mike wondered what the hell was going on. Joe was married? To some girl nobody had ever heard of? Joe was his oldest friend. They'd known each other their entire lives. He considered Joe a brother. But he had never heard of Bethany Benson.

He knew of Rosalea, of course...and Greg. Greg was a jerk from what he'd heard. Older than them by 8 years or so, Greg had never been in their group of friends. Plus, he wasn't really a local. Rosalea had been. She had grown up Sally Rose Harris before she married a man from Connecticut and moved away. Greg was only ever around these parts on rare holidays and maybe for a week in the summer. But it was enough to make the kids in the neighborhood dislike him.

Mike could remember when he was 10, and Greg Benson had visited his grandfather, Al Harris. Naomi and Kristin Johnson were riding their bikes past the Pooles' farmhouse where Mike grew up when Greg Benson drove past in his Porsche 911, forcing the girls into the ditch. He swerved to miss them and hit a bush. It barely scratched the paint. But he had both girls in tears.

He stepped through the door of Ravens' Roost and stopped dead in his tracks. He locked eyes with Jillian. Her spine stiffened. She waved awkwardly. God, she was pretty in her purple dress. He always loved her in purple. It was a bewitching color on her.

"Hi, Mike!" Missy exclaimed, rushing forward and hugging him.

"Hey, there, Miss," he said, hugging the girl briefly before turning and following Mr. Morgan into the dining room, ignoring Jillian. It killed him to ignore Jillian. But he'd never make it out if he didn't.

A little girl skipped past him and grabbed Dex Lawson's hand.

"How's Kenny?" Dex inquired after Mike's brother.

"Good. He's good," Mike replied. He looked down at the girl and barely contained his surprise. Holy cow. Bethany Benson was that girl! The girl from the Martha's Vineyard trip. Joe had fallen in love with Greg Benson's wife! And there was no way that child was anybody's other than Joe's…certainly not Greg's. The green eyes were a dead giveaway. He looked back up at Dex, who nodded wordlessly.

Mr. Morgan chuckled. "Don't act so shocked, gentlemen. You never really know what goes on in somebody's life. Trust me. That girl…she's been through hell. But she's going to make him happy. I know it." He picked up his briefcase off the floor by the console and set it on the dining room table. He clicked it open and withdrew several documents. He motioned Mike over. "Here's Melanie's will, Mike. She left everything to Bethany Benson with the stipulation that Greg Benson not be listed on the deed for 10 years after Melanie passes away. Of course, that is not an issue since he, too, has passed away. It makes no such stipulation regarding Joseph Gardner, however. And you know as well as I do that Melanie wanted to leave the property to him. He, however, insists that the property be deeded in Bethany's name alone. You and I both know he talked Melanie into this. Sally Rose has no claim to this property."

Mike examined the documents and handed them back to Mr. Morgan. He nodded. He headed back outside.

"This property was bequeathed and is deeded to Bethany Benson. She and Mr. Joseph Gardner were married earlier today, and he is a legal resident," he announced, glaring hard at Rosalea, whose mouth dropped.

"I'm calling my lawyer!" she screeched.

"Yes, ma'am. You can certainly do that…but from somewhere else. Mrs. Gardner asked you to leave her property."

Bethany crossed her arms and grinned. "Bye," she said sardonically.

"You're that Poole kid, aren't you? I remember you," Rosalea blustered. "You're his friend."

"Mr. Gardner is a friend," Mike concurred. "But are you suggesting I would not perform my duty? I assure you. Mrs. Gardner has the appropriate documentation."

Rosalea pulled her cell phone out of the tote. "George!" she yelled when her husband picked up. "Find me a hotel near this dump!" Another cold gust of wind came up suddenly. Oak leaves that lay scattered across the lawn rustled in the wind and took flight. The gust caught Rosalea's skirt and blew it up, Marilyn Monroe in *The Seven Year Itch* style. The sound of laughter seemed to ride on the wind around them. Rosalea, blushing at having her red Spanx revealed to the group, yelped and pushed her skirt down awkwardly.

She quickly climbed back into the rental, backed out past the squad car, and pulled away.

Joe looked at Mike. "Hungry? We have a ton of food."

"I...I'm happy for you...and I would love to...but...I shouldn't." Mike replied. "Congratulations, by the way. 'Bout time."

Joe nodded. "I understand. That's why I called Dex instead of you." Mike reached out and shook Joe's hand.

"Yeah, I figured that. Um...I gotta go...I...tell Missy goodbye for me." He hurried back to his squad car. He gripped the wheel until his knuckles were white. He closed his eyes and clenched his jaw. He just tried to breathe. "Oh, Jesus, Jillian," he sighed. She had a black eye. She had a fucking black eye.

———

Eventually, the day came to an end, and the new blended family found themselves alone and cleaning up from the festivities. As Joe washed dishes and Bethany dried, he was quiet. He handed her a plate and said, "I don't think Sally Rose will be easily dissuaded."

"Who?" Bethany asked.

"Sally Rose," he chuckled. "That's Rosalea Benson's given name."

Bethany sighed. "You're kidding? That's so... wholesome," she pondered. "And no. No, she won't be," she agreed.

"I think I should start replacin' the windows tomorrow," he said. "I found replacements out in the barn a while ago. They should fit in the existing sills, so we won't need a buildin' permit...and I gotta feelin' she'll try callin' CPS about the house bein' unfit to live in. I also put a call into my boss's brother. He has an HVAC business. We gotta buy a new furnace. He said he'd give us a good price and could come out tomorrow, too. Also, we should go to the grocery store. I bought for two, and five have been eatin' it. They check for things like that."

Bethany nodded. "All good ideas. I can go shopping tomorrow if you want to get started on the windows. The boys can stay and help you, and I can take Meghan with me. I'll help when I get back, but I need to do some laundry, too."

"We should think about getting a washer and dryer," he added. "One of those stackable sets would fit in the downstairs bathroom. It's a pain in the ass to go to the laundromat...and expensive."

"So are a washer and dryer," she replied.

"Hmmm. Yeah, but in the long run, it's the better value."

She was suddenly laughing. Hard.

"What?" he asked.

"We've been married for what? 8 hours?" she asked, nearly doubling over in laughter.

He laughed, too. "Okay. Point taken." Then he splashed her.

"Oh, dang! I forgot about the U-Haul trailer!" she exclaimed. "I'm supposed to turn it into the U-Haul place today!"

"Mason's Garage?" he asked.

"Yeah. Where is it?" she asked, wiping her hands.

"It's where I work," he grinned. "I'll see if my boss can come get it." He took out his phone and walked out of the room. He returned a minute later. "All good. He's on his way."

"Wow. Even if he is your boss, that's amazing. No one would be that nice in Connecticut," she pondered. "I'd be paying a penalty, and I'd have to get it there on my own."

"Well, this ain't Connecticut," he teased.

From the living room, *I Can't Help Falling in Love* started playing again. They both turned to look in that direction.

"Aren't the kids upstairs?" she asked, frowning.

"I thought so," he answered. "Okay, Alec. We'll shut up about mundane things. Should I kiss her again?"

The music got louder.

"Ahhhh!" she said as Joe grabbed her and kissed her. "Great," she said, placing her hand on his chest. "We have a matchmaking ghost!"

"In the words of my beautiful wife to my dog this afternoon...Good boy! I say we listen to the matchmaking ghost." He kissed her again.

Ryan and Jessup came running downstairs and into

the kitchen in time to witness the end of the kiss. "Really?" Ryan scoffed.

"What do you need?" Bethany asked him.

"Who gets the big bedroom downstairs?" he asked.

"What?"

"Jessup's in there now, but it's the biggest room," Ryan said.

"Oh. I hadn't thought. I...uh...we do. I'll move my stuff downstairs."

"Then who gets your room?" Jessup asked.

Joe snorted. "Meghan. Girls need more room."

A tiny "Yay!" erupted from the other room.

"You guys suck," Ryan announced. Then he playfully shoved his new stepbrother's arm. "Come on. I'll help you get your stuff."

"Okay," Jessup said. And they were gone like a shot. Joe chuckled at this turn of events.

"I better get my stuff out of my room before they start tossing it out into the hall," Bethany observed, stepping out of his embrace.

He grinned. "Bethy?" he called after her as she backed up to the doorway.

"Hmmm?" she asked, looking him in the eyes.

"Are we...Um...do I need clean sheets?"

"Oh. Yes," she replied, turning and walking out of the room.

He smiled and leaned back against the farmer's sink. Then he seemed to really grasp her answer, and he ran to his room to change the bedding.

———

At some point in the middle of the great bedroom swap, the doorbell rang as Bethany passed Jessup on the stairs, each with an armful of clothes. It was like a *Keystone Cops* episode as they raced around moving things. They were all laughing. The more they laughed, the faster they moved.

Duke started barking at the sound of the doorbell.

"Welcome to Chaos Central!" Bethany called, laughing, making her way past Jessup to get to the door. She adjusted the clothes in her arms and flipped on the exterior light as she opened the door. A man in gray coveralls and wearing a Mason's Garage baseball cap stood on the porch.

"G'evening," he said, looking up from his clipboard. "Um, are you Joe's…uh…"

"Wife," she finished. "Yes. Are you Mr. Mason?"

"Um…yes, ma'am. Norm Mason. Nice to meet you. I was…surprised…when Joe called. I didn't even know he was datin' anyone."

"Ah, well, it's been a whirlwind kind of thing," she offered.

"Oh. I see. Um…well, congratulations! Um, I dug out your paperwork on that trailer. Just sign here. I'll haul it back for you. Um…Joe around?"

She took the clipboard, adjusting her armload of clothing again. She signed where he indicated. "Joe!" she called.

"Yeah?" he called back from the bedroom they were about to share.

"Mr. Mason's looking for you!" she hollered. She smiled and handed the middle-aged man back the clipboard. Joe emerged from the back room. Meghan came running down the stairs. "Daddy!" she squealed with laughter. "Come see my new room!"

"In a minute, Meggy," Joe replied over his shoulder before turning his attention to the man at the door, who was gaping at the child.

"Hey," he said to Norm. "You need help?"

"Um…if ya don't mind," his employer requested. "Exactly when was this whirlwind?"

Joe followed Mr. Mason outside, and Bethany returned to transporting her clothes.

Within an hour, Bethany had finished and lay back on the bed in her new bedroom. "Whew," she said, closing her eyes.

She shivered as the room seemed to suddenly get cold, though it could just be that she had been working up a sweat and had suddenly stopped moving. "Brrr," she muttered, sitting up. "I think I need a hot bubble bath," she announced. "Alec! Stay out of the upstairs bathroom. And tell your friends," she said, climbing off the bed. She grabbed a nightgown, clean panties, and her robe.

Minutes later, she lowered herself into the tub full of hot, foamy water. She slipped in her earbuds and sang along to Taylor Swift.

———

Joe chuckled as he came back inside to hear Bethany singing from the bathroom upstairs. Otherwise, the house was quiet, the kids having finally gone to bed in the newly assigned quarters. He sat down on the sofa and turned on the TV…his from the trailer, as it was newer and bigger than Bethany's. He scrolled through the options on the guide, selecting a rerun of *The Mentalist,* in which the team investigated a haunted house. "See that, Alec? Nothing more than smoke and mirrors," he snickered.

"I wish," whispered a voice behind him. He jumped and looked around at the empty room and darkness from the foyer beyond. "She woke him."

"Well, that was creepy as hell," Joe said, shaking his head.

As the episode ended, Bethany emerged from the bath, pink-skinned and smelling like lavender. She sat beside him in her robe and set a bottle of lotion on the coffee table. She squirted some into her hand, rubbed her hands together briefly, and lifted one leg, putting her foot on the sofa and applying the lotion to her calf. Then, she repeated the process on the other leg.

Joe sat quietly, not sure whether to look or not. It was torturous. Her robe split and revealed her leg up to her…His breath caught. She smiled and took the tie out of her hair, which dropped like silken ribbons to her shoulders. Having finished her grooming, she suddenly moved, swinging one leg across his lap and turning to stand on her knees on the sofa, straddling his legs. She loosened the tie on her robe and let it fall open. The sheer white nightgown hung to her hips. The white satin thong straps rested low on her hips under the see-through material of the gown. He reached out and gently stroked the crease below the thong's waistband, where a butterfly alighted on a lollipop tattoo that was normally hidden beneath her clothing. He moved his hands to her hips and tugged them toward him as he buried his face in her chest. She lowered herself to his lap and wrapped her arms around his neck. He moved his hand up her side under the gown until he cupped her breast. He sucked on it through the sheer nightgown. She moaned in response.

He quickly grabbed her legs under the buttocks and stood lifting her with him. She wrapped her legs around his waist, and he carried her to the bedroom. "So, ya know, I plan on eating that lollipop," he whispered before he tossed her gently onto the bed.

CHAPTER 9

Bethany awoke to find Joe had already gotten up, showered, and was hard at work pulling the replacement windows out of the barn. She stretched and buried her face in his pillow, breathing in his delicious scent, a mixture of sandalwood and fresh-cut grass. She found she was smiling. She had never awakened smiling in her life.

The room was a little chilly, but the bed was warm and cozy, and the sun was streaming through the window. It was a beautiful, crisp autumn morning.

Gradually, she became aware of the sound of the television in the living room...*Disney Jr.* Meghan must be up. She could have slipped into her robe, but she grabbed Joe's discarded tee shirt from last night and slipped that on instead. She dug through her drawer in the bureau, finding a more practical pair of underwear, and pulled them on before slipping into a pair of sweatpants and going to the living room.

"Morning, Sweetheart," she said to her daughter, who was sitting on the floor in front of the TV, watching *Mickey's Clubhouse*. "Where are the boys?"

"Outside helping Daddy," she answered.

"Have you had breakfast?" she asked.

"I had cereal," the little girl answered.

"Okay then. I'm going to jump into the shower, and then you and I are going to the grocery store. So, go get dressed."

Bethany quickly showered and headed back to the bedroom to dress. She put on a bra but still chose to wear Joe's tee shirt, exchanging the sweatpants for Levis. She ran a brush through her hair and applied some lipstick, leaving the rest of her face clean. She pulled on some socks and put on her Keds. No need to dress up. She planned on working today. It would be a waste of makeup to apply it. Besides, her complexion was good and even. She didn't need much, anyway. She reached for her jacket but saw Joe's cardigan and took it instead. His USMC stocking cap lay on the dresser. She pulled it on and thought she looked kind of cute.

"Ready, Baby?" she called, emerging from the bedroom.

"Yes, Mommy," Meghan answered. Bethany looked at her. She was wearing her leotards and tutu...and had her sneakers on the wrong feet.

She swallowed her laugh. "Okay. You can wear the tutu if you want, but you still need at least leggings...and your shoes are backwards...but you did a good job! Go get some pants."

"Okay," the child said, giggling.

Having sorted out Meghan's wardrobe, the two of them headed outside. Bethany walked around the side of the house and waved to Joe. He looked up at her. "I'm going to the store!" she called.

He nodded and waved.

"Get your booster out of the Olds, Meg. We'll take the Cadillac. It's much nicer," she said, digging through her purse for the keys.

Joe had given her great directions, and she found the Food Lion easily enough. Of course, it was only one turn. Otherwise, it would have been a straight shot. She parked, noting she'd have to get the registration switched to her name soon as the license plate was handicap accessible. She, of course, ignored that and parked in a regular spot. She wanted to get her name changed first. She wanted nothing to do with Benson.

Exiting the car, she took Meg's hand, and they skipped together through the parking lot to the store's entrance. She grabbed a cart, sat Meghan in the seat, and started shopping. Not knowing the layout of the store, she started at one end and worked her way down each aisle.

"Were you a Marine? I don't think so!" a man grumbled as she passed him in the cereal aisle.

"I'm sorry?" she said, turning to address him.

He spun around, angrily. "I asked if you were a Marine!" he shouted.

She blinked at him, stunned.

"No," she said. Then she remembered she was wearing Joe's stocking cap.

"Of course, you weren't, or you'd know to remove your cover inside!" he said, moving toward her.

"Oh," she said, touching the hat. "It's my husband's cap. It's the first cap I found before leaving home. I didn't think it was part of his uniform or anything. Should I not be wearing it? He didn't say anything." She pulled it off and smoothed her hair.

He stopped and stared. "Who's your husband?" he grumbled.

"Joe Gardner," she answered.

"Joe? Joe got married?" he said, blinking back tears.

A woman rounded the endcap and rushed over. "Kenny, you can't go around yelling at people," she exclaimed. "I'm sorry. He...has a traumatic brain injury. He has mood swings and social anxiety."

"He's fine," Bethany assured her. "My husband's hat upset him, but I've taken it off."

"Joe got married," he repeated. "Pam…Joe got married."

"I'm sure you misunderstood, Kenny," she assured him.

"No, he understood. I married Joe Gardner… yesterday." The woman turned and stared at her with her mouth open. "Is there something wrong?" Bethany asked, looking around.

Pam shook her head. "Oh, no. I'm just…surprised. Joe and Kenny served together. I think Kenny just thought he'd be invited to something like that. Does Mike know?"

"Mike? Oh, Deputy Poole. Yes. I mean, it was kind of a spur of the moment, so there was just a civil ceremony. We haven't really talked about a reception or anything. Though Joe sure seems to know everybody around here…so maybe we should have something like that…"

A woman with a Food Lion badge walked by. Kenny grabbed her arm. "Joe got married," he said again.

"Yes. I know. He told me yesterday morning when he came in for flowers. Who told you, Kenny?" she asked.

He pointed to Bethany, who smiled and waved with her left hand. "Hi, I'm Bethany," she said.

The woman looked at Meghan and gasped. She grabbed Bethany, hugging her and then took her left hand and gazed at the rings. She kissed both of Bethany's cheeks. "I'm Bev Howard. I'm Esther's best friend. I've known Joe…well, since he was a tiny little thing. How'd you like the roses?"

"They're beautiful," Bethany beamed.

———

Joe finished installing the front window in Meg's new

room. One down. 7 to go before they finished the top floor. He figured he'd replace them all, even the ones that weren't broken since they were all in the barn. Melanie must have bought them sometime before she passed and had not had the chance to install them. Finding them had been a stroke of good luck.

He started down the ladder when one of the boys screamed bloody murder.

Ryan came running from the back of the house. "Joe! Come quick! Duke dug up a skull!"

"What?" he yelled, hurrying down the ladder and running after the boy.

Jess stood in the barn, holding onto Duke's collar, holding him back from the hole he'd just dug in the dirt floor under where Joe had taken the windows.

Had the dog found an animal's skeletal remains? He stepped closer and gasped, "What the…?"

It was indeed a skull…a human one…with a bullet hole in the frontal bone, the bullet still inside the cavity behind the hole.

He took out his phone and made a call. "Mike? My dog just dug up a skull in the barn at Ravens' Roost. How the hell do I know? It's a fucking skull. The bullet inside it looks pretty modern. Maybe a .45 caliber. Yeah. I'll put him inside. See ya in a few." He disconnected and nodded at Jess. "Take Duke inside." He shivered as a cold breeze blew through the barn.

"She woke him…" echoed in his brain.

———

Bethany pulled into the driveway and exclaimed, "What on Earth?"

There were two Westmoreland County cruisers and

three Virginia State Police Cruisers in her driveway. A State trooper walked over. "You'll need to move along, Ma'am," he said when she lowered her window.

"This is my house," she replied. "I have groceries… and…ice cream…" she added.

"Oh. Of course. Just stay away from the back," he said.

"What happened?" she asked anxiously.

"Your dog dug up human remains. That's all I know," he offered.

"He did what? Oh, my God!" she gasped.

"Uh, oh," Meghan said from the backseat. "That's the bad man."

"What? Who?" Bethany sputtered, looking over her shoulder at her child.

"I don't know. Alec just says there's a bad man in the barn. And I should not go out there."

"Okay. Creepy," Bethany said. She wanted to dismiss it as an overactive imagination. But again, she wondered, if Alec was warm, what was cold?

She got the groceries unloaded from the trunk and put Meghan in front of the TV as she put everything away. She was a nervous wreck. The boys had been sent back to the house but watched attentively from the window in Ryan's room, which looked out toward the barn. She stopped every so often to look out the back kitchen window but couldn't see anything.

Finally, two state police carried a body bag out of the barn, and the police began to disperse. Joe and Mike eventually came into the house through the back kitchen door.

Bethany anxiously threw herself into Joe's arms. "What is it? What happened?" she asked, near tears.

He pulled her close. "It's alright, Bethy. Duke unearthed

a skeleton buried in the barn. I pulled out all the new windows this morning and put the pallet they were stored on in the debris pile. Duke took the opportunity to dig in the freshly uncovered dirt. Whoever it was, he's been out there a long time. There looks to be the remnants of an Army uniform... probably post WWII, but certainly not current. The pallet had a shipping ticket attached dated 1969...so he was probably out there since at least that far back."

"Oh," Bethany sighed in relief. "I mean...it's super creepy and disturbing, but at least it isn't a recent murder where a killer is lurking around our barn."

"True, but it was probably murder," Mike said cautiously.

"Huh?"

"He was shot in the head. The gun was buried with him. A Colt M1911A1. The bullet was still inside the skull," he added.

"Well, thanks for the nightmares," she said, shaking her head.

"I'll protect you," Joe teased, squeezing her waist.

She shivered despite his embrace.

"Cold?" he asked. "I'll stoke the fire. Alan Mason should be here shortly about the furnace."

CHAPTER 10

The rest of the weekend passed as planned. Alan Mason arrived shortly after the police left. Over the rest of the day and the next, he installed a working furnace, and by Sunday evening, they were no longer depending upon the wood stove for heat. Mike helped Joe install the windows. They managed to replace all the broken ones and made plans to start working on the ones that were not broken the next weekend.

Bethany noticed Christmas decorations starting to appear in the community and mentioned it to Joe. He told her he wanted to finish installing the windows first but that he would be happy to put up lights once he had done that. Secretly, he also wanted to start stripping the remaining paint and prepping to paint the exterior before it got too cold. He wanted to replace the porch roof in the spring and wanted the exterior to look more inhabitable before starting that project.

Monday morning, he awoke to the sound of rain on the metal roof. Feeling slightly feverish, he groaned and turned over instead of getting up as he normally would. He shivered uncontrollably and pulled the covers up around his neck.

Bethany felt his forehead and exclaimed, "Joe! You're burning up." She insisted upon taking his temperature. When the thermometer read 102.4 degrees, she ordered him to stay in bed. He had no will to argue. He called off work at the garage.

Before fleeing Connecticut, Bethany had registered Ryan for school in Westmoreland County, and his bus stop was at the end of the driveway. Jess's was technically at the veterinary clinic up the road across from Jillian's with Missy, but since it was the same bus, he'd catch it with Ryan. Bethany would contact the school about the change of address after she got to work. Mr. Morgan had insisted that she bring Meghan with her, so after she and Meg left, Joe was alone with Duke in the house.

He slept on and off most of the morning. The rain continued, and he had to admit the pitter-patter on the metal roof was somewhat comforting.

Bethany had made him oatmeal, but he had no appetite, and it grew cold as he slept.

At around 11 am, his fever broke, and his sleep became more fitful. He dreamt of a dark presence rising out of the grave in the barn. The sense of evil was overwhelming. There had been no smell, the body having long since decayed, but in the dream, the smell of death hung heavy in the barn. There was no definable horror…no monster…no blood…no gore… just the feeling of terror. It was so pervasive it woke him in a panic.

He sat up and peered around the bedroom. Duke lifted his head and wagged his tail. Joe caught his breath, noticing the quiet of the house. He looked at the cold oatmeal on the nightstand as his stomach rumbled.

"Yuck," he complained, climbing out of the bed and picking up the bowl. He wrapped the blanket folded at the bottom of the bed around his shoulders and shuffled to the kitchen. He scraped the oatmeal into the trash and put the bowl into the sink. He'd made turkey noodle soup the night before with the last of the turkey leftovers. He ladled out a serving and heated it up in the microwave. He stared out the window at the barn while he waited for the soup. The feeling of terror was still there. His heartbeat quickened, and his breathing became more shallow.

"Calm down. Just a dream," he said out loud. The lights flickered, and the kitchen suddenly felt ice cold. "What the hell? Alan just installed the furnace!" he said, pulling the blanket around him tighter.

"He's getting stronger," a voice whispered. Joe jumped and spun around. Nothing. Nobody. He must be hallucinating. He was sick. He was hearing things.

The room slowly warmed, and the microwave beeped. He sniffed, his nose feeling suddenly congested. He grabbed his soup and a box of tissues. He took them to the living room and put them on the coffee table. He shuffled to the bathroom, grabbing the trash can, and brought it back to the sofa. He picked up the TV remote, turned on the TV, and browsed through the options on the guide, settling on *The Maltese Falcon*. He ate his soup, blew his nose, and lay down on the sofa. The trash can quickly filled with tissues. He felt awful. His throat started to hurt, too.

The movie had nearly ended when the doorbell rang. He groaned and sat up. The movement made his head hurt. He pulled himself up and shuffled to the door. The rain had finally stopped, but it was still a gray, dismal day. He opened it to Rosalea Benson and a well-dressed man, in his mid-fifties. The man was wearing Italian shoes that he nervously wiped to get rid of the mud.

"Huh," Joe huffed. "What do you want?"

"I told you. I'm here to take my family home. Where are they?" Rosalea demanded, pushing her way inside. Joe didn't have the strength to hold her off. So, he just went back to the sofa and blew his nose again.

"They're not home," he said when Rosalea returned

from searching throughout the house, except for his and Bethany's room. Rosalea grimaced and reached for the door to the bedroom. "I wouldn't go in there if I were you," he warned.

Rosalea ignored him and shoved the door open. Duke barked and lunged, backing her into a corner.

"I warned you," Joe said, coughing.

"Call off this beast," Rosalea demanded.

"Duke! Heel," he said, and Duke came over and sat beside him.

"Where are they?" Rosalea demanded again.

He sighed. "Ryan is at school. Bethy took Meghan with her to work."

"Work? Bethany has never had a job in her life," Rosalea scoffed.

"Well, she has one now. Now go away before I sneeze on you," he retorted.

"Get in here. Take pictures. I want all this documented!" Rosalea demanded of the man.

He stepped inside and gazed around. "What exactly do you want me to document?" he asked. "A clean house? A well-behaved dog? A man with a cold disposing of his tissues in a trash can? A woman with a job? A child in school...on a school day?"

Joe laughed.

"They're living in squalor!" she insisted.

"Squalor: extremely dirty, as relating to poverty or neglect. The house is clean. We aren't wealthy. I am a mechanic and a farmer. Bethy, as you pointed out, has her first job ever. But together, we have some savings and two incomes. The house needs restoring, but we have started doing that. The furniture is old but in good condition. The children are well-fed, clean, and loved. There is no squalor here. Go away," Joe said, coughing again.

"I'll have you know; I have served on our school board and on our town council for 32 years. I am a pillar of our community! You act so superior. What have you ever done to serve your community?"

"I don't know. I was a Marine. I was deployed to Afghanistan twice. I was awarded the Distinguished Service Medal and a Purple Heart. I was given an honorable discharge due to my mother's health with a rank of Master Gunnery Sergeant. Does that count as 'serving'?" he asked, sarcasm dripping.

"Are there guns in this house?" she demanded, the idea apparently suddenly occurring to her.

"There is a gun rack in our bedroom. It is locked. There are two shotguns and a hunting rifle…a real hunting rifle, not an AK-47. My service weapon is kept in a gun safe, with a biometric lock, also in our bedroom. My son has an air rifle. And I think Ryan might have a super soaker."

"Mrs. Benson…you also have guns in your home," the man whispered.

"If he's a lawyer, he really sucks at it," Joe pointed out, shaking his head. "We also have a lawyer. He's been practicing for 54 years and is a Professor Emeritus of law at William and Mary. He doesn't suck at it."

———————

Bethany, meanwhile, was settling in at Mr. Morgan's office. While his office was enclosed behind French doors, her workspace was tucked in neatly just opposite the doors in the foyer, in a nook under the stairs. While her desk was not visible from the entrance, the area was still well-lit and pleasant. She would be acting as receptionist and secretary.

Mr. Morgan's files were upstairs in what had once been a bedroom. Mrs. Smith, who had previously held this job for nearly 35 years, had become less fastidious in filing over the years. This room was daunting and decidedly less pleasant. After acquainting herself with the phone and computer and setting Meghan up on the sun porch with her toys and *Disney Jr.* on the television out there, she transferred all incoming calls to the file room and headed upstairs to tackle cleaning up the mess Mrs. Smith had left.

In one stack, she found a previous version of Melanie Horton's will. Curious, she skimmed it. Melanie had planned to leave everything to…Joseph Alexander Gardner. She stared at it for a moment. Had Joe asked Melanie to change her will? Was it his plan to get her here all along? She smiled, a warm feeling spread throughout her body, starting in her chest. Joe really hadn't given up on her, even after years of not hearing from her. He really did still love her and think of her.

Unsurprisingly, she found a great many of Mr. Morgan's personal documents mixed in with his legal files. She found a large box and put the personal items in there while filing the law office's records appropriately. By noon, she had made a decent dent in the mess. She picked up a stack, thinking it would be the last she did today, planning to go back to her desk after lunch and have Mr. Morgan show her how to schedule appointments and court dates.

Halfway down the stack, she found a journal with a leather binding, the name Margaret Ann Gardner embossed in gold at the bottom. She flipped through it, making certain no wayward papers had made their way between the pages. Finding none, she started to put it into the box, but then she thought better of it. This appeared to be a diary written by Mr. Morgan's late wife. He might want to put it somewhere now, not when she finished filling the box.

She checked her watch and abandoned the rest of the stack. She transferred the calls back to her desk, grabbed the diary, and descended the stairs. Mr. Morgan was on the phone in his office with the French doors closed when she got to her desk, a sign he was speaking with a client. She set the diary on her desk and went to the kitchen.

She made a fresh pot of coffee and took the turkey noodle soup she had brought from home out of the refrigerator. She heated the large bowl in the microwave and set the table before calling Meghan in off the sun porch and knocking on the French doors.

He waved her inside. She pushed open the door and waited for him to hang up the phone. "Joe made turkey noodle soup yesterday, Mr. Morgan. I have some ready for us for lunch," she said, smiling.

"Ah, bless you, Dear Heart. Yes, I am a bit peckish. Thank you, kindly." He stood and stretched and followed her to the kitchen. "It smells delicious," he noted. "Joe really is quite the cook."

"Ha! Good thing. I'm only mediocre. In Connecticut, well…the cook did the cooking. Joe's a better cook than she is, to be honest. I usually didn't much care for what she made. But Greg liked it," she said, pulling out a chair. She lifted Meghan and sat her in it before pushing it back in.

"Begging your pardon, Bethany, but you don't seem to have been very happy in Connecticut," he said, taking a seat.

"No. I wasn't. Greg was a monster. His mother…isn't much better. His father, George…was okay. But he's spineless. He won't stand up to Rosalea. Renee's just like her mother. I never would have believed I could leave like I did. It was… an escape. I think the Bensons…all of them…tried to break me. But in the end, I found I am not so easily broken," she answered, smiling. She sat down and picked up her spoon. "Joe's shown me more love and compassion than anyone else ever has in my lifetime. And you...I love you, Mr. Morgan. I feel like I finally have a father. I'm sorry. Maybe I shouldn't have said that." She offered him her napkin as he teared up at her words.

"I'm old enough to be your grandfather, Child," he laughed.

"Okay. Grandfather, then," she chuckled, touching his hand.

There was a knock on the back door. "Ah," Mr. Morgan said. "There she is!"

"Who?" Bethany asked, rising to open the door.

"Meghan's new best friend," he answered cryptically.

Bethany opened the door to a middle-aged woman and a little girl about Meghan's age. "Oh, hi there!" the woman said. She smiled and reached out her hand. "You must be Bethany. I'm Helen Madison from down the street. And this is my granddaughter, Kelly. Fil asked us to stop by at lunchtime to introduce ourselves." Bethany found her hand being clasped in both of Helen's and shaken.

Helen was a hoot. She had big hair that matched her big personality. She also wore a ring on every finger, big hoop earrings, a fake tan, bright orange lipstick, blue eye shadow, a short mink jacket, a short tight black skirt, and knee-high black go-go boots.

Kelly grinned and giggled. Meghan was out of her chair like a shot. "Hi, wanna play Barbies?" she asked.

"After you eat!" Bethany demanded, pointing at the chair. Then, turning back to Mr. Morgan's neighbor, she added, "Please come in. Have you eaten? I brought some turkey noodle soup my husband made. There's plenty." She retrieved two more bowls and spoons and served up some of the soup for the guests.

After they ate, the girls ran off to play, and Bethany poured out three cups of coffee and cleaned up the kitchen.

She liked Helen. She found herself laughing. Though their styles were different, and she was older, Helen reminded Bethany of Jillian in that both women were bodacious. She wanted to be just like them.

Helen finished her coffee and said, "I am raisin' Kelly. My son went to Tennessee and left her with Beau and me. We own the dairy farm up the road. I stay home with Kelly, and I'd be happy to be your babysitter while you work. I know you're just startin' out. I would only charge ya $40 a day, if you're interested. I don't really need the money, but I'd want to charge somethin' for my time, you know."

"Wow. That's really nice. I'd have to discuss it with my husband first. Would that be okay?" Bethany asked. Kelly and Helen left soon after lunch.

Joe was on her mind when the doorbell rang. She ran to the front door. It had started pouring rain again while they had been eating, and it was pouring as she opened the door to a miserable and soaked Joe Gardner. "Oh, Honey!" she exclaimed, pulling him inside, where he dripped on the floormat. She felt his forehead. "You're still feverish. What are you doing out of bed?"

He sneezed into his elbow. Then he pulled a document out from under his coat.

"I'b bend serbed," he said. "I'b sir you will be too when you ge' hobe."

"Here, take off this wet coat and those wet shoes and socks. Mr. Morgan, can we borrow some clean socks?" she called. She peeled the coat off him and hung it on the rack. "Shoes and socks," she repeated, pointing at his feet.

"If I bend ober, my head will exblode," he complained.

She shook her head and knelt, tapped his right leg, and said, "Lift." He did as she said, and she pulled off his boot and wet sock. "Okay. Other one." They repeated the process.

"Tanks, Mom," he teased, almost smiling.

She led him into the living room and had him sit on the sofa. She wrapped a blanket off the back of the sofa around him. "Stay here. Don't sneeze on anything. I have a face mask in my purse. We don't need to give this to Mr. Morgan."

He nodded. She ran back to her desk and dug through her purse, finding the face mask. Mr. Morgan appeared at her desk, holding clean socks. "Oh, thanks," she said. "Joe's sick. I wrapped that quilt on your sofa around him. I'll take it home to wash it." She grabbed the socks and mask and ran back to the living room.

"Here, put this on," she said, handing him the pink mask. She knelt again. "Foot," she said. He lifted one foot, then the other, as she put on the socks. "What if you have Covid?" she admonished him.

"Not Cobid. I took a test. Negatibe. Flu," he asserted. He grabbed her hand as she stood. "I feel like crab."

"You look like crap," she chuckled.

"I'mba sorry, Baby," he moaned.

"For what?"

"I'd reawy like to kiss you, but I don't want to make you sick, too."

She patted his hand. "You have the rest of our lives to kiss me. We can wait a few days," she whispered. "I'd really like to kiss you, too, but no offense, you're kind of...runny... right now."

He laughed so hard he started coughing.

Filmore read through the summons and shook his head. "Well, they are calling you as a witness for the plaintiff in a request for full custody, alleging Bethany is unfit."

"Day're nuts," Joe croaked in response.

"Can they compel my husband to testify against me?" Bethany asked.

"In Virginia, yes. 'Virginia law provides that spouses may be compelled to testify for or against each other in all civil actions.'[1] He can't be forced to disclose confidential correspondence, but he can be made to testify as to your fitness."

Poor Bethany buried her face in her hands.

"Bethy...you're nob unfib," Joe insisted.

"What do we do?" she asked, looking up at Filmore. He hadn't counted on the Bensons being this ruthless.

"They can't compel him to testify against *himself*," he suggested after a moment. "Initiate the adoption process. If he is a legal parent, they'd have to sue him for custody as well."

They stared at him for a moment.

"He is Meghan's father," Bethany told Mr. Morgan.

"Pardon?" the older man asked, blinking.

"Joe is Meghan's biological father. We had an affair...5 years ago," she repeated.

"Yes, Dear Girl. I think everybody knows that. Is he listed as her father on her birth certificate? Has he paid child support?" Mr. Morgan asked, picking up a pen and taking notes.

"I didden know she existed until free days ago," Joe

---

1 https://wblaws.com

answered.

"I see. Well, we'll have to file for a revised birth certificate, for which we should certify paternity...DNA test would be the way to go. That certainly helps with Meghan. There's still Ryan, though, and the affair...hurts."

"I'mbe willin', but he has to want it. I won't force 'im. And if I adopb Ryan, Bethy should adopb Jess. Noboby shou be left out," Joe said finally.

Filmore nodded. "Understood. Uncontested adoption is generally an easy process. I can pretty much guarantee any judge in this case is going to issue an Order of Reference, though, due to your recent marriage. Basically, that means the Department of Social Services would be required to assess the home and adoptive parent and issue a 60-day report. That means adoption is going to take several months. But should you decide to go this route, I can file a continuance at the custody hearing on the grounds of pending adoption. Go home. Talk to the kids. But make up your minds quickly. The quicker, the better."

They both nodded.

"I'd suggest taking Helen up on her offer for childcare as well. The more ducks you have in a row, the more your fitness is apparent," he added.

"Hewen? What offer?" Joe asked.

"Helen Madison offered to watch Meghan during the workday for $40 a day. I told her I needed to discuss it with you," Bethany told him.

"Oh. I know Hewen. She's good peeble. I tink it's a good idea," he said, nodding.

"I'll tell her yes, then," she agreed. She paused for a moment. "How's the skeleton being found in the barn going to affect all this?" she asked.

"Par...pardon?" Filmore sputtered.

"Duke dug up skeletal human remains in the barn yesterday after Joe pulled out the replacement windows that he found out there. It looks like a murder victim, but it had been out there since probably the late 1960s," she answered.

He felt the blood drain from his face. He clasped his chest.

"Mr. Morgan!" she gasped, standing and grabbing him to keep him from falling out of his chair. "Are you alright? Do you need help?"

He steadied himself. "Oh, no. I'm fine, Dear Heart... Just shocked. God! What did they do? What did they do?"

She sat back down. "I forgot for a minute. Your late wife grew up at Ravens' Roost, and Melanie was your stepdaughter. I shouldn't have sprung that on you like that. I'm so sorry."

"It's alright. Really. In answer to your question, it shouldn't be relevant, but your mother-in-law is incorrigible. Just be honest if it comes up. Maggie kept journals. You should probably read through them at that time period to see if she can...explain...The more you know..."

"Oh...I found one this morning in the file room. It's on my desk. I meant to give it to you thinking it might be special..." Bethany told him.

"Yes. Good. Take it home. Read it...but please bring it back," he pleaded.

Mr. Morgan also suggested that Bethany sign up for her GED online. He even offered to pay for the coursework and test as a benefit of her employment, emphasizing that she could start working toward an associate's degree at Rappahannock Community College as early as next semester if she could obtain her high school equivalency within a month's time. He suggested getting her GED and working toward a degree while gainfully employed would also look good to any judge.

Having given them both a lot to think about, he let Bethany leave early. He also told her to come in late the next day, that she should take the morning to change her name, get her Virginia driver's license, and register the Caddy in her name.

CHAPTER 11

On the way home, with her following Joe, they stopped at Madison's dairy farm. Helen came out to greet them.

"Holy crap!" she exclaimed. "Your husband is Joe! Oh, my God!" She pulled out her phone and called her husband. "Where are ya, Beau? Well, get over to the house. You'll never guess!"

Moments later, a man emerged from a nearby barn. "What, Woman?" he yelled teasingly.

She danced a sort of jig and yelled, "Joe Gardner got married!"

Bethany laughed as Joe wrapped his arm around her waist. She whispered, "This seems to be big news around here."

"Hmmm," he affirmed through the pink mask. "Mos peeble had dismissed me as a loss cause, I tink."

"I didn't know I was getting Oak Grove's most eligible bachelor," she giggled.

"Choo should hab. I eben got choo roses," he said, sniffing.

"Oh, Honey. You sound awful. Do you want me to stop at the Stop In and get you some cold and flu medicine?"

"Ah, Baby, dat would be grape," he said, laying his head on hers. "Don't come too cose, Beau. I'mba sick as a dog," he said as Helen's husband approached.

"I coulda warned ya marriage makes you sick," Beau teased, laughing at his own joke.

"Mind yourself," Helen said, smacking him on the arm. "I'm gonna babysit their little girl. She's Kelly's age. Bethany is workin' for Fil."

"Well, that sounds good," Beau said. "Congratulations to you both. We'll have to have a celebration at the VFW soon. Poor Kenny must be beside himself not being part of the wedding."

"Oh, I met Kenny. He was quite upset. I forgot what with…" Bethany said to Joe. He nodded.

"Sure. I gotta get rib of dis firs, dough," Joe agreed.

The couple wished them well, and they left. Bethany stopped at the Stop In while Joe continued on home. She got two boxes of chicken and some sides as well as the cold and flu remedy because she didn't want Joe to feel he had to cook, and she lacked confidence in her skills without him just yet. She let Meghan pick out a candy bar. She smiled wickedly, grabbing a cherry lollipop for Joe.

"Hey, Girl," Jillian greeted her as she placed the items on the counter. "What on earth was goin' on at your place yesterday? Kristin Johnson figure out she lost her chance with Joe?"

"What? Who's Kristin Johnson?"

"Oh, just a skank who's been sniffin' around that boy for years. Oh…and she's my stepsister. So, if not her, what happened?"

"Call me tonight, and I'll tell you. I'd ask you to stop by, but Joe's sick," she said, smiling. "And you can tell me more about Kristin."

Jillian laughed heartily. "Sure thing, Doll. I'll talk to ya later. Tell Joe to feel better. You want your lollipop, Sweetheart?" She started to hand it to Meghan.

"No. That's for Joe," Bethany said, blushing. "The

Snickers is for Meghan."

"Oh, there's a story there from that blush," Jillian said, winking and throwing the lollipop into the bag.

Bethany had plenty of time before Ryan and Jessup's bus would drop them off. Joe was already asleep on the sofa when she walked in the door. She put the chicken in the oven at 200 degrees to keep warm and got Joe a bottle of water from the fridge and two of the cold and flu relief capsules. She stuck the lollipop into her jean pocket and went into the living room. She sat on the edge of the sofa by his knees and gave his hip a quick shake.

He opened his eyes.

"Here, Honey. Take this," she said, handing him the capsules and water. He sat up on his elbow and took the medicine.

"I just got some chicken for dinner," she said, as he lay back.

"Dat's okay. I'mba not hungwy, anyway," he sniffed.

"You should go to bed," she suggested, feeling his head again. "You're still warm."

"No. I'wl slweep out here. Choo tabe da bed. I pulled da sheets offb before I went out. Choo might wanna let Duke out."

She smiled coyly. She pulled the lollipop out of her pocket and held it up. "I got you this to hold you over," she said suggestively.

"Oh...Oh, my God," he sputtered, laughing and coughing. "I'wl neber be able to go true a bank drive-true abin...wibout...choo know." He took the lollipop from her and opened it, popping it into his mouth. "I like da ober one bedder."

Joe was soon sound asleep. She let Duke out and

put clean sheets on the bed. She stared at the growing pile of laundry in the hamper that was starting to overflow and thought Joe was right about needing a washer and dryer. She grabbed clean pajama bottoms and a tee shirt for Joe. He had to be uncomfortable in his wet jeans and shirt, she thought.

She gently woke him again and coaxed him off the couch with the promise that a hot shower would help his head, handing him the clean, more comfortable clothing. She took the opportunity to run the vacuum in the living room while he was in the shower.

The boys got home just as she finished, bringing a wet and muddy Duke inside with them. She screamed in horror as the dog tracked mud all through the foyer before Jessup caught him and picked him up.

"Oh, God," she moaned. "Give him a bath, but clean my tub after you're done!"

"Yes, ma'am," he answered, carrying the dog upstairs.

She started cleaning up the mud when Joe emerged from the shower. "Oh damnb. Duke mabe a mess. I'mba sawry."

"I got it. Go lie down." The strangest thing happened as she cleaned. She was humming, suddenly realizing it was an old song from the 50's called *Lollipop*. What's more, she was happy.

Joe was back asleep as soon as his head hit the pillow. He was vaguely aware of Bethany covering him with the blanket. He heard the kids arguing over what to watch. He sort of recognized the sound of the TV show. At some point, Bethany asked if he wanted anything to eat, offering scrambled eggs and toast, which he thought he refused.

Eventually, though, the house grew quiet and still, and

he slept soundly.

At around 2 am, he awoke feeling much better. His head was no longer congested, and his sinuses no longer ached. Even his throat had stopped hurting. He opened his eyes groggily and closed them again, still caught between awake and asleep. As his mind came awake, he realized that he had seen a young man sitting on the coffee table, staring at him when he'd opened his eyes a second ago. He yelped and sat bolt upright. There was nobody there. Thank God. He'd been dreaming. He caught his breath and laughed at himself. "Geez. Ya gave me a start there, Alec," he said to the empty room.

He noticed that Bethany had left a bottle of water and two cold and flu capsules on the coffee table for him with a note that read, "Take these. Feel better. Love, Bethy."

"Love, Bethy," he repeated, touching his hand to his chest. He smiled and took the medicine as instructed.

He got up, used the bathroom, and returned to the sofa. Even though he was feeling better, he didn't want to disturb Bethany. Plus, he was kind of enjoying the quiet. Knowing she was asleep in his bed was enough for tonight. He lay back down, pulled the blanket back over himself, and closed his eyes.

He wasn't sure how long he had been asleep, but he came semi-awake to the young man's voice in his ear...or was it just in his head? He wasn't sure which, to be honest. The voice said, "He's feeding off that woman, and she's feeding off him. Take care of your Bethy."

"Mmmm. My Bethy," he mumbled, falling fully asleep again.

As the sun rose and light streamed through the easterly window, he awoke again. His arm was around Bethy's waist, her head on his shoulder, as she slept beside him. He held her hand in his, over his heart. One of her legs was draped over his. He had no idea when she had come into the living room, but he didn't care. He pulled her closer and went back to sleep.

———————

Rosalea watched her grandson and that…half black… kid get on the bus from her spot behind Alec's old '49 Ford, where it had been abandoned in the copse of trees on the edge of the field by the road. She had parked her rental on Harris Lane and hiked along the edge of the field behind the thicket that hid her from anyone who might be looking from the road. She knew the truck would still be there. Melanie couldn't ever let go of anything that had belonged to Alec. Sentiment had always been Melanie's biggest weakness.

The past held no appeal for Rosalea. She preferred Connecticut and high society to this place. Being here brought her no feelings of nostalgia, even if she could find the hidden turn onto Harris Lane without even thinking about it. How sad was that? So little had changed in the last 40 years that she could find a single-lane dirt track that was little more than a long driveway without even having to think about it.

She was more focused on Ryan than the fact that she was actually comfortable in jeans and hiking boots. Ryan looked…happier. He and that little…oh, what was the PC term for it…she wanted to call him a mulatto, but that wouldn't stand with the Connecticut crowd…mixed-race…that was it… He and that mixed-race boy seemed quite chummy. To her recollection, he hadn't been chummy with any of the kids at Greenwich Prep. She had to get him away from this place. Her son's son needed to be friends with a better class of people than this.

Minutes after the bus pulled away, Bethany, that bitch, emerged from Ravens' Roost with that man and Meghan. Dear Lord! What was Meghan wearing? Was she actually taking the child out in a pink tutu over rainbow leggings? What was she thinking? She peered through the binoculars hanging from her neck to get a closer look. Holy crap! Meghan got into the car dressed like that.

She hadn't noticed before that Meghan looked like Joe. Or she had pretended not to. It was hard to deny with them side by side. It was true. Bethany, the cheating whore, had slept with Joe Gardner at Renee's wedding 5 years ago. She might need to write off Meghan and just focus on Ryan.

She focused her binoculars on the man's face. He was a good-looking boy. She leaned against the old truck. Come to think of it, he resembled Alec…those same green eyes, same dark curly hair, same nose, same mouth. Gardner through and through, she thought. He threw his head back and laughed at something. Bethany wasn't that funny, nor was she that interesting. Why did it look like he couldn't take his eyes off her? What could he possibly see? Granted, like Alec, he was just a farmer and mechanic, but Bethany did not stand out in any way. Odd that…Joe not only looked like Alec, but he also did the same mundane work…

She adjusted the binoculars to look at Bethany. Wait. She was practically glowing. She was pretty. Her smile was enchanting. Her figure was…perfect. How had Bethany gone from a dowdy, mousy housewife to a sexy, carefree beauty in a week's time?

Rosalea lowered the binoculars as they drove away.

"Oh, God! I have to rescue my grandson before he ends up a farmer," she said to a squirrel who was foraging acorns beneath the oak she was standing near.

The truck's door unexpectedly popped open, knocking her back. "What the hell?"

CHAPTER 12

Joe was feeling much better. He wasn't scheduled at the garage until the next day, so he was able to go with Bethany to get her name changed and to the DMV.

After the boys got on the bus, they dropped Meg off at Madison's dairy farm. Joe drove as he knew where they were going.

"Is Fredericksburg a large city?" she asked.

"Large is subjective. Compared to Oak Grove and Colonial Beach? Yes. Compared to anywhere else? No." he said, laughing.

"You're making fun of me," she pouted.

"Maybe a little," he said fondly, taking her hand and kissing it.

He flipped on the car's radio and searched through the stations, landing on a country music station.

"I remember you like country," she said.

"I guess," he answered. "I like certain artists. Chris Stapleton is good."

"Oh. I don't know who that is," she said.

He laughed. "I'll play you some tonight," he promised.

He thought back to Martha's Vineyard. "What kind of music do you like?" he had asked as they had walked together along the beach.

"Pop, I guess. I like Taylor Swift," she had said.

"That it?"

"No. I like Ed Sheeran, Niall Horan...um, and it's a

little weird…"

"What?"

"I like…Irish Folk Music," she had blurted out, blushing adorably.

"I'm not sure how to respond to that," he had replied, laughing.

"I took 'Riverdance' lessons as a kid. It was one of the few things my parents let me do that I actually enjoyed," she had confessed.

He had looked over at her, and she had blushed again under his scrutiny. He had smiled. "*Riverdance,* huh? I'd like to see that."

"Michael Flatly?"

"No," he had chuckled. "You."

Bethany, with sun-kissed cheeks, had kicked off her flip-flops and had run to the water's edge, where the last remnants of the waves had surrounded her ankles and where she had proceeded to splash out the steps to an Irish reel. She had laughed, carefree and happy, in a way he hadn't seen her act since he'd smiled at her days before. He had laughed, his heart given to her in that moment. He ran out to join her, finding her in his arms. He had lost the battle to respect her marriage and had kissed her.

She'd pulled away in a panic, breathless, tearful.

"I'm so sorry," he had sputtered. "I shouldn't have done that. You're married. I…Forgive me."

But she had suddenly thrown her arms around him and had kissed him again, deeper, longer. When they had finally separated, she had clung to him, eyes closed, chest heaving, body trembling. "Is that what a kiss is supposed to feel like? Is this what love is supposed to be? Warm, tender… exciting…good?" she had whispered in a barely audible tone.

"What?" Joe had asked. "Haven't you ever been kissed, Bethy?"

"Not for real," she had said, whispering still. "I'm going to fall in love with you, Joe Gardner. And it's okay. It's okay to love me back. Any vows I took were under duress. They don't count. What I'm feeling now...this is real. This counts."

He hadn't understood, but he had started to suspect, and with that suspicion, he'd begun to despise Greg Benson. Later, when she'd refused to leave with him, he'd gone to the police, who did a wellness check. They had told him she had simply decided to stay with her husband. He'd left, gone back to Martha's Vineyard, and picked up Duke, the puppy she had picked out, who was meant to be hers. He had returned home broken-hearted. He wondered again what she had been through in his absence, whether he should have ignored the subsequent restraining order. Was this his fault now, too?

He shook his head, returning to the present. "You still like Irish folk music?" he asked.

"Oh, God," she laughed. "Yes. I do." She smiled. God, she was too beautiful, as beautiful as she had been that day, as beautiful as she'd forever be in his eyes.

She pulled Maggie's diary out of her purse. "I read some of this last night," she said. "Do you know how Ravens' Roost got its name?"

"No. Is it in there?"

"Yes, it's kind of romantic. Want to hear it?" she asked.

"Sure," he said, turning down the radio.

She opened the diary to the page she had marked. "Boxing Day, 1957," she read, "I asked Granddaddy why he named the farm Ravens' Roost last night. He had been drinking a bottle of scotch that Mr. Hawke gifted him. He is ever so much more expressive when he's been drinking. He said, 'Quoth the Raven 'Nevermore.' I was confused, but Granddaddy explained he was quoting a poem called *The Raven* by a gentleman named Edgar Allen Poe. 'Why would you name the farm for a poem?' I asked him. He smiled at me and explained that the narrator in the poem is pining for his deceased lady love. I still didn't understand. He laughed and asked me Grandma's name. 'Lenore Mae Gardner,' I answered proudly. 'Jacobs before she married.' He patted my cheek and said that the lady love in the poem was named Lenore, too. 'Your Grandma loved that poem, dark though it be, because her name was used. She thought it grand that the poor man was so distraught that he should be haunted by a raven until his end, pining for his sweet Lenore. I promised my sweet Lenore Mae that I would build her a place where a whole unkindness of ravens could roost ...that's what you call a flock of ravens... an unkindness...and when she was gone, our children and grandchildren would remember her name kindly,' he said. He laughed at his pun. 'She liked that, did my Lenore Mae...an unkindness of ravens reminding our descendants to remember kindly.'"

"Old Zach Gardner was a bit cheesy," Joe laughed. "Anything in there about the body?"

"Not so far. She talks about the old barn burning down in the summer of 1957, which would be in the journal before this one. This one starts in October of 1957. She does talk about the barn being built, though."

"Does she talk about who Melanie's father was?" he asked.

"I...I don't know. I don't know who her father was," she responded.

"Oh. Um...his name was...I don't know the first name,

but...he was one of the Harris boys. The trailer Jess and I were living in was where the Harris farm used to be. That dirt lane...That's Harris Lane. There were two brothers, and the house was a duplex...kind of odd for around here. The only one I know about around here. It was torn down about 4 years ago. They each lived in half. They farmed together. The older brother is named Al. He's still around. He's like 90 now, though. He lived in the house until it was torn down. Now he's in the nursing home in Colonial Beach."

"Oh...that's Mrs. Benson's father! Melanie was her cousin. So, the brother must have been Melanie's father. It's easy to forget Mrs. Benson came from here."

"Yeah. God, what was his name? Vince! I think that's it," Joe continued. "Al was married with kids...stable. Vince was kind of a wild child. He denied being Melanie's father and ran off with a girl from Roanoke. He showed back up several years later married to another girl. She moved into the other half of the house with him, but when she got pregnant, he ran off again. He joined the Army but then went AWOL. She stayed there in that house, though. Her daughter was my landlady."

She was quiet. "Joe," she said after several minutes. "I have a stupid question. What if he didn't go AWOL but was buried in Ravens' Roost's barn?"

He didn't say anything. Was it a stupid question? Then he pulled over and took out his phone. He made a call. "Hey, Mike. Bethy just had a thought. Could that body be Vince Harris? He disappeared in the late 60s. He supposedly went AWOL before shipping out. Yeah. Meredith Mason's father. The uniform...the gun...the location. And it was rumored he was Melanie's father. Yeah. Well, let us know. Thanks." He disconnected and pulled back onto the road. "That was a good thought, Honey. You might be right."

———

They quickly finished their business in the city and stopped at Walmart on the way back. Their new debit cards hadn't arrived yet, but Joe said he'd use his credit card to get some Christmas decorations. He personally only had a small box, and Bethany had left Connecticut with as few items as she could from the Bensons, so she had none.

Bethany picked out a nice pre-lit artificial tree, enough ornaments and garland to decorate it, and an angel for the top. She told him she'd rather come back after they got their debit cards to shop for the kids, not wanting to accrue debt on his credit.

They were home by 1 pm. He unloaded their purchases from the trunk, and she left him at home while she went to work.

"Mr. Morgan!" she called, walking through the front door.

He came out of his office and greeted her. "Ah, there you are, my dear. Did you get your business completed?"

"Yes, thank you. I registered for my GED courses last night as well," she responded, hanging her coat on the rack on the wall by the door.

He seemed so sad. "Oh, yes. Well, that's good. I'm happy to help." She took his arm and walked with him into his office.

She sat down across from his chair at his desk. He took the hint and sat in it.

"Are you okay, Mr. Morgan?" she asked.

"I don't hide my emotions very well anymore, do I?" he said, patting her arm. "Well, I am old. I'm entitled, I suppose."

"What's the matter? Even if I can't do anything, I can listen," she offered.

He was silent, but his eyes were teary. "I can't help but worry...about that body..." he said after staring at the family portrait hanging on his office wall.

"Are you worried the body is Vince Harris?" she asked.

He looked at her, surprise registered on his face. "You know about Vince Harris? Yes. That is my fear," he answered.

"I know the gist of it," she said. She was genuinely worried about him. This melancholy mood was unlike him.

"He raped Maggie," he said. He allowed the tears to come. He sobbed heavily. Bethany stood, walked around his desk, and hugged him impulsively, but he did not push her away. Instead, he clung to her as if he would drown if he let go. When he had cried himself out, he let go and leaned back. "It was a brutal rape...out there in the new barn. Al Harris is a decent man. Hard working. Honest enough. Vince...was not. He was spoiled and greedy...and angry that he wasn't born an aristocrat. He thought he was too good for Oak Grove. But he was more than just...There was something evil in him. I believe he was a psychopath."

"When did he disappear?" Bethany asked.

"The first time...1959, when Maggie started to show... she was only 14 at the time," he said. "We both were. Alec was only 12. But God, he was so angry. It was good Vince left. I think Alec would have killed him if he hadn't."

"How old was Vince? I mean, Greg was 26 when..." she started, stopping as she realized what she was about to admit. "How old was Vince at that time?"

"Vince was 20. Bethany, did Greg...?" Mr. Morgan gasped, grabbing her arm.

She felt her lip quiver, and she fought back the tears.

"It doesn't matter."

"It most certainly does," he assured her.

"I don't know," she answered, a tear rolling down her cheek, but she did know. "Somebody put something in my drink. I woke up in Greg's hotel room. I was beaten up. He said he rescued me from someone…but I don't know. My father made me marry him. Greg had to comply, or my dad would call the police." It was Greg's version of what had happened. She knew what had happened, but she wasn't ready to share it yet.

"Jesus," Joe's voice sounded behind her. He was standing there with a Tupperware bowl. "You forgot your lunch," he said as she spun quickly to see him. He held it up.

"Joe…I," she started, but she really didn't know what to say, so she just let the silence hang there.

He stepped inside the office, put the Tupperware on the desk, and took her into his arms.

Mr. Morgan told them that was enough dwelling on the past for one afternoon, and they spent the rest of the afternoon putting up his Christmas decorations.

Joe made the conscious decision not to leave. He wouldn't have left even if Bethy asked him to. Mr. Morgan seemed to understand and suggested that he would pay Joe to do the decorating. Joe knew they didn't need the money, but if it gave Bethy comfort to accept payment as an excuse for his presence, he was fine with it. His guilt was palpable. He should never have given up. Whatever hell she had lived through since Martha's Vineyard was his fault. End of story.

When they left at 4 pm, Mr. Morgan handed him $100 and said quietly, "Hold your temper, Joe. She needs your support, not for you to vent your anger. And remember, there's a child who was born out of very tragic circumstances. He is innocent...and he loved his father. She hasn't told him. She doesn't want him to know."

Joe had no idea what to say. It was good advice. He hoped he could follow it. He knew he had to protect Ryan at all costs. God, he was so angry, but not just at Greg. He nodded.

"I know what you're thinking, boy. I thought the same thing. It's not your fault. I promise you that," Mr. Morgan assured him. He fought back the tears as he bravely nodded in affirmation. He'd try to convince himself, but he wasn't sure he'd be able to.

Bethy stopped to pick up Meghan. He went straight home. He took Duke out before Bethy and Meg got home. While he was walking the dog, Mike called. He verified the weapon found in the grave was Vince Harris's service weapon. The State Police had contacted Meredith Mason to request a DNA sample to compare with the remains.

When Meredith and Rosalea Benson pulled into the driveway, he sighed and walked over to the car.

He held securely onto Duke's leash as the women exited the vehicle.

"Hello, Joe," Mrs. Mason said.

"Hello, Mrs. Mason," he replied.

"Is it true? Did you find my daddy's body?" she asked.

"I found a body. Evidence seems to point to it being your daddy, but I suppose we won't know for sure until the police check the skeleton's DNA against yours," he agreed.

"I understand. I'd...can I see where?" she asked.

He glared at Rosalea, but he held his temper. "Yeah, sure," he replied. "Let me put Duke inside. I'll take y'all back to the barn."

Bethany pulled in as he unhooked Duke's leash.

"Grandma!" Meg exclaimed excitedly, jumping out of the car and hugging Rosalea, who visibly flinched, Joe noted.

"Hello," Rosalea said coldly. "What are you wearing?"

"Me and Kelly was ballerinas," she giggled.

"Kelly and I *were* ballerinas," she corrected.

Joe gritted his teeth. He motioned for the women. "Come on," he called.

"I'll go with you, Grandma!" Meg announced, taking her hand.

"No!" Joe and Bethany yelped.

Joe said sternly, "Meg, you stay out of that barn. You understand? Your grandma can come into the house and visit after we get back."

Bethany's back stiffened, but she nodded. "Thank you," she mouthed.

He led the two women back to the barn. A shiver ran up his spine, and all the hairs on the back of his neck and arms stood on end as he opened the door. "Brrr," he said. "Gettin' cold."

Rosalea laughed.

Mrs. Mason simply said, "Not especially."

"Oh…well, I'm getting over a cold. Maybe it's just me," he explained. "Over in that corner," he said, pointing. "There was a pallet covering the ground, and the windows were on the pallet. I pulled out the windows to install them, and the pallet was just old and rotted…so I pulled it out to put in the debris pile. Duke dug in the freshly uncovered earth and… dug up the skull."

Mrs. Mason moved closer. "To think he was in view of the house all this time," she said. "Probably."

"Would you like some…time?" he asked.

Mrs. Mason laughed. "My daddy was a son of a bitch. If that was him, he got what he deserved. I just wanted to see." She paused briefly. "I hope it was him. I hope Betty or Maggie shot him dead and buried him."

"Jesus, Meredith," Rosalea protested.

"Shut it, Sally Rose. You know he deserved it. He did the same to your mama that he did to Maggie. He was probably your daddy, too."

"My name is Rosalea."

"Get down off that high horse. Your name is Sally Rose," Meredith Mason affirmed.

"It's not true!" Rosalea...Sally Rose...Mrs. Benson said, pointing at Joe. "My father is Al Harris."

He smiled mirthlessly. "Yeah. I don't believe that. And I think you know exactly why I don't think that. But understand, I don't really care except for as it pertains to my wife. I *will* protect her...at least from now on. I'll not fail her again. I promise ya that. Otherwise, I'm not the kind to spread tales."

They returned to the house. Megan was crying. Ryan was upstairs throwing things in his room. Jess, sweet boy, was sitting quietly on the sofa beside Bethy. Bethy was calmly drinking a cup of her really good tea. As Joe came through the door, with Mrs. Mason and Mrs. Benson behind him, he knew something was very wrong.

Bethany stood. "Your process server just left. Your grandchildren are devastated. Congratulations. You've sure made an impression on them," she said coldly.

Meghan looked at her grandmother and screamed, "I hate you!" She ran from the room. Jess stood and followed her.

"It's okay, Meggy. Don't cry," Joe heard him say as he

went up the stairs behind her.

"Do you think I care that they are angry? Ryan is all that matters. Meghan is where she belongs...the little bastard child...but Ryan belongs with better people." Mrs. Benson retorted.

"Better people? Better than Joe? Joe's the best man I've ever known. My husband was an asshole. My father-in-law is a spineless sap. My father...oh, my God. My father is an emotionally abusive, controlling narcissist who forced me to marry my rapist to protect his precious image. I choose Joe. For me. For my kids. We'll be applying to adopt each other's kids. I'll fight you to the end. And if I have my way, *my* son will *never* see you again," Bethany said, calmly and evenly. "Get out."

Joe pointed at the door.

Mrs. Benson said, "I'm still asking for custody."

"And you're not welcome here," Joe said. "Mrs. Mason, you may come back anytime...without your...sister, is it?"

Bethany rose and walked to him, hugging him. "My father is a prominent minister in my hometown. His image and his family's image were always of utmost importance. We were not permitted to embarrass him," she said. "My... situation...embarrassed him." She sighed and looked him right in the eyes.

"I...I should have made you come with me. I'm so sorry, Baby," he replied, holding her close. He was suddenly terrified. Nothing had terrified him since...Afghanistan, to be honest. He couldn't really explain what was terrifying him, though. Was it what Bethany had endured? Was it that she might hold him culpable? Was it the thought of losing Ryan? Or was it something else, something worse, something evil?

"It's never been your fault, Joe. What were you

supposed to do? Kidnap me and Ryan? Greg had the upper hand. There was no winning. Now…now we have the upper hand. Don't blame yourself. And please, don't blame me. Okay?" she said, squeezing his waist.

CHAPTER 13

Bethany had been looking forward to putting up the Christmas tree. After a near-silent dinner at which the children barely spoke, and when they did, it was only to ask to pass an item, she suggested they play Christmas music and decorate, hoping it would brighten the mood.

Joe smiled and picked the music. "Trace Adkins. *The King's Gift*," he said, winking. "A blend of Country and Irish folk." He quickly set up the new Christmas tree in front of the window in the living room and plugged it in.

This man had shown her what love looked like. He was a pillar of strength, a refuge in the storm. She knew beyond any doubt she would never leave him.

He clicked through the different light settings with the remote for the tree. "Which one do you like, Meghan?" he asked the little girl, who was holding the angel tree topper in anticipation.

"The pretty colors!" she exclaimed.

He set the lights to the multicolor mode.

"Do we want steady lights or blinking, fast, medium, or slow?" he asked, looking at the remote.

"Flashing!" Meghan exclaimed happily.

"Medium," Ryan added.

Joe set the option.

"Joe," Bethany said, gazing at him adoringly.

"Yeah?" he responded, still looking at the tree.

"I love you," she whispered.

He turned his gaze toward her then. He lowered the remote and made eye contact. "I love you, too." He sat beside her on the sofa and draped his arm across her shoulders, pulling her toward him and kissing her head.

She lay against him. "I'm yours. Now and forever," she whispered.

"Hmmm. Same, my Love. I'm never letting go," he whispered back to her. Then, aloud, he announced, "Have at it, kids! Decorate it!" He laughed as the three children enthusiastically started hanging ornaments.

Bethany wrapped her arms around his waist, laid her head on his shoulder, and sighed deeply. She felt that warm, comforting sensation again.

"Hey, guys. I'm going to adopt Jessup. Joe's going to adopt Ryan. We aren't doing this to replace your mom or your dad, but so that you are protected. And it will help fight Grandma getting custody. Is that okay with you guys?" she asked suddenly.

They paused for a moment but then continued to decorate the tree.

"I'll do anything to fight Grandma," Ryan assured them. "And it's not like Dad was ever much of a dad anyway."

"I finally have a mom," Jessup said wistfully.

"I'm not getting adopted?" Meg asked.

"You are already my daughter. I don't have to adopt you. You and I just have to take a test to prove it, and then, I'm legally your parent, too."

"What kind of test, Daddy? Are the questions hard?" she asked, looking frightened, but Joe was steady and calm.

"It's not that kind of test, Honey," he explained. We just have to run a cotton swab, like a big Q-Tip, on the insides of our cheeks. We send the swabs to a lab, and they test the material from our mouths to see if our DNA matches."

"What if it doesn't?" she asked.

"It will," he promised, smiling.

———

With that decision, they settled into their new lives. Joe returned to work at the garage the next morning. Bethany worked hard to learn her duties at Mr. Morgan's. Mr. Morgan filed the petition for adoption and a continuance in family court on the custody suit. As he expected, an order of reference was issued.

The week passed quickly. The boys attended the Lock In as they had requested. Meg had her first sleepover at Madison's Dairy. Joe and Bethany took the opportunity to go Christmas shopping and out for dinner. Bethany was happy. Really happy.

"Where are we eating?" she asked as they loaded their purchases into the trunk of the Caddy.

"It's a surprise," Joe answered cryptically.

"Can I have a hint?" she asked, moving close, batting her eyes at him, and gently laying her hand on his chest.

"Flirting will only get you kissed," he said, grabbing her hand. She had started to trail it down his chest toward his abdomen.

"Hmmm. Sounds like I win anyway," she teased.

He grinned and pulled her to him, kissing her deeply.

"Joe?" came a confused and hurt-sounding feminine voice.

"Huh, crap," he muttered. "Kristin."

"Kristin? Kristin…Johnson?" Bethany said out loud, pulling away and turning toward the voice. Kristin was in her early to mid-thirties. She wasn't unattractive, though she wasn't stunningly beautiful either, though that was perhaps because of her clothes being too large for her frame, her hair being pulled back so tight that it pinched her face, and her makeup being the wrong color palette for her skin tone. Her expression was haughty. She held her mouth and nose in a perpetual sneer...as if she found everything unpleasant. She had all the appearance of a spinster librarian. Bethany wondered if it was her or life in general that Kristin found so distasteful.

"Who is *she*?" the woman asked, pointing at Bethany.

Joe smiled and pulled Bethany even closer. "She's my wife," he said, looking at Bethany and ignoring Kristin.

Kristin stepped toward Bethany. "Wait. Joe and I have known each other since grade school. Who are you?"

"I'm the woman he loves, and you're someone he went to school with," Bethany said wryly.

"We have dinner reservations. Let's go," he said, smacking Bethany's ass. Then he shut the trunk and got into the car behind the wheel. "Come on," he called to Bethany. She hurried and got into the car. They pulled away, leaving Kristin standing there, wearing that same disappointed expression.

He took her to the Colonial Tavern, an Irish pub, where an Irish folk music group was performing Christmas music live. Bethany clapped excitedly as they were seated.

As they enjoyed their dessert and an after-dinner Irish coffee, the singer announced she would be taking a break but introduced Bridget McIntyre, a dance instructor at a local dance studio. An immigrant from Ireland, Bridget explained in a heavy Irish brogue that she was going to teach the audience to do a simple Irish jig. She demonstrated the dance on the dance floor as the group played the jig. It, of course, did not look so simple, but Bethany followed the steps in her memory. Bridget asked for volunteers.

Several people raised their hands, and Joe grabbed Bethany's arm, forcing it up.

"Oy, ye're quick to volunteer yer lady dere, ye are!" Bridget heckled him.

"You betcha," he answered, unashamed.

"I'll do it," Bethany said, laughing.

"Ah, dere's a good sport," Bridget praised. "Give 'er a hand."

The ensemble played the jig again, and the group tried the jig with Bridget. Only Bethany performed the steps correctly. Bridget broke into applause as she and Bethany finished the jig in step with each other. "He sent in a ringer, he did!" she joked.

Bethany laughed and curtsied as the audience and her fellow volunteers applauded. Joe stood and whistled as he applauded. She flung herself into his arms, kissing him. He swung her, holding her and kissing her as he spun her in a circle. "You're so great!" he exclaimed proudly. It was the best date she'd ever been on.

She should have known the intense cold just inside the front door when they got home was foreboding, but she was so happy that she willfully ignored it. She made love to her husband and slept happily in his arms.

———

Joe was working on replacing the living room front window with Mike when Bethany returned from picking up the kids. Ryan raced into the house, slamming the front door behind him as Bethany was still getting Meg out of the car.

"What's with him?" Joe asked Jess, who shrugged on his way inside.

Bethany ushered Meghan inside. "He...um...had

a noticeable...um situation when he woke up, and he's understandably embarrassed."

"A noticeable situation?" Joe repeated, not understanding. She lowered her eyes to his jeans zipper. "Ohhh!" he yelped, covering the area with both hands.

Mike snorted. "Sorry. I didn't mean to laugh," he coughed.

"His first?" Joe whispered to Bethany. She nodded. "Um, can we take a break, Mike?" Joe asked.

"I'm here all day," Mike replied casually.

"I'll be right back," Joe assured him, heading inside.

He walked through that cold spot again and shivered but ignored it, climbing the stairs and knocking on Ryan's closed bedroom door.

"Ryan!" he called. "May I come in?"

"Do whatever you want!" came the anguished response from inside.

Joe entered to find Ryan lying face down on the bed, his face buried in the pillow.

"It happens to everybody," Joe said, sitting beside him on the bed. "I know that's not much comfort right now."

"Why did it happen in front of...everybody?" Ryan wailed.

It occurred to Joe that while it was embarrassing that it had happened in front of "everybody," there might be a specific somebody that made it seem worse.

"Everybody?" he asked. "Or Missy in particular?"

"God, even you know! I could just die."

"I promise you won't die. At least not from this," Joe assured him, rubbing his back. "Do you want to talk about it? Or anything? Do you have any questions?"

"No," Ryan answered quickly.

"Okay. But I'm here if you ever do…okay?" Joe said. He stood and started to walk away.

When he reached for the doorknob, Ryan sat up. "Am I going to be like my dad? Am I going to…make girls…like Dad did Mom?"

"Jesus," Joe said, taking his hand off the doorknob. "I didn't know you…knew that."

"I'm not stupid," Ryan replied, tears in his eyes.

Joe walked back and sat beside him again. "No. You're not. First, what happened this morning…that was a biological thing. It really does happen to all boys. You're starting puberty. It's perfectly natural. What your dad did…that isn't natural…or even a result of sexual desire. It was more about control than anything. That's not you, Ryan. Just understand that what you want and what any girl you are interested in wants might not be the same. Respect that. No means no. An inability to say either…means no. Sometimes, yes means no. If she's not into it wholeheartedly, just don't. I don't think you'll have a problem with that, though. From what I know about you, you're very respectful of others."

Ryan nodded. Then he flung his arms around Joe's waist, hugging him tightly. "Thanks, Daddy."

"You bet," Joe answered, rubbing his head gently. Then he just hugged the boy.

When Joe finally stood to leave, Ryan added, "Daddy, could you not tell Mom? It would make her cry to know I know. She's cried enough."

"I think you should let her know…because she worries that it will hurt you, but I won't say anything. I think it should come from you."

———

Bethany handed Mike a mug full of steaming hot tea,

her really good tea from a teahouse in Manhattan.

"Hey, that really is pretty good," Mike said, taking a sip.

She beamed. He was the first person to accept her offer of the tea. "How long have you and Joe been friends?" she asked, taking a sip from her own mug.

"Oh, we've known each other all our lives. We're cousins somewhere along the line," he quipped, winking.

"Of course you are," she laughed.

"Yeah, my great-grandmother and his great-grandfather were siblings or something like that," he explained. "On his mother's side. She was a Rosewood. So was my mama." He nodded at the house. Then he pointed across the street beyond the trailer and behind a small grove of trees to a farmhouse. "That was my great-grandmother's house. My grandmother's nephew lives in that trailer there."

"What does that make him to you?" she laughed.

"Um...related," he joked. "I don't know. I get lost after first cousin."

"Me too," she giggled. "It seems like everybody is 'related' around here."

"Um. Yeah, pretty much," he agreed, chuckling.

"Maggie's mother was Betty Gardner, right? What happened to Betty's husband? This was his family's farm, wasn't it? I've been reading Maggie's journal. She never talks about her father," she asked, taking another sip.

"He was killed in a farming accident. He rolled a tractor out there when a sinkhole opened around that natural spring up on that hill. It crushed him to death. In 1950, I think," he said, pointing out into the field at a spot with a lone tree and an area of bushes.

"I was wondering why that was in the middle of the

field," she said as a car with a Hertz sticker on the windshield pulled into the driveway.

Before she knew what was happening, Reverend James West had jumped out of the car and was bounding toward the two of them. Her father came at them like a bull, grabbing Mike and punching him in the face before either of them could even react. Mike's tea went flying. The mug shattered against the side of the house. "Uncultured, backwoods cretin! How dare you interfere with my daughter's family!"

"Father!" Bethany yelled.

Mike, being an experienced officer of the law, grabbed her father and pinned his arms behind his back, slamming him against the house just as Joe came out the door.

"What the hell?" Joe exclaimed, startled by the unexpected scuffle.

"I could arrest you for assaulting an officer," Mike yelled. "But seeing you're Bethany's father, I'll let it slide… for the moment!"

"Father?" Joe asked, looking at the man.

"Yeah, Joe, meet my father, Reverend James West. Father, *this* is Joe Gardner, my husband." She leaned forward to look her dad in the face, which Mike was holding against the side of the house.

"Then who's this restraining me?" her father grunted.

"Deputy Mike Poole, Joe's friend," she answered. She hated to admit it, but it was gratifying to see her father like that.

"Deputy?" her father groaned.

"Westmoreland County Sherriff's Department," he answered.

"My apologies. I mistook you…"

"For Joe. Yeah, I've pieced that together. Even so,

you're a man of God. You shouldn't be assaulting people," Mike said, releasing his grip on the Reverend West.

"Is your mother going to get out of the car?" Joe asked, sounding stunned and pointing at the car.

Bethany turned to look. She sighed. "Not until Father tells her to."

"What century do your parents live in?" Joe asked incredulously.

"Um, 19th?" she chuckled.

"And he called Joe an uncultured, backwoods cretin. Jesus," Mike added.

"Mother! Get out of the car!" Bethany yelled. "Come in the house." Her mother didn't move. "Tell her to get out, Father," she said, resigned to her mother's unwavering obedience.

"Ruth, come say hello to your daughter," her father said. She could swear he sounded proud of his control over his wife.

Bethany grabbed Joe's hand. "Father, you broke the mug. You clean it up. Before you step foot in my house. Mike, come in, and I'll fix you another cup of tea. Mother, would you like some tea?" With that, she pulled Joe inside. Mike followed. She went to the kitchen and put on the kettle.

When she turned around, her mother stood in the door between the kitchen and dining room, clutching her purse in both hands. She peered cautiously into the kitchen.

"Bethany, this…is quite nice inside. Your floors need sanding and staining. And you could use some new appliances, but it's…homey. From the outside, I thought it would be…"

"It's all cosmetic, Mother. The house is actually in good shape. Joe is replacing the windows. He's going to try to prep for painting the exterior before it gets too cold, and in the spring, we plan to paint and put a roof back on the porch. I think we are going to add some shutters too…and I want to plant some flowers."

"Rosalea led us to believe you were living in a shack that was falling down around you," her mother said.

"Mother, Rosalea is a bitch," Bethany retorted.

Her mother smiled. Mother never smiled.

———

Joe and Mike sat down in the living room. After a moment, rather sheepishly, James West came through the door with the pieces of the broken mug. Joe pointed to the trash can, and his father-in-law discarded them.

"Aren't you going to welcome me?" James asked.

"No," Joe responded.

"Why not?"

"Why not? Are you kidding? You attacked my friend, thinking you were attacking me. And that doesn't even scratch the surface of what you've done to my wife," Joe scowled, crossing his arms across his chest and resting his right foot across his left knee.

There was also the whisper only Joe could hear. "He's feeding him. Don't let him be here." Joe was pretty sure it was in his head, though it felt like it was external. It was disarming. It had him questioning his sanity, but he still believed the whisper.

His dislike for his wife's father was strong, even before meeting him, based on what he had done to Bethy. The manner of their meeting had certainly not improved his opinion.

"Regardless of my behavior, which I admit was less than stellar, I have Bethany's best interest at heart. You have nothing to offer her. She has no future here," James West said, sitting, uninvited, in an armchair.

"No future? She's taking courses to earn her GED. She has a full-time job in a law office. She's planning on attending college next year. I have nothing to offer? How about my heart, my undying love and devotion. I love her. Do you?" Joe huffed, shaking his head in disbelief. "Unlike Greg, I'd never hurt her."

"We won't consent."

"I don't give a damn. She's an adult. Your consent isn't required this time."

James West turned bright red. Joe was unmoved. Mike excused himself and walked back outside.

CHAPTER 14

James knew his anger was misplaced. There wasn't one word that hillbilly spoke that wasn't true. He had forced his daughter to marry a man who had raped her. He'd even handed her over for it to happen. And when she'd gotten pregnant as a result, he'd used the rape as a way to get out of a lawsuit and hand off Bethany to someone else. The man was a lawyer. He could provide for Bethany. And it didn't take much to persuade him. Bethany was gorgeous.

He'd practically jumped at the offer that James had made him. James agreed not to involve the police or sue in civil court if he married her. Additionally, James agreed to settle his church's lawsuit against Greg's client, a ministry administrator who had recruited several young women in his congregation to travel to Africa and allowed them to be abused at the training facility in New York, where the organization was headquartered. That was the real clincher. James valued his reputation far more than money, far more than his daughter, and far more than a few stupid girls who had gotten themselves into a bad situation. He'd wanted to sweep it under the rug anyway.

His motives had been selfish. He knew that. Bethany had always been...an obligation. The simple truth was he didn't much like Bethany.

Blake, his son, had been in the seminary at the time, and Penelope, his eldest child, had recently married his associate pastor. They were older than Bethany by several years. And she was more rebellious than they were.

Gaining an attorney as a son-in-law and getting rid of Bethany had been too good to pass up. He was almost happy she had gotten pregnant.

It was clear Bethany's new husband hated James, thoroughly. It was also clear he was a working class nobody. He'd never be more than a farmer and a mechanic. And Bethany, through that damned rebellious spirit of hers, was throwing away a life that freed him of the obligation. He didn't want her back. Rosalea did.

His anger grew as he cleaned up that mug. Then, as he entered that house, he felt a dark presence begin to feed on his anger and hate. The more it fed, the angrier he became, and the more he hated Bethany and the hillbilly. It felt good. He felt empowered by the dark presence.

"We're staying here," James announced, arms crossed. He was used to being obeyed.

"Like hell, you are," Joe replied, standing in indignation.

James didn't care. The house had been left to Bethany. Bethany would obey.

"Tell this cretin we are staying, Bethany Elaine," James demanded.

"No," his daughter replied. She sighed. "The simple truth is Mrs. Horton left me this property because he asked her to."

"That's not tr…Okay, that's true, but she did leave it to you and not me, so your father is right. It's up to you, not me," the cretin told her.

"I put your name on the deed," she said suddenly. "You own this property as much as I do. I saw her old will, Joe. She would have left it all to you. The only reason I was able to escape was because you asked her to give it to me."

"I...I just wanted you to have a way to escape if you wanted it. That's all," he said, pulling her close.

"This is our home, Joe. Together," she assured him. "That said, if you really don't want them to stay here, they won't. But for my part...they are my parents."

He nodded. "Fine, but I won't tolerate his hurting you, Bethy."

She smiled and stood on her tiptoes to quickly kiss him.

James heard every word, but all he felt was vindication. "We'll take the master..." he started.

"You'll take Meggy's room," Joe said with authority. "She can sleep in our room."

————

Ruth, unlike her husband, saw Bethany in a new light. Their daughter had persevered and had blossomed. And, unlike her husband, Ruth recognized they had not done anything to benefit Bethany. They had, in fact, irreparably damaged her. They had no right to make any demands of her. And yet, there he stood, demanding Bethany and her husband allow them to stay in their home...and it was their home. They both had a vested interest in the place. They both took pride in its upkeep and had plans to make it their own.

Ruth laid her hand on James's elbow. "Perhaps we should get a hotel," she offered meekly.

"Absolutely not," he said, standing. "We don't have any real evidence that these two are really even married. I will not permit them to sin around these children."

Bethany's husband turned bright red. But he calmed under Bethany's loving caress of his shoulder.

"Sit down, Father," she said calmly. She walked out of the living room. She returned moments later with a framed marriage certificate. "Here you are. Proof. Now, if you want to stay, you will stay in Meghan's room…top of the stairs, to the left. That's your choice. Meghan's room or go to a hotel."

Ruth had never been prouder of Bethany. She wished she possessed half of the fortitude of character that Bethany had. "I'll get our bags, Dear," Ruth offered.

Joe blustered. "Please. Sit down, Mrs. West. I'll get 'em." He strode toward the foyer. He opened the door, and his friend jumped up from where he sat on the porch, waiting for Joe's return. "Help me get their bags, will ya, Mike?"

"Sure thing, Joe. Whatever ya need," the friend replied.

Ruth turned to look at James. He was seething. Bethany had bested him, even if he had gotten his way about their staying here. But she had allowed it on her terms. Nobody did that to James West. Nobody. A deep, bone-chilling, cold filled Ruth as she looked at him. She'd have liked to have said she didn't recognize him, but, unfortunately, she did. Still, he didn't quite look like himself for half a second. Then the cold passed, and James was just James again, though maybe slightly paler.

Joe and his friend came in through the front door with the Wests' bags in tow. They started up the stairs. Joe led the way, calling, "Meggy, you'll be sleepin' with Mommy and me tonight. Your grandparents will be in your room." James stomped after them, and Ruth followed him.

A beautiful little girl emerged from her room. She had brown curly hair and striking emerald, green eyes. She looks just like her father, Ruth noted, suddenly realizing she meant Joe, not Greg. James seemed to have the same thought. He stopped short upon first seeing his granddaughter. "Adulterer," he hissed.

Joe twirled to face them. He hissed back, "Judge not, Reverend," he growled as he glanced over at the child who was so obviously his and clamped his mouth shut. "Just judge not."

The room grew exceedingly cold again. Ruth could see her breath, and puffs of frozen breath spewed from James's mouth like smoke rising from the bellows of hell. His face did not look like his own, and the words that he spat out with the smog made no sense. "I hate you, Alec. I really do. I will not rest until you are driven from this place!"

"Alec? I'm Joe. What do you know about Alec?" Joe asked, obviously confused.

"What are you talking about?" James replied coldly, though his face and the room's temperature had returned to normal.

"You said you hated me and called me Alec," Joe said, more and more confused, as was Ruth. What was happening? She shivered uncontrollably.

"I did no such thing," James asserted. But he had. She'd heard him. Hadn't she?

The child looked up at James with fear in her bright eyes. "Daddy," she cried, grabbing Joe's leg. "That was the bad man from the barn." She burst into tears.

Joe quickly and lovingly picked her up. "It's okay, Meggy. I won't let the bad man hurt you," he comforted her, hugging her to his chest. "Your grandfather didn't mean it."

"I didn't say it," James insisted.

"Um, yeah, ya did," Joe's friend interjected.

With that, the two men dropped their bags and headed back downstairs, Joe carrying *his* daughter.

"Our daughter is going to hell," James said as they walked away.

"Oh, shut up, James," Ruth exclaimed. It was the first time she'd said anything against him in 42 years, and it was long overdue. She picked up her bags and carried them into the bedroom. "What a lovely room," she said, lifting her bags to the double-size brass bed placed opposite the window, complete with a lovely window seat. Roses graced the wallpaper. It was old and faded but sweet. It felt like a room in a B and B.

———

While Joe and Mike finished installing the new front window and moved to the next one on the side of the house, Bethany gathered the laundry.

"Mother, Father, I'm going to the laundromat!" she called up the stairs. "Do you have anything you want me to wash?"

"You have to go to the laundromat?" her father called back down to her derisively.

"Yes. I have to go to the laundromat," she replied. God, her father was exhausting. Her mother, at least, was making an effort and called that she would bring down the clothing from their drive out from Illinois.

Bethany pushed open the front door to find Missy about to knock. She had a friend with her. "Oh hey, Missy," she greeted her friend's daughter. "Who's this?" She shifted the laundry basket on her hip.

"Good morning, Mrs. Gardner. This is Carly. She's my best friend. She lives in Placid Bay. We were wondering if Ryan and Jessup would like to go on a bike ride with us?"

"Do kids still ride bikes for fun?" she asked, staring at the pre-teen girls who entirely looked like teens. Missy was blonde, unlike her mother, with big blue eyes. Carly was dark-haired with brown eyes. They both blushed as Missy asked about the boys. Jesus, they're twelve, Bethany thought, chuckling. "I'm sure they would, but Ryan doesn't have a bike. We moved kind of…quickly. The bike didn't make the trip," she explained.

The girls looked dejected. "My mom says that I can't play inside your house until she's met you," Carly said sadly.

"Ah. Well, I appreciate that. How about if I pay you four to rake the leaves for us? That way, you'll be outside, you'll be able to hang out, and you'll make a little money… say $10 each?"

Missy's eyes brightened, and she elbowed her friend, who smiled prettily and nodded.

"Joe," she called. "Do we have four rakes around here?"

Joe appeared around the corner wearing a quizzical expression. "Sure, what for?"

"Missy, Carly, and the boys are going to rake the leaves for $10 each. You have cash?"

He nodded and said, "I'll get the rakes," and walked away. Mike waved and winked at the girls. Missy gave an excited jump and ran to hug the deputy.

"Hiya, Mike," she said, grinning. Bethany wondered if she might have a little crush on the handsome man.

Bethany smiled and leaned back inside, and called for the boys. "Ryan, Jessup. Come outside and help the girls rake the leaves while Meggy and I go to wash clothes."

At the word "girls," the boys' bedroom doors upstairs burst open, and the two of them came bounding down the steps. James West appeared at the top of the stairs, scowling disapprovingly. His wife pushed past him with their laundry and followed the boys down the stairs.

Bethany walked out to the Cadillac. She opened the trunk, put the clothes basket in, and walked to the driver's side door. Ruth added her bag to the trunk and closed it.

Meghan ran out and jumped into the back seat. "You coming with us, Mother?" Bethany asked.

"I wouldn't mind," Ruth said, smiling. Bethany unlocked the door, and Ruth got into the passenger side. With that, they left just as Joe reappeared to hand out rakes. Bethany saw her father glaring out of the upstairs window as she drove away.

————

James was almost impressed that the teenage harlot wouldn't come into the house with the boys, but he became thoroughly convinced that the girls were agents of evil as he watched them flirt with the boys. Their jeans were too tight. Their shirts were too short. They wore those puffy little vests unzipped, their breasts not hidden at all. It disgusted him. And he wasn't really sure why he was thinking this way. His own granddaughter, Laura, was about these girls' age. She dressed much the same way. She acted similarly around boys. Other than being Penelope's daughter, there was little to make his opinion of her any greater. Of course, Penelope was his pride and joy. Of his three children, she was the only one that he truly loved. Bethany was an obligation. Blake was a disappointment. Penelope...could do no wrong. And her daughter and son were the only grandchildren he could stomach.

He seethed, watching the pre-teens act like pre-teens.

Further, Joe seemed to be enjoying having those kids around. Both he and his friend laughed easily and often, even while supposedly working on replacing windows.

All James felt was vitriol.

He didn't notice the cold.

————

Joe smacked his hands together, calling the window

replacement work done for the day. He nodded toward the sound of the children laughing in the front yard, remembering his own childhood in this blessed region. It had been a good childhood despite the hardships. Though his biological mother had died, he was raised by a wonderful, loving stepmother who filled the role of mother perfectly. Though his father had been unable to keep the farmland, he'd been raised in the house where his father had been raised. He had a real sense of belonging here. And though Ravens' Roost wasn't that property, it had been the house where his grandfather had been raised, built by his great-grandfather for his great-grandmother, and he felt a part of the land and even the house. He had close friends he had spent his childhood with, gone to kindergarten with, played football in high school with, and joined the Marines with. Westmoreland had blessed him and his life. He hoped he blessed it, too. And so, as he rounded the house to witness his own son take a running jump into the giant pile of leaves that he and the other pre-teen children had worked so hard to rake up, Joe couldn't help but laugh. The leaves scattered. Then, the other three did the same, and the pile obliterated. He and Mike gleefully helped them re-rake the leaves.

He watched Mike with Missy. He recognized what Mike was feeling. It had to be hard. He'd never said anything, but Joe could tell he suspected the girl was his child. The relationship between Mike and Jillian was complicated. Seeing Missy always put Mike in a good mood, though. Joe was glad to allow his friend some time with the pre-teen, who did remarkably resemble Mike. Jillian knew Mike was helping today. She'd obviously allowed the girl to come, knowing it was a workaround for her mother's disapproval of Mike spending time with Missy. He decided that it was their business and that he wouldn't confront either of them about it. It was rough enough to deal with Jillian's family without Joe sticking his nose in it. They'd talk to him or Bethany if they wanted to.

His joy only increased as Bethany returned from the laundromat. Meghan ran to him, and he lifted her high in the air, kissing her rosy little cheeks before kissing his beautiful wife as she struggled with the laundry basket, now full of clean, folded laundry.

His mother-in-law smiled at him and held up a bag of groceries. "I bought ingredients for Italian beef sandwiches," she announced. "A little piece of Chicago."

"Sounds great," he said, putting Meg down and taking the laundry basket.

He opened the door, and the chill hit him in the face. "Jesus," he swore. "What the heck?" It was frigid in the house, way colder than it was outside. He put down the laundry and headed to the thermostat, which read 42 degrees, though it was set at 68 degrees. He tapped it, knowing full well that would have no effect.

He took out his phone and called Allan Mason.

CHAPTER 15

Allan examined the newly installed furnace and saw nothing wrong with it. In the end, he pulled off the thermostat and installed a new one. The furnace instantly kicked on, and within minutes, the house began to warm up. "I'm sorry, Joe. I don't know what was wrong. The thermostat just didn't seem to work. I just replaced it," he said, coming into the living room where Joe and his new father-in-law sat, the latter disapproving of everything. Allan could tell from the expression on his sour face.

"Hey, I just need a workin' furnace. Whatever it takes," Joe replied good-naturedly, shaking Allan's hand. The father-in-law grimaced. The hostility coming off that man was white hot.

"Yeah, I don't know. It was workin' just fine when I installed it, and I can't see anything wrong. Just gonna say it's bad and leave it at that. Let me know if ya have any more problems," Allan replied, looking not at Joe but at the cranky man beside him.

"I knew it. Rosalea was right. This place isn't fit to live in," the old man grumbled.

"That's a bit harsh," Allan interjected. "It's just a bad thermostat. I just put in a brand-new furnace for them. I know the exterior is a little rough, but the house is actually pretty nice. Joe and Bethany are doin' their best to make this place a real home."

Joe was a nice kid. He clearly was mad about Bethany.

And no, the little girl hadn't escaped his notice. Greg Benson was not a Gardner. He was a Harris. But that little girl... she was Gardner through and through. This was obviously not a brand-new relationship. Allan could do math just like anybody else. It was clear that there had been extramarital activity before Greg Benson died, but that was none of his business. And he liked Joe. He did not like Greg. Greg had been, to put it simply, a psychopath.

Allan was not a Harris, but his Uncle Larry was married to Meredith Harris, and as such, his path and Greg Benson's had crossed on more than one occasion. He was a good ten years older than Greg, but he wasn't ashamed to admit that Greg scared him. There was the time Greg got a hold of a BB gun and shot Aunt Mere's old Pekinese with it... by holding the gun against the poor thing's head, killing it, claiming he thought the gun was a toy. Then there was the time Greg had cut Trudy's hair while she slept. Trudy, Allan's baby sister, had long golden hair that fell nearly to her waist. She fell asleep at a New Year's Eve party when she was 13, having been given cold medicine earlier in the evening. She awoke to Greg's raucous laughter while he snipped the last of her golden tresses less than an inch from her skull. There had been something wrong with Greg Benson. Bethany was far better off with Joe than that little monster. How could her father possibly be blind to that?

"Mind your own business," the old man muttered.

"Alrighty then," Allan responded. "Just let me know if ya need anything else, Joe." With that, Allan took his leave, but he decided on his way out that Joe's concerns about the exterior of the house were not unfounded. He made a call to his brother as soon as he got out of the truck.

———

There was a daybed that Joe had dragged around with him for years, that he had stored in the barn when he had moved his stuff from the Harris Farm to Ravens' Roost. He and the boys dragged it into the house after dinner and set it up in the dining room under the window. Bethany put on clean linens, and Meghan set up her bed tent on it. The bed upstairs was too big for the tent, and she was excited to get to use it. She took as many stuffed animals and dolls with her to bed in the tent as she could and was asleep by 8 pm.

Bethany breathed a sigh of relief as she sank into the sofa beside Joe. He pulled her close, and she laid her head on his shoulder. "Whew, what a day," she huffed. "I'm going to sleep tonight."

"Hmmm. Me too, Babe," he concurred.

Her mother, sitting in the armchair, crocheting, smiled. Her father, in the recliner, scowled.

"I promise you, your mother and I will not give you one red cent towards repairs on this shack," he grumbled.

"I don't believe we asked," Bethany replied. Joe chuckled. Why did such a little thing as his warm laugh make her heart soar? "We have our own money, Father."

"How much could you possibly have?" he scoffed.

"Well, Joe had close to $50,000 saved when we got married. And Melanie Horton left me nearly that much. We spent around $5,000 on the new furnace. And between us, we still have over $90,000 saved. Plus, Joe has applied for a VA loan. We don't need the newest and fanciest, Father. I've had that, and it was a prison. I love this old house with its creaking floors and cold drafts. And it's a bit rough looking on the exterior right now, but inside it's home. So, we don't need or want your money," she said, leaning forward, her hands on her knees. "I'm going to take a bath." And she stood and walked into the bedroom to get her pajamas before heading upstairs.

Later that night, after everyone had gone to bed, Joe checked on the boys, finding them sleeping soundly in their rooms. Then he checked on Meghan, who woke as he walked into the dining room.

"Sorry I woke you, Baby," he whispered as she sat up.

"It's okay, Daddy," she said sleepily, lying back down amid her stuffed animals. "Alec is right there. Nothing will hurt me." She pointed to the dining room table and a single empty, out-pulled chair near the wood stove.

"Ah, that's good, then," Joe whispered, smiling. Whether Alec was there or not was immaterial. Meghan felt safe and cozy with the belief. And Joe was beginning to think there was more to this world than could be seen. Had he not himself often spoken to Jemma? And he had believed she heard and saw. Why couldn't Alec be sitting in that chair? "Goodnight, Angel. Goodnight, Alec," he said quietly and turned to join Bethany in bed.

He slept well, believing, like Meghan did, that Alec and maybe others as well were watching over them.

He was in a deep sleep when Bethany's blood-curdling screams for help woke him with a start. He sat up in the bed beside Bethany, who was sitting up herself, screaming. "Help! Help me! Joe!" It wasn't even a yell. It was a scream. Primal. Terrified. Terrifying. He reached out and grabbed her as she blindly fought him.

"Bethy, it's me. Bethy. Stop. I've got you. You're okay," he bellowed, trying to interrupt the scream.

She hyperventilated, trying to catch her breath, recognizing his voice at least, and clung to him instead of fighting against him. Slowly, she calmed down and started to cry. "I'm sorry," she wept. "I sometimes have night terrors. I should have warned you."

"I already know that, Baby. It's okay. I have you."

"Oh. Did I have them back then? Already, I've forgotten how long I've lived with them."

Yet again, his heart broke for her, for having abandoned her, even though there was nothing he could have done. She was right that Greg had had the upper hand. The pandemic had aided that bastard as well. Joe had hit one brick wall after another trying to get to her. Then, when Melanie was so ill after her stroke and knew that she wasn't going to live long, he had asked her to leave Ravens' Roost to Bethany, and only Bethany, as a way to offer her an escape should she choose it. It had been his last-ditch effort. He had never expected Greg to die before she took it.

Yes, she had night terrors back then, though not this intensely. She also talked in her sleep. And the things she'd said haunted him.

She hadn't recognized him, even back then, though she was still drawn to him. The secret that they had known each other, however briefly, was one he had not had the chance to reveal back then. And he wasn't sure how to broach it even now. She had been on a class trip to Washington, DC. He had been 19 years old and on his way home on leave when he had decided to stop to see Rolling Thunder in DC on Memorial Day weekend. She had gotten separated from her group, and he had helped her find them, but not before spending a great day with her.

She'd been different then. Carefree. Innocent. That's how he knew Greg couldn't have thought she was 21. She looked 16. And he, at 19, had been acutely aware of it and had been careful not to confuse matters.

He still saw glimpses of that girl. He hoped he could somehow bring her back, even if it took the rest of his life.

For now, he held her tightly until she stopped trembling, and they both fell back to sleep.

CHAPTER 16

The longer he stayed at Ravens' Roost, the stranger the house felt to James. That night, he heard the water turn on in the bathroom at 3 am. He climbed out of bed, walked out onto the landing, and knocked on the bathroom door. No one answered. But the light shining under the closed door shut off. The water was still running, though. After knocking several times, he tried the doorknob, and it turned freely. He pushed the bathroom door open. The sink and tub faucets were both running, but there was no one in the bathroom. He turned off both faucets and went back to bed, puzzled.

Sunday morning, he awoke, planning to demand that Bethany take them all to church. He found a note instead of his daughter. She, Joe, and the children had gone to Mass at the Catholic Church. She left directions to and service times for Trinity Methodist Church in King George, advising it would take 20 or so minutes to get there. He sputtered in anger.

From the living room, there was a crash, sounding like the window had fallen out of the frame and crashed to the ground, breaking. That sound was followed by a growling and howling as things crashed to the floor around the room, like an animal had jumped through the hole where the window had been and was running around the living room, crashing into furniture and knocking things over. He could swear he heard the television hit the ground and break. But when he rushed to the room, the noise ceased, and there was nothing amiss. The window was still in its frame, and the television was still on the entertainment center. The dog was sleeping soundly in its bed in the corner.

As the week passed, and while Bethany and Joe went to work, the boys to school, and Meghan to the sitters, Ruth slept in late, and while he was alone, he constantly heard an unintelligible murmur in another room. It sounded like a child's whisper. But it was constant. If he was in the living room, the murmur sounded like it was in the bedroom. If he was in the kitchen, it came from the dining room. If he was in the foyer, it came from the living room. It stopped the moment Ruth woke up and joined him downstairs.

The house was making him crazy until, on the morning of Thursday, December 19, when James opened his eyes to look into the face of a demon. He tried to scream, but he was unable to make a sound. He was unable to move. The demon was the shape of a man, but his face was contorted in pain and hatred, and he was transparent. James could see the roses on the wall through the demon. There was a putrid smell that filled the room. And though the man looked to be on fire, the room was frigid. It had been the cold that woke him. He'd been about to get up to yell at Joe that the furnace wasn't working again.

The demon came closer, reaching out for him, grasping and clawing at him, unable to actually touch him, but with murder in its eyes. James gasped. Ruth turned from where she stood, oblivious to the cold and the demon. Her voice sounded far away and like it was underwater, "What is it, dear?" She grew pale and stepped closer. "James? Oh my God! James! Joe, Bethany! There's something wrong with James! Help!"

Through the transparent demon, which grimaced at him in glee, discovering that it could squat on top of his chest, crushing his lungs under a tremendous weight, James saw his daughter and her cretin husband rush into the room before the demon crushed the air from him, and he surrendered to the encroaching darkness.

He came to later in a bright white room to the sound of beeps from a hospital monitor.

"Father?" Bethany's voice, as if from a great distance, said. "Father?" she repeated, sounding more like herself and leaning over him. "He's awake, Mother."

"James?" Ruth said, appearing beside Bethany. "You had a massive heart attack. You need a triple bypass. They'll be taking you back for surgery soon. Thank God Joe was there. He performed CPR on you until the ambulance arrived. He saved your life."

He tried to speak and found he was still unable to.

"Don't try to speak, Father. You've been intubated. I called Blake. He's not able to get away right now. But he'll come after Christmas. And Penelope said Silas needs to tend to your congregation," Bethany said, taking his hand.

Wouldn't you know it? Bethany was the only one who had time for him. Wasn't that just ironic? He slipped back into unconsciousness, clinging to his daughter's hand. The terror was real. The demon was real. It squatted in the corner of the room like a toad, waiting to pounce again. And when it did, it would take his life. He knew it beyond any doubt.

———

"Do you want to stay with your father tonight?" Joe asked.

"No. The doctor said he should be out for the night... and he needs rest. Do you want to get home?"

"Yeah. I don't want to take advantage of Mike's goodwill," he teased. They had left the children with his friend 12 hours ago. He was genuinely concerned about the kids taking advantage of Mike. True, his friend was a deputy, but kids could be scarier than criminals when you weren't used to dealing with them.

She stood and walked over to shake Ruth. "Mother," she whispered.

Ruth stirred and looked up at her. "We're going home for the night. You should come with us. I'll bring you back in the morning."

Ruth nodded and gathered her purse. "James, get some rest," was all she said to her sleeping husband. Joe didn't understand this family.

He and Bethy walked arm in arm while Ruth trailed ghostlike behind them. She never spoke. He left Bethy and Ruth at the door to go retrieve the car. They stood silently beside each other as he walked away. When he pulled up, they were standing exactly where he had left them in the same position, still not speaking. He scratched his head. Bethy opened the passenger side door. Ruth climbed mutely into the backseat. Bethy got into the front seat and closed the door. In unison, they fastened their seat belts.

He loaded a CD into the radio/CD player and grabbed Bethy's hand. Music filled the silence, and he pulled away.

"Mmmm. This is good," Bethy said, swaying to the bluesy riffs. "Who is this?"

"Chris Stapleton," he answered.

"I like it," she said, closing her eyes to feel the music.

"Yes, it's quite nice," Ruth said from the back seat.

That was all they said. Not a word of comfort to each other, not a single expression of worry over James. He knew they both cared. He'd seen Bethy cling to her father's hand. He'd seen Ruth wiping his forehead tenderly. He was completely baffled by the dynamic.

That was it. They were silent for the rest of the ride.

———

Ruth sat in the back seat, watching Bethany. It had been over twelve years since she had last seen her daughter. Rosalea and that Greg had spirited her away and kept her from even talking to Ruth without supervision. Bethany. Her Bethany. Her last hope. Gone. James and those people crushed that girl's spirit. She had receded into her shell.

But as she watched her now, she saw her daughter. The calm smile graced her face as if it had never vanished. Her body swayed to the music as if it were free to dance. Her hand reached for the man's as if it belonged in his. This Bethany was the same girl who had begged for dance lessons despite James's objections, who excelled in school, and who laughed. She hadn't been crushed. She'd merely been sleeping, awaiting an opportunity to awaken and break free.

When they arrived back at the house, Bethany exited the car and ran to the man's side as if even a few seconds out of his reach were too much to bear. He laughed and pulled her close, kissing her cheek and, unsatisfied with that, her neck. He was captivated. He was…in love. Ruth was certain. That man loved Bethany. What's more, Bethany loved him.

Rosalea had claimed that Bethany had gotten married as a means to thwart her mother-in-law from taking rightful claim to the property and bringing her and the kids home. She claimed the man had married Bethany to get her money and the farm. But that was not what Ruth saw. Those might be benefits to both of them, but they were married to be with each other, to be partners to each other, to bolster each other. Her Bethany had awakened. Damned if she was going to let anybody put her back to sleep.

"Joe?" she said as she got out of the back seat. "May I speak to you for a moment…privately?"

He stopped, releasing Bethany. "Um. Okay," he replied, walking back toward her. Bethany continued up onto the porch and opened the front door. Once she had disappeared inside, Ruth grabbed Joe's arm.

"Do not give up. James…the Bensons, they'll urge you to leave. They'll offer you money. They'll threaten you. But don't give up. She's…better off with you. No matter what they say." she pleaded.

"Mrs. West…" he started.

"Ruth," she corrected him.

"Ruth, I have no intention of giving up," he assured her. "You shouldn't, either." He smiled and took her arm, leading her up the porch steps.

She laughed. She hadn't laughed in a long time. It felt good. She took his elbow, and he led her inside.

"Duke, you're so pretty," Bethany said as they walked through the door.

Joe looked into the living room. "What did you do to my dog?" he exclaimed. The dog was wearing a tutu, a tiara, and several long, beaded Mardi Gras necklaces.

"More importantly, what did he do to earn those necklaces?" Bethany cooed, scratching the dog on the jowl. "Such a pretty boy." The dog wagged his tail and panted.

"Boys! Don't let your sister dress the dog," Joe said, shaking his head. "Duke, you don't have to put up with this. Good boy." He reached down and took off the tiara and necklaces and petted the animal. "Bad children." He shook his finger at them and then winked.

The three children burst out laughing.

"Where's Mike? Have you tied him up in a closet?" Joe

asked the children.

Meghan ran to him, wrapping her arms around his legs. "You're so silly, Daddy!" she giggled. "He's in the bathroom, of course."

He growled playfully, reached down, and scooped the child up in one arm, slinging her over his shoulder. "Gotcha!" he laughed. Meghan giggled.

"Is Granddaddy okay, Granny?" the boy called Jessup asked.

Ruth wanted to cry. He called her Granny. Like it was nothing. Only it was everything.

"Thank you, Jessup. He's as well as can be expected," she replied, smiling.

Bethany stared at her with her mouth open. "Mother, you answered to 'Granny'!" she said in amazement.

"I like 'Granny.' Grandmother is so stuffy," she announced, sticking her chin in the air.

"'Granny' it is then," Joe concurred.

A warm feeling spread over her...like the house was welcoming her. She sang *Hound Dog* softly under her breath as she climbed the stairs. She hadn't listened to Elvis in years, but he'd been a favorite of hers when she was a child. She didn't know why that song popped into her head. Maybe because of Duke...

CHAPTER 17

Joe, having taken the day off at the garage because the kids were off for Christmas break, awoke to the smell of bacon and coffee. He felt behind him to discover that Duke occupied Bethany's side of the bed. "Get down," he grumbled. This was Bethany's doing. She had been letting Duke on the furniture. "Where's Mommy?" he asked the German Shepherd. The dog looked at the bedroom door. "Big help. I can see she's not in the room," Joe chuckled.

He climbed out of bed and followed the smell to the kitchen, Duke on his heels. There was Bethany standing over the stove. "How do I know when they're ready to flip?" she asked, holding a spatula in the air.

"You see the bubbles? When they pop and leave a dimple, instead of closing up, you flip the pancake," Ruth instructed her.

"Oh, like that?" Bethany asked, pointing at the pan in front of her.

"Yes, exactly. Flip it," Ruth told her.

She flipped the pancake and laughed. "Look at me. I'm making pancakes," she squealed, seeing Joe in the doorway.

"I see," he said, grinning. "I smell bacon and coffee, too."

"Oh. Look. Look at my bacon! I only burned a few pieces," she giggled, holding up a plate full of bacon. "I can officially cook more than just scrambled eggs and oatmeal for breakfast now."

"That's great, Babe. Because, to be honest, you can't really make oatmeal," he teased.

The doorbell rang. Joe turned around and went to answer it. Mike stood on the porch, ready to work on installing the windows.

"G'mornin'," Joe greeted him. "Come on in. I just got up. Bethany and her mom are makin' breakfast if you'd like some."

"I could eat," Mike replied, sniffing the air.

"You usually can," Joe laughed.

Soon, they were all seated around the table. The kids were laughing. The adults were talking. The mood was pleasant. Joe felt a cold chill creep over him. Goose pimples formed on his arms. He rubbed his arms to warm them.

Bethany's phone rang. She looked at the caller ID. "The hospital," she said. They had left her number as her mother did not have a phone; only James did, and Ruth did not know his passcode to open it. Bethany accepted the call and held the phone to her ear. "Hello," she answered. "This is his daughter. Um…code 5421. What?" Her mouth fell open, and a gasp escaped from it. She closed her eyes and frowned. "I understand," she said, tears falling down her cheeks. "Yes. Thank you for calling." She grabbed Ruth's hand. The room fell quiet in dread. She disconnected and laid her phone on the table. "Father suffered a fatal heart attack about 20 minutes ago," she announced, her lip quivering. She sniffed and started to sob.

Joe pushed back his chair and was beside her in seconds. "I'm so sorry, Baby," he said, pulling her to him and hugging her.

Ruth looked at her hands. Oddly, Joe thought, she looked…relieved. Maybe it was just resolved.

She calmly patted Bethany's hand. "May I use your phone, dear?" she asked.

Bethany nodded, locking her hands together behind Joe's back as she held onto him for dear life.

Ruth took the phone and typed "nearby funeral homes" into Google. She called the number that came up and walked out of the room when they answered.

Joe and Mike headed outside to finish installing the windows after Joe dressed quickly.

He offered to go with Bethany and Ruth to the hospital to pick up James's effects, but Bethany said he should stay with the kids and finish the windows. She wanted some time with her mother.

Bethany and Ruth left at 8 am.

Missy walked down the street from her house to see if Jess and Ryan wanted to play Minecraft. Joe was pretty sure Ryan would play anything Missy asked him to. While the pre-teens played on the PS5, Meghan sat cross-legged on the ground with Duke next to her, watching Joe and Mike work.

When they got to Joe and Bethany's first bedroom window, they made quick work of getting the old window out, and Joe discovered some wood rot on the sill. "Crap," he complained. "Looks like it's just the sill, but I'm gonna need to run to the hardware store. Can you watch the kids for me again really quick?"

Mike laughed. "You know I'll do anything for you. No matter what or when."

Joe smiled. "Thanks, Mike, but that's overkill. I didn't bring him home in one piece like I promised." Joe didn't feel like Mike owed him anything at all. He felt he owed Mike... and Kenny so much more.

"Joe. You threw yourself on top of him. Nobody could

have done more. Kenny is alive…and mostly alright. He's a little slower, a little more childlike. But he was childlike already. We owe you everything for what you did for my brother. We'll never forget it. I'll watch the kids," Mike assured him.

"Can I go with you, Daddy?" Meghan asked, standing.

"Did Mommy leave your booster?" he asked.

She nodded.

"Alright, then," he agreed.

"Yay!" she exclaimed, running off to retrieve her booster.

———

Mike took a break while Joe and Meg went to the hardware store in Colonial Beach. He gazed lovingly at Missy for a moment while no one was watching. Then he went to the kitchen, looking in the refrigerator. "Iced tea," he said, taking the pitcher out. "Do they got any lemons?" he asked the room after he set the pitcher on the counter. He turned to look in the fridge again, and the pitcher crashed into the wall opposite where he had placed it. He straightened and looked back to where he had set the tea and then at the wall. 6 feet… at least.

Jessup, Ryan, and Missy came running. "What happened?" Ryan asked.

Mike pointed to the counter and then the wall. He was having trouble comprehending what happened. "I…uh… something threw the tea across the room," he said, mystified. "Is there a ghost?" he asked, unable to think of a reasonable explanation.

Ryan laughed. "Meggy says there's a ghost named Alec," he teased. "Did you make Alec mad, Deputy Poole?"

"I…I don't think so," Mike replied. "I'm sorry, Alec, if

I offended you somehow."

He felt his hair stand on end as a voice hissed, "I'm not Alec!" He jumped. It sounded like...James West.

"Did you hear that?" he yelped.

"Hear what?" Jessup asked.

Ryan shrugged. Missy shook her head. "I didn't hear nuthin', Mike," she said, hugging him around the waist.

"I'm losin' my mind," Mike said sardonically, hugging her back.

———

Bethany reached across the table and took her mother's hands. "Isn't this place great? Joe brought me here last week."

Ruth smiled sadly. "Yes, dear. You always liked this Irish stuff."

Bethany breathed in happily through her nose, sighing contentedly. "I always wanted a claddagh ring," she declared. She held up her wedding set and gazed at it adoringly.

The waitress who was nearby overheard and offered, "There is a really cute shop on Caroline Street called Irish Eyes. If you like this kind of stuff, it should be right up your alley."

"Oh, thank you," Bethany replied.

The waitress nodded and went to get their lunch.

"I want to stay with you," her mother said, abruptly.

"I'm sorry. Wh...what?" Bethany asked, choking on her Coke.

"I don't want to go back to Illinois," she clarified. "I would like to find an apartment or something near you and the children. Your sister and her husband will be moving into the parsonage, anyway. I won't live with that, Kyle. He's a little monster." She dropped her voice to a whisper as if Kyle might be listening.

"I don't think he can hear you from Virginia, Maaaaaa...mom," she sputtered.

Ruth beamed. "You called me 'Mom.' You haven't called me Mom in years."

The waitress returned with their grilled chicken salads. Ruth dug through the greens in front of her with her fork. After several minutes, she said, "I'm so sorry, Sweetheart. I failed you. I didn't protect you from your father and the Bensons. I didn't think I had the strength. Maybe I didn't. But you do. You are so strong. I...I don't expect you to forgive me. I can't even forgive myself. I love you, Bethany. You...you were my hope. And I let your father nearly destroy you. But instead of...becoming like me...you became...everything I hoped for you. A great mother, a strong, intelligent woman, happy. Ohhh...that man loves you...so much. He's a good man."

Bethany chuckled. "I love him, too, Mom. It's like I've known him forever."

"You never loved Greg?"

"No. How could I?"

"Bethany, who's Meghan's father?" her mother asked.

"Can't you tell?" she chuckled.

They finished eating, and as they stood to leave, Bethany said, "I want you to stay, too. And I *do* forgive you."

———

Joe and Meghan quickly found the supplies Joe needed to repair the rotting windowsill. He bought extra, in case the other windows had the same problem, with the manager's assurance he could return any wood he didn't cut. As he turned to leave, Kenny Poole approached him.

"You got married," Kenny said sadly.

"Hi, Kenny," Joe said. "Yeah, I did. But I promise,

when we have a wedding in a few months, you'll be a part of it. It was just the spur of the moment. You'll like her, Kenny."

Kenny nodded. "Where's Mikey?" he asked, looking around for his brother.

"Where's Pam?" Joe asked. That was the more important question. Pam took care of Kenny. She appeared around an endcap, and Joe sighed in relief. "Ah, I see her. Mike's at my house." He thought for a second and then asked, "Do you want to come over and help, too?"

Kenny's face lit up, and he turned to look at Pam Poole. "Can I?" he asked, like a child asking permission from his mother. The fraternal twins, Mike and Kenny, called her their sister. Fifteen years older than Kenny and Mike, she had practically raised them. Everyone suspected she wasn't really their sister, but no one said anything.

"Mike can bring him home, Pam," Joe said, and she nodded. Kenny bounced up and down with excitement.

Joe paid for his items, and he, Kenny, and Meghan climbed into his truck.

Back at Ravens' Roost, he unloaded the supplies while Meghan took Kenny by the hand and showed him around.

Mike was sitting on the porch, smoking a cigarette.

"I thought you quit," Joe laughed.

"I did. But the ghost of Reverend West threw a pitcher of tea at me in your kitchen, so I started again," he retorted.

"Pardon?" Joe asked, taken aback.

"Yeah. I know. I'm losin' my mind, but the pitcher flew across the room on its own, and I swear I heard that asshole's voice."

"What's in that cigarette?" Joe teased.

"You're right. It's crazy. The kids didn't hear it...so maybe the tea just spooked me. I wish I could explain it. Let's just get done. I don't want to still be here after dark." He was joking. But he was spooked for real. Joe could tell.

———————

Bethany and Ruth got back to the house at quarter after 3 in the afternoon. She found Joe and Mike hard at work replacing a windowsill. Meghan and Kenny were sitting across from each other cross-legged on the ground, playing jacks.

Bethany waved at Kenny and called to Joe, who was up on the ladder about 6 feet up, "Hi, Honey!"

"Hey," he responded cheerily. "Hold on." He set down his hammer and climbed down to kiss her.

She returned the kiss and turned to go inside.

Kenny laughed and clapped. "Bethany and Jag...sittin' in a tree k...i...s...s...i...n...g..." he chanted as Joe climbed back up the ladder.

She whirled back around, her heart in her throat. "What did you say?" she exclaimed, a little more loudly than she'd intended. Kenny jumped back. "I'm sorry. I'm not yelling at you. I...what did you call him?"

"Jag," he answered.

Joe laughed. "It's okay, Sweetheart, it's just a nickname. It's my initials. You remember that old TV show?"

"Jag?" she repeated in shock.

"Yeah," he said, winking.

"Ahhh," she squeaked, backing up.

His eyes clouded over; his brow furrowed. "What?" he asked.

"That was you?" she said. "In DC." She stepped back. "Oh, my God."

Joe swallowed hard. "Bethy?" he whispered. He already knew. She could see it in his eyes.

CHAPTER 18

Joe followed Bethany into the house. "You are Jag?" she said, turning to face him. "Why didn't you say something?"

"Does it matter? You didn't remember me. It was just a few hours. What's important is what came later," he said, taking her hand. "You didn't know me yet. It was nothing."

"It wasn't nothing, my Darling. It was a great day. It's a cherished memory. And I'm glad it was with you," she smiled sweetly. She paused a moment before taking his hand. "I'm not going to break, Joe. I know I seem weak, but I'm not."

"I don't think you're weak. Not at all. You're the strongest person I know," he proclaimed. "I just don't know what is painful for you and what is not. I don't know what pain I caused, what pain your family caused, or Greg caused. And I'm trying to navigate it in the dark. But I'm not trying to keep things from you. I swear."

She nodded and sighed. "If I want you to tell me everything, I should tell you everything, too. I get it. But it's a lot, Joe." She bit her lip nervously, the way she did when she was trying to make a decision. "Let's go to our room. Not here in the foyer…okay?"

Holding her hand, he allowed her to lead him into their bedroom. He closed the door behind them. There was a soft scent of rosewater in the room he had never noticed before. "Hmmm. It smells like Melanie," he noted.

"Does it? I found a hope chest in the closet. This quilt was in it. It smells like rosewater. Everything in the chest

did," she said, sitting on the quilt, which was spread out on
the bed. "It still smells of it even after I washed it." She ran
her hand over it.

Joe sat beside her. "It's nice, though. The smell, I mean.
The quilt is nice, too…oh, geez. I don't know what to say."

Bethany laughed softly and kissed his cheek. "I met
you on my junior class trip. It was one week before I met
Greg. I'm going to start there, okay?"

He nodded again.

She laughed as she began, "First of all, no way were
you this tall."

He laughed, too. "No. I wasn't. I grew three more
inches that year."

"See, there are very good reasons I didn't know it was
you. You went by Jag. And you were three inches shorter.
Those eyes, though. I should have known."

She lay against him before she continued. "My father
never liked me. I suppose he loved me. I don't know. I was
never good enough. Penelope was his pride and joy. Miss
Perfect," she sighed. "Blake tried really hard, but he could
never measure up. I…I wouldn't say I didn't try. I just never
understood what I was supposed to do. I got good grades. I
attended church. I participated the way I was supposed to, but
the things I enjoyed…well, he always deemed those things
as sinful. The shows I watched, the books I read…Harry
Potter was a whole catastrophe. My music. My dance classes.
Pom. Glee club. All sinful. I meant it when I told Jillian I was
the black sheep…because I was unwilling to give up those
things to get his love. I settled for his disdain. We fought over
my going to DC. He refused to let me. Penelope signed my
permission slip. I thought she did it because she believed I
should go, but no. She…she likes me even less than Father

did. She did it to drive a wedge even further. I went against his wishes. So, when I got home, he was so angry. The thing was, Penelope went…as a chaperone. He wasn't even a little mad at her."

"I'm sorry, Bethy. It must hurt to have a parent treat you that way."

"Mmmm. I was used to it, Joe. But as punishment, I was sentenced to service. I had to stay by my father's side for a month. And my father had court in Chicago the next week, so I went with him. He was a witness for the defense. Three girls from our church had signed up through a ministry presented during a service, endorsed by my father and the church council, to go on a mission to Uganda. The training was provided by the mission at a facility in New York. While at the training facility, the girls claimed they were sexually harassed and assaulted in varying degrees. Their families were suing the church and the missionary organization. And at first, I had fun, just to spite Father. I even wrote Jag a long love letter." She batted her eyes.

"Stop it," Joe whispered.

"No. I did. But Father found it and tore it up. He burned it in the trash can on the balcony of our hotel room with me watching. Then he made me stand…as in I was not allowed to sit…on the balcony for two hours in prayer. Hands pressed together in front of my chin. Eyes closed. I was very dizzy. I fell coming in off the balcony and scraped both my knees and my palms. Anyway, I missed lunch, and I was feeling lightheaded from the standing with my arms up, and eyes closed. He told me to put on a pretty dress that he bought me."

"Wait. What?"

"I thought it was an apology."

"Bethany," Joe gasped.

"I know. But I was still a kid...for a few more hours anyway. And it was a pretty dress, unlike anything he'd ever bought me before. It was red, and it had straps instead of sleeves. And the skirt was just above my knees."

"God..." Joe sobbed.

"He took me to dinner, and Greg was there. And I was starving because I hadn't eaten. And he ordered a Shirley Temple for me. Then he got a call from a parishioner and asked Greg if he'd mind keeping me company." She kind of laughed as a tear rolled down her cheek. "This is where I've always said I stopped remembering. But that isn't true. I remember it. I was just unable to stop it...to fight. Greg didn't save me from anybody. He beat me himself before...during... after...I was...so ashamed."

"Why? You didn't do anything wrong."

"Yeah, I know. But I was still a child. I believed I did. I believed that I should have been able to fight." She took a sharp, jagged breath. "The worst thing was Greg gave him money...right in front of me. He took me back to our room in that torn...red...dress and knocked on the door. My father answered. And Greg handed him $200. I was worth $200." She buried her face in her hands.

Joe pulled her to him and smoothed her hair as she cried into his shirt. He was trembling in anger and in grief. But he held her, and they both cried.

From upstairs came a loud bang...as if all the doors on the second floor slammed shut at once.

"What was that?" Joe asked. "Our ghost sure has been angry today." He laughed nervously. James West, is that you, you bastard? he thought, looking around the room.

After everyone had gone to bed, Joe sat up. The house

grew quiet. He sat watching the fire through the wood stove's glass door. "If you'd asked me 12 years ago if I believed in ghosts, I'd've told ya no. Then Jemma died. And I never saw her or experienced anything like I have since being in this house, but I knew…just knew…her spirit was with us. So, I'm gonna tell ya, Reverend West…I'm not sorry you're dead. I'm happy if you're stuck. I'd be happier if you were burning in hell. You brought it on yourself. But I acknowledge that God commands love and forgiveness. It's not my place to forgive you. Bethy hurts from what you did, but she does forgive you. So, why shouldn't I? I'll offer you some advice. Don't let your anger keep you here. Because…we're goin' to be happy regardless of how many doors you slam or pitchers of tea you throw. I love Bethy. Meghan is my daughter. I'm goin' to adopt Ryan. Bethy is goin' to adopt Jess. We're a family. And you can accept that and rest in peace or not and slam a few doors. In the end, you'll either be welcomed by love or consumed by hate. Your choice," he said to the night. The night was quiet in response.

———

Bethany was roused by Joe's lowering his weight onto the mattress beside her. It occurred to her that this was the moment she had always feared while married to Greg, whereas now, she awaited it with anticipation. She felt no fear. In fact, she couldn't wait for Joe to lie down beside her. And when he did, she felt safe. What a juxtaposition!

She moaned contentedly and reached out to lay her hand across his chest. He grabbed her hand and kissed it. "Sorry I woke you, Baby," he whispered.

"Mmmm. That's okay. I don't mind your waking me," she mumbled, snuggling in closer. She sighed. "You know that day…that night…it doesn't define me anymore. You know what I wrote about in that letter? Dancing with Jag at a staging area for Rolling Thunder. Some bikers were playing music, and we danced. Right there on the sidewalk."

He coughed.

She smiled. "The song was *I Can't Help Falling in Love* by Elvis Presley," she said, patting his chest.

He was stifling his laugh. "Yeah. You got me. I *did* add that song to my playlist. I just didn't want to explain why. Happy?"

"Hmmmm, yes. Very," she giggled. He rolled to face her, pulling her close.

"I'll never dance with anyone else to that song."

"You'd better not," she whispered huskily. He kissed her, and she wrapped herself around him…blissfully.

In the distance, she heard a door slam.

CHAPTER 19

Saturday, December 21, Joe was scheduled to work at Mason's garage. He left after breakfast. Bethany took Meghan to play with Kelly Madison and was then going to do laundry. Ruth went with her, but the boys stayed home.

As she pulled into Madison's Dairy to drop Meg off, her phone rang. She put the Caddy in park and pulled the phone out of her purse. Blake's name appeared on her caller ID. She sighed and accepted the call. She pasted on a smile and greeted her brother, "Good morning, Blake." She held the phone away from her ear as Blake lambasted her. "I didn't convince Mom to hold the funeral here. That was her idea. No. Of course, I will come home for the funeral if that is what Mom wants. She says she wants it here. I don't know. She's right here. Would you like to speak with her? I'm…Blake… Blake. I have to take Meghan in to the sitter. Here, talk to Mom." She handed the phone to her mother and opened the door with attitude. "Come on, Meg. Mrs. Madison is waiting."

When she got back to the car, her mother handed her the phone, having disconnected the call. "Blake and Trudy are on their way. Your sister still insists that she is not coming and that the funeral and burial will be in Sterling. I told Blake she'll miss her father's funeral in that case," she told Bethany. "Your brother and sister do not take me seriously."

"I'm sorry, Mom. I swear, if you want to take him home, we'll go with you, and we'll bring you back if that's what you want," Bethany assured her. It was reasonable, after all, that his congregation would want to say goodbye. But Ruth was adamant.

"I don't have anything against Sterling...or the congregation," she explained. "They're good people. I just never want to go back to that house where I...ceased to matter."

Bethany spent the morning doing laundry at Hall's Laundromat on Route 205. She drove back to Madison's Dairy to pick up Meghan before heading home.

Shortly after 4 pm, Bethany took Duke out. It was a brisk December day. She sat on the porch step and hugged her knees for warmth, letting Duke run free, chasing squirrels around the yard. He never came close to catching any, but given the dog's speed, she suspected Duke wasn't really trying to catch them. He was just having fun. Why had she ever been afraid of dogs? Duke was amazing. He was her "widdle baby boy," and she laughed at the German Shepherd's antics.

She saw the car coming down the street. She called Duke to her side and grabbed his collar as the vehicle slowed and turned into her driveway. She slipped on his leash and stood to welcome her brother and his family.

"What a dump!" Blake proclaimed, exiting the rental car.

"It's just cosmetic," Bethany said, trying hard to maintain her smile. "Joe just finished installing all new windows, and we just replaced the furnace."

"Joe?" Blake said with a sneer, feigning ignorance. "Oh, that man who conned you into marrying him to get the farm."

"That's not what happened," she returned, dropping all pretense now, sneering back at him.

"I'm sure it's very nice inside," Trudy, his wife, said,

climbing out of the passenger seat. The words were polite, but Bethany wondered if she was sincere.

"Whatever. Bring the kids inside," she said. "You got here fast."

"We were already at the gate at O'Hare when I called this morning," Blake said.

"You're not taking that...dog...into the house, are you?" Trudy blanched.

"Of course I am. He lives here," Bethany retorted. Petting Duke's head, she cooed, "Don't you, sweet widdle boy?"

"Little?" Trudy whispered to her husband. They helped their kids, Tiffany, 10, Peter, 8, and Michelle, 2, a pandemic baby, out of the backseat. Trudy, carrying the toddler, with the other two trailing behind her, followed Bethany inside.

Blake stuffed his hands into his pants pockets and begrudgingly came in last.

"Meg, put Duke in my room, and then come say hi to your cousins and aunt and uncle," Bethany called from just inside the door. Oddly enough, she didn't feel the cold spot just inside the door as she usually did.

"Oh, it's not that bad," Trudy muttered, looking around.

"Good enough that a farmer would covet it," Blake asserted.

Eight years older than Bethany, Blake had always resented resigning his position as the baby. Not that Bethany benefited from being the baby. Their father clearly favored Penelope over both his younger children. Given Penelope was 4 years older than Blake and 12 years older than Bethany, she wondered if her father had even wanted her and her brother at all. Still, Blake at least grew on the reverend as he had followed in his footsteps. Bethany had never made any headway in garnering her father's affections.

"That's just not true, Blake," Bethany assured him. "I know you won't believe it, but we're actually in love."

"Impossible," he responded.

Meghan, having emerged from her bedroom upstairs, descended the staircase. "Hi!" she said excitedly, happy to meet her extended family.

Bethany handed her the dog's leash.

"Do you trust that animal around her?" Trudy asked.

"Yes" was the only answer offered. Nothing more. Bethany didn't need to explain anything to these people.

Meghan put the dog in her parents' bedroom. When she returned, Bethany asked, "Is Granny upstairs?"

"Uh-huh," Meg answered. "She's lying down because she has a headache."

Outside, Jessup and Ryan appeared from the backyard, where they had been playing football, and ran toward the house, coming through the door at full speed.

"I win," Ryan said, raising his arms over his head like Rocky.

"You're pretty fast," Jessup admitted. "But you did have a head start."

"I am the wiener!" Ryan sing-songed, dancing in a circle.

Jessup laughed.

It brought a smile to Bethany's face, replacing the fake one she'd been wearing since her brother had arrived. She sat down in the old leather recliner Joe had brought with him and reclined, closing her eyes.

"Are you tired, Mama?" Jessup asked, coming into the living room,

"Mmmm. Yeah, I'm a little tired. I spent all morning at the laundromat. I've made a dent in the laundry, but I think Daddy is right about our needing a washer and dryer. And I'm getting a headache, too. What do you need?"

"I don't need anything. But I can rub your head for you if you like. My Grandma Esther used to like it when I rubbed her head when she had a headache," he offered.

Bethany smiled and took the boy's hand. "Thank you, Jessup. That might help," she said. Mostly, all Jessup wanted was a mother's love, and she had that in abundance. She had never really been a fan of being rubbed, but Jessup needed to feel needed, so she let him.

Trudy, being nosy, dug through the study guides on the desk in the corner.

"You're taking your GED exam?" Trudy inquired.

"Yeah. Next week," she answered. "My boss is paying for it and wants me to start college in January."

"Where are you working?" Trudy asked conversationally.

"Filmore Morgan, Attorney at Law. He was Melanie Horton's stepfather and the executor of her will. He's a very kind man."

Her brother grumbled unintelligibly.

"What'd you say, Blake?" she asked.

"Nothing. Where's Mother? I want to discuss the funeral arrangements and go check into our hotel room."

"She has a headache. Why don't you go check into your hotel? And we'll meet you for dinner at 7."

He sighed heavily. "Where?"

"There's a restaurant called Raven's Point over by the hotel on Washington Ave.," she said, smiling smugly.

"And you'll bring Mother?"

"Believe it or not, Blake, I agree with you. I think he should be buried in Sterling, and the funeral should be in his Church," she told him.

She felt a warm, comforting sensation, similar to the one she had felt before...but different somehow. The lamp beside her seemed to burn brighter for a second. Then the sensation was gone, and the light bulb's incandescence returned to normal.

Outside, the barn door swung in a sudden wind, and the large oak tree behind the house groaned and toppled, its roots breaking free from the ground, leaving a large hole. The massive trunk came crashing into the barn, completely destroying it.

Bethany jumped up and ran to see what had happened. Her brother followed.

As she rounded the house and saw the destruction, she gasped, covering her mouth with both hands. All of Joe's farming equipment was in that barn.

"Wow," her brother said. "Good thing the tree fell away from the house."

"Yeah. At least nobody was hurt," she agreed.

———

Joe stared at the wreckage. He shook his head. "The equipment is insured, but even so, I'll have to take out loans to replace everything. I'll never get approved for that. My wheat will rot in the field. I'm...done." He'd cry if he could. But the devastation was so overwhelming that emotion was beyond his ability. He was numb.

"There wasn't that much wind today. How did this even happen?" Norm Mason asked, standing beside his employee. He'd followed him out of concern when Joe had, out of character, left work after a call from his wife.

"My brother suggested a micro downburst. I didn't notice any thunder or lightning though, just a sudden, strong wind. It blew over the tree and then was gone. That's weird, right?" Bethany explained, standing on the other side of Joe.

"Jesus, what a mess!" Joe muttered.

"I'm so sorry, Honey," Bethany said, sniffing.

Joe draped his arm around her shoulders and pulled her to him, kissing her on top of the head. "Thank God it fell on the barn and not the house. We'll have to get a tree guy out here to check the big oak out front that lost a branch before Thanksgiving. We don't want that one coming down on the house," he suggested.

"That's probably a good idea," Norm agreed.

He looked at Joe, concerned, but Joe looked okay. The girl might have something to do with that, Norm mused. Joe had seemed happier since she had come into his life. Even this didn't seem to break that happy bubble that had encased him these last few days. Sure, Joe recognized the seriousness of the situation. This would surely set his dream of farming back by at least a year, but he was okay.

"We'll get through it," she said. "We might exhaust our savings, but that's what savings are for."

"Mmmm," Joe answered. "You're right, Mrs. Gardner. Hey, Boss…I'll take as much overtime as you can throw at me." He laughed, but he was serious. Joe was one of his hardest workers. He absolutely would take as much OT as Norm could give him.

The hair on the back of Norm's neck stood on end, and he felt a sudden chill. The corner of the barn, still standing, suddenly fell. He jumped. Was that a scream?

"Is there somebody in there?" he yelled.

"There shouldn't be!" Joe replied, removing his arm

from Bethany's shoulders and running toward the collapsed structure. Norm ran after him. "Call 911!" Joe yelled at Bethany.

————

Bethany was on the phone with 911 when Jillian pulled into the driveway in her minivan. She lowered her window and called, "Hey, is Missy here?"

Bethany lowered her phone in horror. "Missy!" she screamed. She turned back toward the barn and ran toward it. "Joe! Joe!" she yelled. He was climbing carefully on top of the debris. He looked up at her. "Missy is missing!"

"Missy!" he called. "Are you in there? Can you hear me? Missy!"

Jillian had climbed out of her car when Bethany had turned away like that. When she saw the barn and heard Joe yelling for Missy, she screamed. "Nooooo! Missy!"

Bethany held her back.

Suddenly, Blake was running toward the barn, too. "Tell me what to do!" he called up to Joe.

"I'm goin' to start shiftin' debris. I'll hand it down to you. Keep listenin'. Let me know if you hear her!"

Jillian collapsed into Bethany's arms. "It's not certain she's in there," she said, trying to offer some hope to her friend. But as soon as she'd seen Jillian's vehicle, she'd known that had been Missy's voice she'd heard.

Trudy came around the house and helped to bolster Jillian up. "Hi," she said, wrapping her arms around Jillian just like Bethany was. "I'm Trudy West, Bethany's sister-in-law. You don't know me, but I'd like to offer a prayer for your daughter if you'd let me."

Jillian, tears in her eyes, just nodded.

"Dear Heavenly Father, please watch over Missy. Let

us find her safe and bring her back to her mother's arms. Wrap her in your loving embrace, Lord. Guide those trying to rescue her. In Jesus's blessed name, we pray. Amen."

"Amen," Bethany said tearfully.

Poor Jillian wasn't able to speak, but she mouthed "Amen."

The Oak Grove Volunteer Fire Department responded. Soon, the barn was surrounded by men and women. Calls of "Missy!" filled the air.

Colonial Beach Fire Department and Rescue Squad also responded. Neighbors came by the dozens. The refrigerator filled to the seams. Jillian's car was also filled with food. It seemed that those who couldn't help dig through the rubble took to their kitchens instead.

As the light waned, the firetrucks positioned themselves and turned on their lights, and spotlights were set up. A crane was brought in to lift the giant oak off the barn.

Finally, it was Joe who yelled, "Missy! I found her! Keep talkin' to me, Sweetheart. I'm coming!"

It seemed the world held its breath. There must have been sound, but all Bethany heard was her own heartbeat. Jillian clasped her arm so tightly, though she didn't feel it. Everything seemed to move in slow motion. Joe disappeared down into the rubble. And then suddenly, there was sound again, and the world returned to regular speed. Joe emerged, carrying Missy.

Jillian ran toward Joe and Missy. The EMTs rushed forward with a board. Joe gently knelt and placed the child on it. He stepped back as Jillian and the EMTs surrounded her. The spotlight shone on Joe like a halo. Bethany's heart was in her throat. She was relieved Missy had been found, of course, but all she saw was Joe. "He's so cool," she whispered.

Trudy, still beside her, smiled and half hugged her. "Yeah, he really is. He's cute, too." She winked at Bethany.

The air filled with applause as Missy held a thumbs up when the EMTs lifted the board onto the gurney, which they loaded into the ambulance.

Before Bethany knew what was happening, portable tables appeared on her lawn, and food was brought out of the house. Paper plates and sodas appeared from nowhere. All the volunteers were fed.

Joe disappeared into the house.

————

Joe didn't want to be rude, but he needed a moment alone. The whole scene hit a little too close to home and reeked of painful memories.

He took a moment to catch his breath and a shower... just to settle his nerves. When he emerged from the bathroom, he found Ryan sitting on the floor outside the bathroom door, hugging Duke and crying. He squatted, leaning his hands on his knees in front of the boy. "What's the matter, Ryan?"

"It's all my fault! I told Missy about the skeleton, and she wanted to see it. I told her we weren't allowed in the barn, but she must have snuck in..." he sobbed.

"It's not your fault. But I know how you feel. When I was a senior in high school, I decided I wanted to be a Marine. I told everybody I was going to enlist. My buddy, Mike, had a fraternal twin, Kenny. Kenny was a skinny, little shy guy who followed me and Mike around wherever we went. Kenny declared he was going to enlist, too. And when that recruiter came to our school, he signed right on that line, just like I did. I told his family he'd be fine. I'd take care of him. And I did. We went through basic training together and ended up in the same unit. Lo and behold, we ended up in

Afghanistan. He was driving a Humvee and went off the road. The vehicle flipped, and…he wasn't wearing his helmet. I… uh…I managed to get him out, but we fell under heavy fire. I had a broken leg, but I shielded him until our unit rescued us. I got a Purple Heart and a Medal of Valor. My leg healed. And…well…you've met Kenny. It wasn't my fault, but it sure feels like it was. Missy is goin' to be okay. She was real lucky. The tree missed her, and though she was trapped, she was in a pocket. The barn fell around her, not on her. She's got a few bumps and scrapes, but she was lucky. And it's not your fault," Joe said softly, looking Ryan in the eyes throughout.

Ryan hugged him around the neck. He hugged the child back, tears in his own eyes.

"Thanks, Joe," Ryan whispered into his ear.

"You bet," Joe whispered back.

Ryan let go and stood. "I'm going to go get something to eat," he said, standing.

"Sure," Joe replied, standing as well.

As Ryan walked out the front door, Joe felt a warm, comforting sensation. The foyer light burned brighter for a second. Joe couldn't explain it if he tried, but he felt he was being entrusted with something. He looked at the light.

The front door opened and closed. And Joe knew a presence had left for good. But he was beginning to believe there was more than one presence still in the house. "Good job, Alec. You turned him," he whispered.

A voice sounded in his head. "No, you did."

———

Mike heard the call over his radio. Unfortunately, he was already on a call in Kinsale, 40 minutes away. Even if he hadn't been in the middle of taking a statement from the proprietor of the hamburger restaurant reporting a robbery, he'd never be able to get there in time to help, despite his concern for his friend. He'd nearly finished when Janine Hendricks, the dispatch officer, announced that the girl trapped in Joe and Bethany Gardner's collapsed barn was Missy Lowe, age 12. His knees buckled. He gasped audibly, and his blood ran cold.

"Are you alright, Deputy?" Mrs. Dixon, the restaurant owner, asked. "You went pale."

"Um, yes. Sorry. I…um, think I have everything I need for now. I'll…um…sorry. That's my…I mean…I think…it's complicated. Do you mind if I…" he stammered stupidly.

"Oh. Gotcha. Go. I understand. I have your card. I'll call if I have any questions," the woman said kindly. He'd gone to school with her son, Drew Dixon. They'd been on the football team together. There was a very good chance she understood exactly why he was reacting the way he had. Her knowing smile supported that theory.

He ran to his squad car in a near panic. He flipped on his siren and took off like a shot. He drove as fast as he could. He was halfway back to Oak Grove when Janine called him.

"They got her out, Mike. You can slow down," Janine said soothingly.

"Is she okay?" Mike asked. His heart was still in his throat.

"She's responsive. They're taking her to Mary Washington Hospital," Janine replied. Her voice was calm and even.

"Oh, God," Mike sobbed.

"You'd think she was your kid, not just your ex's," Janine chuckled.

"I do," he mumbled.

"I'm sorry, what?" Janine asked after a pause.

"I think she's my kid," he confessed.
"Oh," came the quiet reply.

CHAPTER 20

Bethany sat down beside her mother on the sofa and closed her eyes, resting her head on her mother's shoulder.

The volunteers had all finally left. Lyle had declared Missy wasn't his kid, so he didn't care if she was in the hospital, but Jillian's mother followed the ambulance so Jillian could stay with Missy. Jillian asked Joe to make sure Lyle left her house before she got back. She was no longer interested in sharing her home with him. It wasn't necessary, though. His new girlfriend picked him up before the ambulance was halfway to Mary Washington Hospital.

"Mom," Bethany said. "We really should take Father home. Let his congregation say goodbye. I promise, you can come back with me. You can live here if you want. But you should take Father home."

"Please, Mother," Blake added, sitting in the armchair. "I'll bring you back myself if that's what you want."

Ruth West sighed deeply. "I'm not going," she said, resolved. "He'll be cremated Monday. You can take him home if you want."

"Mom," Bethany argued.

"Bethany," her mother retorted. "It's 3 days before Christmas. I'll revisit having a funeral after Christmas."

———

In the morning, Joe rose early and left before sunrise. He needed to get in as many hours as he could since he was going to have to replace all his farming equipment, so if he could work on Sundays even, he'd do it.

Norm was surprised to see him so early. He assured Joe, "You're the best mechanic I got, Joe. You can have all the hours you want."

"Thanks, Norm. I need the money," he replied.

"I understand," Norm said. "Have you heard how Missy is doin'?"

"Hmmm. Yeah, Jillian called Bethy last night. They kept her overnight for observation, but she just had a few bumps and scrapes. I don't know how she got that lucky. I'd have sworn no one could have survived that tree hittin' that barn," Joe mused as he got to work replacing the brake pads on a late model Ford Expedition.

He worked steadily throughout the morning, finishing up at just after noon. As he prepared to head home, Norm handed him an envelope full of cash. "I can't take this, Norm," he protested.

"Don't be stupid. Take it. Call it your Christmas bonus," Norm insisted.

Joe shoved the envelope into his pocket and shook Norm's hand.

———

Bethany sat reading Maggie's journal.

This one was dated July 1965 through May 1967.

Page one: "Alec shipped out for Viet Nam this morning. He's with the 173rd Airborne Division…whatever that means. He's proud of it is all I know. Mama won't come out of her room. Mellie and me are so scared for him, but he promised to write to Mellie all the time. I got a job at Oak Grove School in the cafeteria, so I can help pay the bills at least while he's gone, but Mama is convinced we'll all starve. Granddaddy just sits in the dining room, drinking from his mason jar of moonshine. We're all just lost without our boy."

Page 27: "We got a letter from Alec today. He is doing well. He has made a few good friends; brothers in arms, he called them. He says the Army is good for him. He sent his love and told Mellie to behave herself. He sent home some money, too. Granddaddy said we need to use it to buy some new chicks, as our laying hens are getting too old. Fil came home for a visit. He took me to the church picnic. We both missed Alec and ended up cryin' on each other's shoulders all afternoon."

Page 86: "We got the telegram today. Alexander Joseph Gardner was killed in action on November 8, 1965. He's not coming home."

"His name was Alexander Joseph Gardner!" Bethany gasped, tears streaming down her cheeks.

"What?" Ruth asked, sitting beside her and setting a cup of tea on the coffee table in front of her.

"Oh, nothing. Joe was named after a boy who was born and raised in this house. He died in Vietnam. His name was Alexander Joseph. Joe's is Joseph Alexander," she responded, wiping her eyes with the back of her hand.

"Is Joe related?"

"Um...Yes. From what I've pieced together, Zach Gardner had 6 kids. The oldest was Daniel, Alec's dad. Then there was Hazel, Violet, Samuel, Joe's grandfather, Ben, and Francine. So, Alec would be Joe's father's first cousin." Bethany sniffed and nodded. "Alec died in Vietnam on November 8, 1965."

"He did? Was he in the 173rd?"

"Um...yeah, how'd you know?" Bethany asked.

"I knew someone in the 173rd," was all she said.

"You did? You were just a toddler, Mom," Bethany

pressed.

"My father, Bethany. Your grandfather was in the 173rd," Ruth finally answered. I haven't spoken to my parents since I married James," she said sadly.

"I thought they were dead," Bethany said. She was shocked.

"No. They live in Maryland...Not far from here, actually. In Waldorf. Fred and Hillary Hampton. My father is 85, and my mother is 83 now," she sighed mournfully.

"Why haven't you ever spoken of them?" Bethany asked.

"They didn't like James. I chose him. It was the wrong choice, but it was my choice. Your father and I eloped. Didn't you know?"

"No. I didn't."

———

Joe pulled into the driveway as Blake pulled in right behind him.

"Hey," he said, climbing out of his truck.

"Hey," Blake replied, climbing out of the SUV he'd rented. "I guess we're early."

"For?" Joe asked.

"Oh, we're going to Waldorf, Maryland...apparently my mother...our mother's parents are alive and well and living 45 miles away from here," Blake told him.

"Ah...um...alrighty then. I need a shower and clean clothes," Joe said, pointing at the house. He flashed a smile.

Blake laughed. "Yeah. I'd recommend it. And perhaps a shave."

"Y'all might want to come in while I get ready," he invited as he opened the door.

He was greeted by Bethany from the living room,

where she was sitting on her knees on the floor, wrapping a box in bright red Christmas wrapping paper.

"Hi, Babe," she called. "Hurry and get cleaned up. We need to get going."

"I heard," he said. "Blake told me."

Blake, Trudy, and their kids followed him.

"It's funny. My grandfather was in the 173rd Airborne, the same as Alec Gardner. Isn't that weird? What if they knew each other? Wouldn't that be cool?" she asked excitedly.

"That would be unlikely. The 173rd was a brigade. That's between 3,000 and 5,000 men, Hon, but yeah, it would be kinda cool. What are you giving them?"

"I just don't want to go empty-handed. I got an American flag throw from the Mercantile," she answered. "Hurry!" She waved him off.

He laughed and headed off to the shower.

CHAPTER 21

Fred Hampton and his wife, Hillary, had been living in the assisted living apartment for 2 years. They were still quite active and "spry," as his wife teasingly told him regularly. He still drove. She still participated in the church, a devoted member of the Alter and Rosary Society. They took most meals in the community dining hall, but she still cooked breakfast in the morning and made special dishes for their family. Their daughter Grace, their grandkids and great-granddaughter, 4-year-old Amanda, lived nearby. Their lives were good. They were happy.

And yet, there was a huge hole in their family. They had not seen nor heard from their eldest daughter, Ruth, in 42 years. And that reality left a void in their hearts that was ever-present.

Ruth had fallen in love with a protestant seminarian. Fred didn't really care that he wasn't Catholic, but he really disliked the boy's self-righteous, bigoted attitude. He couldn't see his daughter being happy long-term with that boy, and he'd told her to stop seeing him. He'd only managed to push them together, and he'd ended up losing his daughter.

He thought about it often, especially around the holidays. Today, he'd thought about Ruth a lot. He wondered if she was happy. Had he been wrong?

Dinner in the dining hall was early, even for him. Old people ate so early, he often noted. So, at 4 pm, he and Hillary locked arms at the elbow and shuffled their way to the dining hall.

"It's nearly Christmas," he said. He sounded sadder than he had intended, so he forced a smile. "I've been thinking of Ruth all day."

"I know, Dear," Hillary replied. "I can tell when she's on your mind."

They took their seats at their regular table with Howie and Fiona Rogers, one of the few other married couples living in the facility. Sadly, most of the residents were widows or widowers. Belinda, an orderly, placed their meals in front of them.

"Meatloaf tonight. Everybody's favorite," she said with a smile.

The dining hall was adjacent to the lobby, and they heard the door open. A man's voice asked for Fred and Hillary. The couple looked at each other and turned to see a large group standing at the reception desk; two men, two women, 3 children, one toddler…and behind them all…

"Ruthie!" Fred shouted, standing. "Hill! It's our Ruth!"

––––––––

Joe rushed forward to catch the old man, who too quickly moved toward his long-absent daughter, tripping over his own feet. Thankfully, Joe was quick, agile, and strong. He easily prevented the man's falling.

"Whoa, I gotcha. You okay?" he asked, helping the man regain his balance.

"Yes, I…Alec?" the old man sputtered. "Have I died? Ruth's here…with Alec?"

"Um…no. I'm Joe, not Alec," Joe responded. "You actually knew Alec Gardner?"

"He saved my life," Fred said, staring until Joe was slightly uncomfortable. "What's going on?"

"Hi, Daddy," Ruth said, stepping forward. She smiled nervously. Her voice drew the old man's attention away from Joe and back to her. Joe was thankful. Being looked at like he was some kind of ghost was unsettling. Did he really look that much like his father's cousin?

Fred reached out and grabbed Ruth by the shoulders, looking at her before he pulled her close, kissing her on both cheeks as tears rolled down his own.

Joe took a step back.

Hillary Hampton pushed her way into the throng of people and grabbed Ruth's elbow. Ruth pulled out of her father's embrace and turned to her mother, being embraced by her as well.

"Well, I know he's Joe…Gardner…who are all of the rest of these beautiful people?" Fred laughed.

Joe grinned.

Ruth laughed with her father. "Well, this is my son, Blake. He's 37. This is his wife, Trudy. I won't disclose her age. These are their kids, Tiffany, 10, Peter, 8, and Michelle, 2. And this is my youngest daughter, Bethany. She's 29. Her husband, Joe, whom you seem to know somehow, and their kids, Jessup and Ryan, both 12, and Meghan, 4," Ruth said, pointing to everyone.

Hillary smiled and nodded at everyone. She looked up at Joe. She was a small woman, just under 5 feet tall. "Wow. You're a tall drink of water," she said, laughing.

"Um…thank you," Joe stuttered. He never understood that idiom, but he thought it was meant as a compliment. She smiled and touched his arm, so he thought he'd guessed correctly.

"Is this everybody?" Fred asked, hugging everybody in turn.

"Oh, no. My eldest is Penelope. She's 41. She's married with 2 kids, Laura, 12, and Kyle, 10. They're in Illinois," Ruth said.

"Where's...James?" Fred asked.

"Oh...well...he died a few days ago," Ruth said sadly. "I'm not sure how I feel. I mean, I'm sad. I've been married to him for 42 years. But I'm relieved...because, oh boy, were you ever right. I don't even want to take him home for a funeral."

Fred pulled his daughter close again. "Come on back to our apartment, Ruthie. Let's talk."

Joe looked around. There was a large Christmas tree in the lobby. To the right of it was a baby grand piano. He hadn't played in a long time, but he sat at it and fingered a couple of notes as Ruth walked away with her parents. Wanting only to keep the kids from getting restless, he started playing *Jingle Bells*. Meghan clapped and jumped up and down excitedly as Joe started to sing.

———

Bethany was blown away. She had no idea Joe knew how to play or that he had such a good voice. She shouldn't have been surprised, she guessed. He never did anything halfway. If he did it, he did it well. She sat beside him and started to sing along in harmony. Soon all of them were singing and throwing out Christmas carols for Joe to play. The residents, as they finished their meals, came into the large lobby, sat in the various seats around the piano, and joined in with the caroling.

"Did I know you played?" she whispered to him, doubting herself, knowing what Greg and Dr. Ramayan had done to her, knowing even her recovered memories had false memories, like Joe's murder, implanted. She was finally starting to put things straight, but she thought she'd always be asking about that time. The only thing she was certain of was that she loved Joe.

He had a strange look on his face. His bright eyes, which usually sparkled with joy, turned sad and cloudy. "No. I haven't played in years," he whispered. Then he smiled a smile that was somehow really a frown and played a couple of chords of Beethoven's 5th Symphony.

"How many years?" she asked. "Eight?"

He gasped out a breath. "I told him that I'd play when he got better."

"Has he asked you to play?" she asked.

"All the time," he answered. "But…"

"But nothing. How do you think that makes him feel, Joe? You don't think he's better. I love you. I'm saying this from a place of love. Kenny needs you to say he's better. He knows he's not what he once was. And it frustrates him. But if you can't even acknowledge that he's okay, how can he? You can't let whatever guilt you feel about his injury affect him like that. Just play the damn piano." She smiled and kissed his cheek.

He nodded, the sparkle returning to his eyes. "You're right."

"It's okay to be happy, Joe. You're one of the most optimistic people I've ever met, except when it comes to yourself. You blame yourself for everything. You're not to blame. Not for Kenny. Not for me. Remember that, Babe. Okay?" she pressed.

The front door opened, and a woman resembling her mother rushed inside, looking around furtively. She rushed down the hall and knocked on the door her mother and grandparents had gone into to talk.

Blake walked up behind her and Joe and leaned down

between their heads. "She looks like Mom. Do you think she's our aunt?" he asked in an excited whisper.

"Probably," Bethany replied, equally excited. She'd never been close to either her brother or sister, but over the last day or so, she'd seen a different side to Blake. He, like their mother, seemed freer now, like a weight had lifted. "Blake...do you think we could be friends?"

He looked at her and suddenly hugged her from behind. "Nope. You're my baby sister. You're stuck being my family," he groaned. Then he kissed her cheek. "I'm sorry, Beth. I've spent a lifetime resenting you when I should have cherished you. I won't make that mistake anymore. I think we're friends. I even like this behemoth," he joked, elbowing Joe.

"Haha. Watch out, or I'll squash you, pipsqueak," Joe teased back.

"I think I might actually miss you when you go home," Bethany added.

"Yeah. Did Father tell you my latest indiscretion?" Blake asked, taking a seat in a nearby chair. "I left the Methodist church. I...I am converting to Catholicism."

Joe sputtered. Bethany laughed.

"What?" Blake asked.

"Joe's Catholic," Bethany chuckled.

"Really?"

"Sacred Heart tattooed on my chest, Catholic," Joe snickered.

"Wow. That's Catholic," Blake laughed.

"Why the change? I mean...weren't you a pastor?" Joe asked.

"Yeah. And the more I read, the more I subscribed to Catholic doctrine...until I...left my congregation."

"What are you doing for a living?" Bethany asked.

"Living off our savings until I figure it out. I was guaranteed I would not be given one red cent to help us survive the transition."

"What do you want to do?" Joe asked. "That's the question."

"I always just kind of wanted to be a teacher," Blake proclaimed.

"So, teach. You have a college degree. How much more do you need to be a teacher?"

"Well, not a lot. I...I've gotten my master's in education a few years ago. But Father never approved, so I kept it to myself. I...I applied to Westmoreland County online this morning. Nothing may come of it..."

"Blake! That would be so great!" Bethany exclaimed, jumping up and hugging him.

"Really? You'd like us to be near?"

"I'd love it," she said, hugging him again.

———

The door to Bethany and Blake's grandparents' apartment opened, and Fred, Hillary, Ruth, and the woman who resembled her came out, rejoining the group in the lobby. Ruth and the woman walked with their arms around each other. "Come meet...well, most of my family. Penelope and her husband Silas and two kids aren't here, but the rest of them are."

The woman laughed. Bethany and Blake, hand in hand, stepped forward with big, goofy grins on their faces. Joe had to smile. It was cute. Their aunt was named Grace, apparently. She was married and had two daughters, one still in college and one married with a 4-year-old daughter herself. Meghan about peed herself, learning there was a little girl her age in the family.

Joe and Trudy kind of moved to the background, letting Blake and Bethany get to know their newfound grandparents and aunt.

"Joe," Trudy said, sitting beside him.

"Hmmm?" he answered.

"You're alright," she said, winking.

"You're not so bad either," he chuckled.

"James…and Penelope…they're cut from the same cloth."

"You don't care much for Penelope?" he asked, grinning.

"You're astute," she laughed. "James was a…"

"Son of a bitch," he finished for her. "Jackass," he suggested. "Mother…"

"Yes," she interrupted. "I take it Bethany has told you some things."

He nodded.

"Blake didn't believe me back then. I don't think he really believed me until the pandemic. We couldn't get in touch with Bethany for a year, Joe. Greg usually let us talk to her some. But the entire year, she was unavailable. And then, she had a baby. He never told us she was pregnant. She just suddenly had a baby…and the baby looked nothing like him," Trudy said.

"She does look like me," he replied, the sob escaping before he could control it.

"Do you know what happened?"

"No. I only knew she was going to leave him. We had a plan. And then she told me to get lost. She even got a protective order against me. I never knew she was pregnant. I never knew Meghan existed. And when Bethy finally showed up last month, she didn't even remember me. It's come back, but she has some weird false memories…horrible things like Greg murdering me…that came back with the real ones. She says she'll tell me, but she can't handle it all at once. And I honestly don't think I can either. I'm liable to…" He sighed. "How do you manipulate someone's memories like that, Trudy? I can't even fathom it."

"I don't know. Drugs. Hypnotism. Psychological torture. None of it's good. And I promise you, James knew. Heck, Penelope probably knew."

"How'd you know? About what James did?" he asked, turning to look her in the eyes.

"Oh, I've been with Blake since high school. I was one of the girls who…the lawsuit…I know what rape looks like after…and I saw it all over her face in court, in her body language. Blake didn't believe it. Not that I blame him. He was a victim, too. James was not a good man."

"We can have Christmas at our house!" Bethany exclaimed excitedly. "Can't we, Joe?"

"Um, sure, Babe. Whatever you want," he said, smiling.

CHAPTER 22

The next morning, Joe awakened to the sound of voices coming from outside. He got up, threw on some clothes, and opened the front door. He stared slack-jawed at the hub of activity around the house.

Alan and Norm Mason were up on ladders, painting the exterior of the house. Beau Madison was replacing the last of the pillars to hold up the new porch roof that was laid on the front lawn, completed and ready to place once the pillars were up. The sound of several chainsaws buzzed from the backyard, where half a dozen friends and neighbors were removing the tree that had fallen. Mr. Morgan sat in the yard on a glider for the porch, going through dozens of boxes of Christmas decorations for the exterior of the house.

Joe called, "Hey! What's this? A drive-by home repair show filming or something?"

"Or something," Norm laughed. "You could stop gaping and grab a paintbrush."

"Um…okay…let me put on some coveralls."

Meredith Mason, Joe's previous landlady, Vince Harris's daughter, drove up in a pick-up truck with a load of appliances in the back. "Appliances weren't included in the sale of the trailer. I got no use for 'em. I figure they were newer than yours, and they aren't worth nothin', so I brung 'em over. Where do you want the washer and dryer?"

"I told ya, Aunt Mere, he said the downstairs bathroom!" Norm called down to her.

Joe silently laughed and shook his head. "Jess! Ryan! Come help," he called upstairs.

"What about me, Daddy?" Meghan asked, appearing beside him and pulling on the hem of his shirt.

"You, too," he said, nodding.

"I'll get breakfast ready to feed this bunch," Bethany said happily from the bedroom door as she tied her robe closed. "Duke! Come to Mommy!" The dog ran to her with his tail wagging and leapt into her arms. "Dat's my widdle baby," she cooed, kissing the dog's head right between his ears. "Does you need to go outside? Such a good boy."

"You've convinced that dog he's an infant human," Joe chuckled.

After changing, Joe, Ryan, and Jess joined the Masons in painting the exterior of the house. Mr. Morgan approached Joe as he dipped his brush into a can of white latex.

"I got wind that Mrs. Benson was at the County Land Use office asking about building codes and requirements for occupancy. I know you were working on it, but I asked Norm if he could help make it look more...inhabitable. Meredith donated the appliances of her own accord."

Joe nodded. "Thanks, Mr. Morgan."

"Anytime," he said, cleaning his glasses.

About an hour later, Bethany and Ruth called everyone in to eat.

As the men finished filling their plates and milled around eating, Jillian and Missy knocked on the door. Joe opened it to them, balancing his plate and his drink as he let them in.

Missy nearly knocked everything out of his tenuous grasp as she flung her arms around him. "Thank you so much, Mr. Gardner!" she exclaimed. "I was so scared. Did the boy get out, too?"

"Boy? What boy?" he asked.

"There was a boy in the barn with me," she said, releasing him from the sudden hug.

"Missy, there was no one else in the barn. We checked," he told her.

"Yes, there was," she insisted. "He was like a high school boy. Real cute. Dark hair. Green eyes. He looked a lot like you…only not old…"

"Thanks for that," he chuckled. "Seriously, Sweetheart, you were alone."

"No. He was in a Boy Scout uniform."

"Boy Scout?"

"Yeah. I mean, I think it was a Boy Scout uniform. It was green," she informed him.

She caught sight of Ryan and Jess and was off like a shot.

Joe looked at Jillian, who shrugged. "I think she imagined him. She was really scared. You rescued her, so the boy looks like you," Jillian offered.

"Sure. Maybe," he agreed, but he knew Missy hadn't imagined the boy. "Thanks, Alec," he said when Jillian walked away, patting the door frame.

As he closed the door and turned, he saw him standing at the top of the stairs. Alec smiled and saluted. He returned the salute, and Alec faded to nothing, but the scent of Old Spice filled the foyer.

"Did you see Alec, Daddy?" Meghan asked, taking his hand. "It looked like you did that soldier wave at him."

He looked down at her. "I saw him, Meggy," he said, squeezing her hand gently.

After breakfast, Joe, with his friends and sons, finished

painting the front of the house. As he moved to start the side of the house, Ryan picked up a can of paint and followed Joe. He stood there silently, watching Joe for a minute.

"Something on your mind, kiddo?" Joe asked, positioning the ladder against the house.

"I know, I called you 'Daddy' when I...was upset... Was that okay?" he asked, nervously.

"Of course. Ryan, you can call me whatever makes you comfortable. I personally like 'Daddy,' though," he said, winking.

Ryan grinned. But his smile faded quickly. "Is it weird that I hate my dad, my real one, I mean? I mean, I hated him as long as I can remember. He was...mean. Not just to Mom but to all of us. He...never mind."

Joe had an overwhelming feeling of dread flood his body.

"What do you mean, Son? What did he do to you?" he asked.

"Nothing," the boy answered too quickly.

Joe got on one knee and grabbed the boy's shoulders, searching his face for the answer he didn't want to find. "What did he do to you, Ryan?"

Ryan's eyes dropped so as not to look into Joe's, and Joe let go of his shoulders. "Oh, God," he muttered.

"I'm glad the car wrecked. He was starting to look at Meggy," Ryan said before he ran off. Joe just knelt there in shock.

"Shit," he said finally as he rose. The words echoed in his head: "I'm glad the car wrecked. I'm glad the car wrecked. I'm glad the car wrecked. I'm glad the car wre..." His heart was pounding out of his chest.

They got the roof on the porch installed. Mike Poole

called and volunteered to help finish painting since he had a day off. He said he didn't know how much help his brother might be, but he'd bring Kenny, too. Joe laughed good-naturedly and said he was sure Kenny would be a big help.

When Mike and Kenny arrived, Mike smiled at Jillian and waved. "Mike," Joe warned, "be careful there."

"I know, Joe. I know. She needs to get a divorce first. Believe me. I won't cross that line," his friend assured him before getting to work.

Norm helped Joe load the old appliances into the back of his old truck. "I'll go to the dump with you in the morning to get rid of this stuff," Norm offered.

"I don't know how to thank you," Joe said, shaking his hand.

"Come to work on Saturday," Norm replied. "Skip doesn't know a carburetor from an intake valve."

Jillian watched Mike work. She didn't know what she expected. All she knew was when she had climbed out of the ambulance the other night, he had been standing there waiting for them. He was there. He was always there whenever she or Missy needed him.

Missy had seen him standing there. She had called out for him in fear as the EMTs moved her from the ambulance to the Emergency Room. But she hadn't said his name. She'd called him "Daddy." He'd stepped forward and clasped her hand.

"It's alright, Sweetheart," he'd assured Missy. "You're okay. I'm right here with your Mama. We aren't goin' anywhere."

And he had stayed. He had stayed through her mother's protestations. He had stayed after Rich, Jillian's first husband

and Missy's father, as listed on her birth certificate, had finally showed up with his new wife, Kierra, and his stepdaughter, Dahlia. Mike never said a word. He just stood there, taking all the abuse Jillian's mother could dish out.

When Jillian had broken down, overwhelmed, he'd taken her into his arms and held her until she was calm. Mike protected her...always.

Jenny, her mother, had told him to leave, that he wasn't welcome, but Missy had asked for him, not Rich. He had walked back to Missy's room, leaving Jenny and Rich to stew.

Today, he acknowledged her presence but nothing beyond that. She knew he wouldn't be the one to come to her, but somehow, she expected something more than a nod and a wave.

Eventually, she couldn't take it. She marched over to him as he painted his section of the back of the house.

"Mike," she started.

He put down his paintbrush and turned to face her, giving her his full attention. "Jillian," he replied.

"I..." she tried again. She wanted to tell him how much she loved him. But she remembered why she had left him to begin with. Her reputation had prevented him from receiving a promotion he deserved. He was better off without her.

He smiled, and her heart felt like it might burst.

"Sort it out, Baby. I'm always here. But it won't go anywhere until you work out what you want. Understand?" he whispered, leaning toward her, his mouth just inches from her ear. He filled the air in and around her. He was the oxygen she breathed for a second, and she trembled under his intoxicating presence.

She nodded. He winked and went back to painting. In the end, she walked away.

———

Bethany had worked as hard as any guy after lunch, painting the side of the house almost entirely on her own as the men installed the roof. She was adorable, covered in white paint, sitting hugging her knees on the third step in the foyer. She smiled at him as he shut the door. He groaned as he lowered himself to sit beside her. "God, I'm sore," he said, leaning his elbows on the step behind him.

"The kids are completely occupied watching television. I think that tub is big enough for both of us," Bethany whispered suggestively.

"I'm totally into it, Babe," he flirted. "As long as you do all the work. I'm beat."

She sighed. "Oh, I know as soon as we got in, all three would come knocking."

He chuckled. "Yeah, sounds about right." He grabbed her and pulled her against him, kissing her. "Go soak, Babe. You know you want to."

"You don't have to tell me twice," she answered, pulling herself up and bounding up the stairs.

He closed his eyes as he heard the water start to fill the tub upstairs. He heard the stair creak and felt the presence sit beside him. The foyer filled with the scent of…rosewater.

"Melanie?" he said, opening his eyes.

He was alone, but he knew he wasn't really.

"I like her," said Melanie's voice inside his head.

"Me too," he said out loud. "Thanks for your help."

The scent faded, and he knew he was alone again.

He could hear Rudolph's nose growing brighter from the television in the living room. He groaned again as he pulled himself to stand and joined the kids in the living room. They were all scrubbed clean and dressed in pajamas while

Joe was still grimy and covered in paint.

"You're dirty, Daddy," Meghan snickered as he sat in his recliner.

"Yeah. I'll take a shower when Mommy gets out of the tub," he said, winking at his daughter.

On the television, *Rudolph* ended, and *Frosty* began.

Joe drifted off to sleep.

He didn't know how long he'd slept, but Bethy awakened him with a kiss and said, "Go get cleaned up, Honey. The kids are in bed, and I'm lonely."

"Oh, okay," he yawned, smiling at her pretty face.

He showered and joined his wife in the bedroom.

CHAPTER 23

Bethany awoke to the sun streaming in the window. She pulled the comforter up over her head and ran her foot up the inside of Joe's leg. He moaned and ran his hand up the back of her thigh to the sweet spot. She giggled as he rolled, pinning her under him as he kissed her deeply.

Unfortunately, that was as far as it went. The doorbell rang. "Damn," Joe cursed, burying his face in the pillow. Bethany laughed and smacked his ass.

"They're here to help," she said, with a genuine smile.

He nodded and climbed off her. He made a few adjustments and said, "You'd better get it."

She snorted and covered her mouth with both hands. "Sorry," she said. Then she pulled on his tee shirt and a pair of sweatpants. She ran to the door while he disappeared into the bathroom.

"Hi, Mike. Hi, Kenny," she said, opening the door. "You're here bright and early."

"There are enough Christmas lights out here to go full Clark Griswold," Mike observed, pointing to the dozens of boxes on the front porch.

"Yeah. We'll be visible from the space station," she affirmed. "I'm about to start breakfast. Any requests... keeping in mind I know how to make scrambled eggs, bacon, and pancakes...and nothing else."

"How about scrambled eggs, bacon, and pancakes?" Mike replied, grinning.

"It's a good thing that's what she knows how to make!" Kenny said, unironically.

"Ain't it though, Buddy?" Mike laughed, slapping his brother on the back.

The twins followed her inside and to the kitchen.

"Joe awake yet?" Mike asked, peering into the kitchen cautiously.

"What are you looking for?" Bethany whispered.

"Um...anything flying through the air," he replied.

"Huh?" Bethany asked, grabbing a skillet and a spatula.

"Uh. Nothing. Unimportant. Can I help with anything?" he asked.

"No. You're here to help us. The least I can do is make a mediocre breakfast," she said, grinning.

"Well, me and Kenny wouldn't mind some of that really good tea of yours," Mike requested.

"Coming right up," she said, smiling big and kissing his cheek.

"How about me? I want the tea, too," Kenny interjected.

She kissed his cheek as well, and he giggled and blushed.

Mike and Kenny sat down at the dining room table, and she heard Joe emerge from the bathroom, calling from the bottom of the stairs, "Jess! Ryan! Get up!" Then, turning to his friends, he said, "Give me a minute. I'll get dressed and be right with you."

———

Joe quickly dressed and put on his paint-covered coveralls. He joined his friends in the dining room just as Bethany placed the food on the table.

Jess was the first of the children downstairs. He hugged Joe's neck and kissed his cheek as Joe was sitting in his usual chair, about to take a bite of pancakes. "Ryan is in the bathroom, throwing up," he announced. "I mean, it's like *The Exorcist.*"

Joe set his fork, still full of pancakes, back down on his plate. "Thanks for that, Jess," he said, shaking his head. "What do you know about *the Exorcist?* Excuse me, y'all. I'll go check on Ryan. Jess…Eat."

He wiped his mouth with his napkin, set it on the table, and rose from his seat. He climbed the steps, noticing the cold spot at the top of the stairs. He shivered as he passed through it. Ryan's bedroom door was slightly ajar. It swung slowly open and slammed shut.

Joe jumped. But ghosts simply did not scare him. It was creepy, sure, but it elicited more curiosity in him than terror. "That all you got? Slamming a few doors? The dream that night was scarier," he told the…cold.

He knocked on the bathroom door. "Ryan? You okay, Kiddo?" he called. From inside, behind the closed door, he heard Ryan wretch and vomit. "May I come in?"

Between heaves, Ryan said, "Yes." He opened the door and stepped inside. He sat on the edge of the tub and placed his hand on Ryan's forehead. Ryan was kneeling in front of the toilet.

"Well, no fever. That's good, but you're clearly sick, so…*oh no*…no forced child labor for you…" Joe teased.

Ryan vomited again. "Ah. Buddy," Joe commiserated, rubbing his back. He waited for Ryan to finish. He cleaned up the boy's face and the toilet. "Come on, Honey. I'll carry you downstairs."

"I'm not a baby," Ryan protested.

"Do you feel like walking?" Joe asked.

"No," Ryan answered, sitting on his bottom on the

tiled bathroom floor.

"I'm a big guy, Ryan. I can carry three or four of you," he winked. "And I won't tell anyone," he added in a whisper.

Ryan surrendered, and wrapped his arms around Joe's neck as Joe lifted him piggy-back style. Joe grabbed the trashcan and handed it to Ryan. "Throw up in that, not on me," he told the boy before carrying him downstairs to the sofa in the living room. He covered the child with a blanket and positioned the trash can strategically on the floor.

The doorbell rang. He winked at Ryan and went to answer it. Norm and Allan stood on the doorstep, hands in their pockets. Jess pushed past him. Carly was walking down the street with Missy toward the house.

"Don't let me get in your way!" Joe called to his retreating back, chuckling. "You'd think he'd never seen a girl before." Then, to his boss and boss's brother, he said, "Bethy made some bacon that's only crisp, not quite burnt, some pancakes that aren't half bad, and her eggs are actually on the good side. Hungry?"

"No oatmeal? It's kind of chilly this mornin,'" Allan teased.

"Trust me. You don't want her oatmeal," Joe chuckled, letting them in. "It's lumpy and oddly…crunchy."

"I heard that!" Bethany called from the dining room.

"I said it out loud," he loudly proclaimed, closing the door.

––––––––––

After they finished eating, Joe and Norm took the old appliances to the dump while Mike and Allan got ready to paint. Kenny helped Bethany clear the table and do the dishes.

"I'm sorry I was mad at you when I met you, Miss Bethy," he said sheepishly. "I sometimes feel mad for no reason. I used to be able to handle it…but not so much since Afghanistan."

"It's okay, Kenny. I didn't think about how my putting on that hat might affect other people. I get why it upset you. Maybe you could have told me without yelling at me…" Bethany said, laughing brightly. She nudged him in the shoulder playfully.

"I used to be smarter than I am. The funny thing is, I remember not being stupid. Isn't that funny?" he asked, tearing up, his voice breaking.

"No. It's not funny," she said, taking his hand. "It's alright to feel sad and angry about that, Kenny. That seems like how anyone would feel. And for the record, you're not stupid. Not even a little bit. I'll fight anybody who says otherwise," she promised. "Do you know I never finished high school? I'm taking my exam to get my GED next Thursday. And then, I'm going to college. Half my life, I've been told I'm not smart enough or interesting enough. But I am. And those people who told me that…they aren't anything compared to you. I'd rather be your friend."

He blushed and snickered.

Mike, from the kitchen door, said, "Hey, Buddy. Pam's outside. Go talk to her."

As Kenny moved past him and out the door, he turned to Bethany and smiled. "He was an honor student in high school," he told her. He paused.

"What's on your mind, Deputy?" she asked with a kind smile.

"You're well suited, you and Joe. I wish you both all the happiness in the world," he said before he followed his brother. She watched him leave and thought he'd be great with Jillian. She should talk to Joe about setting them up.

She finished cleaning up and took out her phone. She opened the fridge and spoke into her phone, "Add to shopping list: eggs, milk, butter, bread, instant oatmeal, since mine is so terrible, pop...no, they call it soda here... soda, bacon, hamburger, orange juice...Pedialyte for Ryan... three rib roasts per Joe, potatoes, green beans, onions, French fried onions, cocoa for the Buche de Noël, raspberries, cream, frosting, oh...yeast rolls..."

After she finished her shopping list, she got Meghan dressed and checked on Ryan, who had fallen asleep on the sofa. She felt his forehead, like Joe had before, and concluded as he had that Ryan did not have a fever. She took her hand away, and Ryan opened his eyes. "Hi, Baby," she said, smiling. "Go back to sleep. I was just checking on you."

"Am I bad, Mommy?" he asked, sounding like a much younger child.

"No. Why would you ask that? You're my savior," she responded, kissing him on the forehead.

When Joe and Norm returned, she asked Kenny to come in and keep an eye on Jess, Ryan, and Meghan while she and her mother ran to the store.

"You mean it?" he asked. "You trust...me?"

"Of course I do. You fought for my country. Certainly, you're capable of watching three kids, one of whom is sleeping, for an hour or so," she assured him.

He beamed and ran into the house. Joe walked over to her and kissed her...one of those bend you over backwards kisses. His friends catcalled. She blushed and waved them off.

She did her shopping swiftly and dropped her mother at Blake's hotel for the afternoon. He had volunteered to take her shopping for gifts for her family. Bethany returned to Ravens' Roost just before CPS pulled in behind her. She was unloading groceries from the trunk as the social worker, a slightly overweight woman in her forties, who introduced herself as Diane Ramsey, got out of her nondescript sedan.

"I'm here because of the order of reference for Jessup Leroy Gardner and Ryan Malcolm Benson. Also, I have a complaint as regards all three children."

"Of course you do," Bethany said, rolling her eyes. "My late husband's mother."

"Why isn't your new husband petitioning to adopt your daughter?" Diane asked, taking out a notepad and pen.

"He's her biological father," Bethany said, with her hand on her hip.

"Oh," Diane said, turning white. "I was unaware. I thought you two had just met."

"No," Bethany said, grabbing two bags of groceries. "Make yourself useful and grab a bag." She walked to the kitchen door. Inside, she called, "Kenny, I'm back. Can you go get the groceries for me?"

"Yes, Ma'am," he replied from the living room.

"A friend of ours," she told Diane. "He suffered a traumatic brain injury while in the Marines…in Afghanistan."

"You trust him around Meghan?" Diane asked.

"Implicitly," Bethany told her.

She quickly put away the three bags she and Diane had brought in before Kenny returned with the last two bags. "Thank you, Kenny," Bethany offered, taking the bags.

"You're welcome, Miss Bethany. Do you need me to do anything else? Meggy and me were in the middle of a game of Candyland."

"You can go play," she laughed. He ran off like the big kid he was.

Bethany finished putting away the groceries and

grabbed the Pedialyte, cracking it open and pouring a glass.

"Ryan was sick this morning. He's been lying on the couch. I need to see if he can get this down," she said, holding up the glass and walking toward the living room. Diane followed.

"Hey, Baby," she said, sitting on the edge of the sofa beside Ryan, who sat up on his elbows and scooted back to lean on the pillow and armrest.

"Hey, Mom," he said weakly but sounding a little better.

"Drink this," she said, handing him the glass and feeling his forehead again. He took the glass and pushed away her hand. "Geez. I don't have a fever. You and Daddy need to chill."

"Daddy keeps checkin' for a fever?" she asked, laughing.

"Every few minutes. It's kind of annoyin'," he retorted. He shivered violently.

"Oh, Honey," Bethany commiserated. She pulled the blanket up around him. "Do you think you could eat something?"

"Not really," he answered.

Diane made a few notes. "Well, obviously, the report is unfounded. But I do still need to talk to the children one on one. I'll come back sometime next week since Ryan is ill, but where is Jessup?"

"He's still outside with Carly," Ryan moaned.

"I'll call him in for you," Bethany offered. "Drink." She pointed at the glass before she stood and made her way to the front door. "Jessup!" she called. He and Carly were going through a box of exterior Christmas decorations. He looked up and came inside when she motioned for him. He was a good kid. She felt lucky he wanted her as a mother.

After speaking with Jessup alone, Ms. Ramsey returned to the kitchen where Bethany was arranging things for Christmas dinner tomorrow.

"My initial impression is good, Mrs. Gardner. Thank you for your time," Ms. Ramsey said.

"Oh, sure. Let me walk you out, Ms. Ramsey," Bethany offered, motioning toward the door.

By lunchtime, the men had finished painting the exterior of the house and had started stringing lights on the front, which had dried. Bethany ordered Domino's Pizza en masse.

As the guys attacked the pizza in the dining room, a woman's voice yelled from outside, "You've got to be kidding me! Agggggggggggg!"

They all turned to look out the front dining room window and saw Rosalea Benson standing in the middle of the yard in front of Ravens' Roost, stomping her feet. Her purse bounced around angrily as she stomped.

"I swear to God, it was a shack...a dilapidated shack."

Joe rose and walked outside, Bethany following him to the door.

"Well, hello, Sally Rose," Joe said sardonically, stepping out onto the front porch.

"You needed a building permit," she screeched, pointing at the man with her. "Right?"

"To paint and repair the roof on the covered porch?" Joe said, smiling. "No."

"As long as the roofing is the same material and dimensions, he's correct," the man agreed.

"I told you it was all cosmetic," Bethany called from the door.

"The windows! You replaced the windows!" Rosalea yelled in desperation.

"Again, as long as they don't add or remove any windows and they do not require altering the size of the existing window frames, no permit is required," the man said.

"No. You have to help me. They're trying to take my grandson from me!" she pleaded, grabbing the man's arm.

"I'm sorry. I'm not with Child Services. I'm with Land Use. And I don't see a problem here," the man said. "I'll do an inspection, but I can tell from here that the foundation is good. I don't think I'm going to find anything."

Rosalea collapsed to her knees. She glared at Bethany. "You…you bitch," she screamed. "You killed Greg, and you want to take his son from me and give him to this…this Alec Gardner carbon copy."

"I did what to Greg?" Bethany asked, flummoxed by the hurled accusation.

"You killed him. Do you think I wouldn't know? He never used GHB himself. He only…" Rosalea said through gritted teeth, pulling herself to stand and taking a step forward.

"He only what? What Rosalea? Secreted it into my drink whenever he wanted to rape me?" Bethany shot back, stepping out onto the porch herself. "I didn't give him GHB. I was locked in my room alone all day and all night until the police arrived to tell me he'd crossed the middle line and driven head-on into an oncoming semi. They had to cut off the padlock to let me out because Mrs. Foster wouldn't get the key unless Greg told her to." She could have been yelling, the way her voice resonated through the silence that had fallen, but she wasn't. Her voice was actually low and even. Still, she could swear Jillian could hear her down the road. It was as if all other sounds ceased.

"Holy shit," Joe whispered hoarsely, staring at Bethany with his mouth open.

"Indeed," said the Land Use Inspector. "Uh. Wow!"

"You really didn't put the GHB in anything and give it to him?" Rosalea asked, tearfully.

"I really didn't. It's in the police report, Rosalea. They found traces in his scotch glass, and only his fingerprints were on the glass. I don't know why he took it. Maybe he meant it for me, and he got the glasses mixed up. I wanted to escape, Rosalea. But I just wanted to leave, not harm him," Bethany explained.

"Bethy," Joe gasped.

CHAPTER 24

Joe was taken aback by her strength. "God, Baby," he whispered, pulling her in close to hug her. The silence from the people around them was...oxymoronically...deafening.

"Sally Rose...get off our property," he announced, holding Bethany tightly in his arms. "Take that evil spirit with you." He had mumbled that last part so that only Bethany heard him. But there was a sudden wind, and the front door blew open and shut, slamming to break the silence.

Rosalea Benson huffed and stomped away, getting into her vehicle and driving off. Joe and Bethany walked arm in arm back inside. The scents of Rosewater and Old Spice mingled in the foyer. The house was warm and cozy.

"Allan and me will finish puttin' up the Christmas lights for you," Norm said awkwardly, making a beeline for the door.

"Yeah," Joe agreed. "Thanks."

"Um...Tomorrow is Christmas," Kenny said. "You said we could come over."

"Y'all are family," Joe assured him, slapping him on the back. "I got something for you tomorrow, anyway."

"Yeah," Mike said. "We're just going to leave." He grabbed Kenny's arm and pulled him out the door.

Joe turned to face Bethany.

"Joe," she started.

He didn't wait for her to say anything. He kissed her deeply. When he pulled away, he said, firmly, "Our lives start from today. Right now. And you never have to live with that kind of…horror…ever again."

She smiled, nodded, and pulled him back into her tight embrace. He breathed in her scent and relished her warmth against him.

"The bad man is gone," Meghan said suddenly, breaking the spell.

"What, Honey?" Bethany asked, stepping out of the hug.

"The bad man…from the barn. He left with Grandma."

"Ohhhh…kay," Bethany said haltingly. "That's good, I guess."

Joe chuckled and winked at Meghan.

The rest of the afternoon passed uneventfully. Ryan started to feel a little better and managed to eat some toast and go back up to his own room. Meghan watched *Elf* on television. Joe showered and emerged from the bathroom smelling of sandalwood and fresh cut grass. Bethany finished reading Maggie's journals.

She closed the book and sighed. "She never wrote anything about the body in the barn…not that I expected her to. She wasn't a stupid woman," she said to Joe, who was watching the movie with Meghan.

"Mmmm. Yeah. I was in the Marines when Maggie passed, and I wasn't that familiar with her before that, but she never struck me as stupid," he replied.

"I think I have a better understanding of Alec and Melanie, though…at least Melanie as a child."

"Melanie was a great lady. And I do miss her," Joe said, smiling.

"She was a spitfire of a little girl," Bethany told him, laughing. "She didn't like to see injustice."

"She was the same as an adult," he chuckled.

"That's why she shot the bad man in the barn," Meghan said, as if it was normal to say such things.

"The things that come out of your mouth!" Bethany mused, getting up and going to the kitchen to start dinner.

"It's the truth, Daddy. She told me. The bad man in the barn was trying to hurt her Mommy again. And she got his gun out of his car and shot him in the head. Alec said he was there in spirit to help...guide her hand." Meghan said earnestly.

He knelt to look her in the eyes. "I believe you, Sweetheart," he assured her.

"She said that's why she helped guide Ryan's hand. It was hard for her to get to us, but she went through the phone call Mean Daddy made to Mr. Morgan that night."

"Guided Ryan's..." he trailed off and looked up. "Keep that to yourself, Meggy. Don't even tell Mommy, okay?"

"Okay," she answered, returning to her Barbie on the floor by the television.

He stood and bounded upstairs. He knocked on Ryan's door.

"Yeah," Ryan moaned.

"May I come in?" Joe asked.

"Yeah," the boy answered.

Joe opened the door, slipped inside, and closed the door behind him. "Um...Ryan...I...what happened the night your dad..."

"Died?" Ryan finished for him.

He nodded.

Ryan sniffed, and his eyes filled with tears. "You'll think I'm a bad person," he cried.

"No. Honey. I won't," Joe assured him, sitting beside

him on the bed.

"He hurt her," Ryan sobbed. "All the time. And I saw him put that stuff in the glass like he did every time he hurt her...so when he got a call...I put on my winter gloves and switched the glasses. I didn't think he would leave the house. I swear. He never did before...but the phone call was from that secretary...and she told him to come over."

Ryan clung to Joe, crying into his chest.

"Okay," Joe said softly, rubbing his head. "Listen to me. That never happened. Do you understand?"

Ryan looked at him and nodded.

"Your dad took that drink of his own accord. Then he got behind the wheel of his car, and he died. The end."

Ryan nodded again.

Joe hugged him again before he stood and left him.

————

Bethany woke the next morning to find Joe had already risen. Duke had jumped into his spot in the bed. She laughed and hugged the dog. She felt lighter. The air in the house felt lighter, too.

When the doorbell rang, she practically skipped to the door. "Good morning, Mike," she said in a sing-song voice.

He laughed. "You're in a good mood, Bethany," he observed.

"Hmmm. I am. Are you here on official business?" she asked, noting he was in uniform.

"Yeah, I guess. I wanted to let you know we got the DNA results back on the skeleton and Mrs. Mason. It was Vince Harris."

"Oh. Well, that's good to know. We pretty much assumed that, anyway," she said, smiling. "Any clues on who shot him?"

"Yeah, actually," he said, shifting on his feet. "Um, based on the angle of entry of the bullet, the shooter would have been kneeling...or about 4 feet tall." He cleared his throat.

"Ah...Melanie. She would have been...what...8?"

"Well, there's no way to say with certainty, but yeah. She would have been living here, and she would have been 8, so probably about 4 feet tall."

"She couldn't have buried him, though...at least not on her own," Bethany pondered.

"Yeah, probably not. My guess is that Zach and Betty buried him and dumped his car somewhere. You just never know what happens in people's homes, I guess. Betty died when I was 8 or 9. But I remember her living alone in this house. She wasn't scary or anything. Just a nice old lady. Funny," he mused. "Anyway...that's all we got." He turned to walk away.

"Hey, Mike, about yesterday...about...me, and what happened to me," she started.

He stopped and turned to look at her. "I can't imagine. I do know of a good crisis counselor if you need someone to talk to about it. I mean, I'll listen if you want me to..." he sputtered.

She smiled and shook her head. "I know. And I might take you up on that crisis counselor...but for right now...I just wanted to let you know I'm strong. I came out the other side, and I'm great...at least for today," she told him.

He nodded, tipped his hat, and walked to his squad car. "You coming for dinner?" she called.

"I get off duty at 2. Kenny and I will be by after I get changed out of my uniform...about 2:30?" he asked, opening the squad car's door.

She nodded and waved. Bethany closed the door and asked Alexa to play Christmas music.

Meghan sat up from her tent bed in the dining room as Bethany walked through to the kitchen. "Did Santa come, Mommy?" she asked, rubbing her eyes.

"He sure did. But Daddy went out for a bit to get one last present...for Kenny. He'll be back in a few minutes, and then we can open presents, okay?" she whispered.

No sooner had she spoken than Joe pulled into the driveway, a piano in the back of the truck. Blake and Trudy pulled in behind him.

————

While Bethany, Trudy, and Ruth held the kids back from ripping into the presents, Joe and Blake got the piano off the truck and into the living room somehow before collapsing onto the sofa. "Okay, who's gonna hand 'em out?" Joe asked, breathlessly.

"I will," Ruth announced, sitting cross-legged on the floor by the tree. "I've been looking forward to this. Meggy and Michelle can help me."

They were in the middle of plowing through the gifts when a car pulled into the driveway, and someone started pounding heavily on the door. "Bethany Elaine. You little heathen! How dare you make me come out here on Christmas. Open the door!" a woman screeched.

"Ah...Penelope," Ruth sighed.

The door popped open on its own; the screen door swung out and smacked the deranged woman in the forehead. "Ow!" she exclaimed.

Meghan giggled. "That wasn't nice, Miss Melanie," she whispered.

"Well, stop screeching like a crazy owl and come in,"

Bethany called to her sister. "Where are Silas and the kids?"

"In the car. We're only here for Mother and Father. We're collecting them, and then we're going home," Penelope scowled.

"You can have your father. He's upstairs in the urn on the mantel in Meggy's room," Ruth said. "But I'm staying here. My parents, sister, and nieces are coming for dinner."

"You can stay, too, if you want," Bethany invited her.

"Blake, tell Mother to get in the car," Penelope demanded.

"Not a chance," Blake retorted.

Penelope turned and stomped back out the door. She returned moments later with Silas in tow. Silas was bigger than Blake at 6 feet tall, but his 260 pounds wasn't muscle. He was on the chubbier side of large as compared to Joe's 6'3" lean, muscular frame. But, as Joe had yet to stand, Bethany had to assume Penelope thought her husband's appearance would be intimidating from the way she grinned as she told him to bring her mother out to the car.

He took one step inside, and Joe rose, godlike, from his seat on the sofa, his stone-cold gaze and enormous size stopping the older man in his tracks. "She said no," Joe said calmly.

"I...Please understand. I had to find a substitute speaker for Christmas service this morning to deal with this mess. We just want to get this settled," Silas stammered.

"She said she'd talk about it after Christmas. It's not after Christmas yet. Now, if you want to stay for Christmas dinner, that's fine. But if you want to force Ruth to do something she isn't ready to do, then you should leave," Joe replied.

"I...uh...what are we having?" Silas said with a smile,

patting his belly.

"Rib Roast, sautéed mushrooms and onions, mashed potatoes with gravy, green bean casserole, fresh homemade biscuits, roasted Brussels sprouts with cinnamon butternut squash with pecans and cranberries, creamed spinach, Virginia ham, and a chocolate raspberry cream Buche de Noel for dessert," Bethany answered seductively.

"You can cook that?" Penelope exclaimed incredulously.

"No. But Joe can, and I can help," Bethany said proudly.

Silas looked around and then leaned back out the front door. "Laura, Kyle! We're staying," he called. "Come on in here."

Penelope stomped her foot.

As the children came in through the door, Ruth pulled their gifts from under the tree, and Meghan ran over to them with their presents.

"We got presents?" Laura asked, taking it with a look of awe on her face.

"I always get you something, Laura," Bethany laughed.

"You do?" Laura asked, turning the gift over.

"Of course. You never got my gifts?" She was hurt. She looked at Penelope with tears in her eyes.

"Your gifts were always inappropriate," Penelope insisted.

"I...I gave her a leather-bound Bible last Christmas, with her name embossed on it in gold leaf," Bethany said.

"I didn't get a Bible," Laura interjected.

"Oh...my mistake...maybe Greg..." Bethany suggested, turning away. "It's just a faith, hope, and charity charm on a gold chain. I hope that's appropriate."

Bethany stood and left the room. Joe followed her. She walked through the foyer and dining room and into the kitchen. She opened the fridge and pulled out the rib roasts, setting them on the counter. She felt his arms encircle her from behind as her tears fell to the counter.

"Why doesn't she like me?" she sobbed. "And why do I care?"

"I don't know why she doesn't like you, Babe, but you care because she's your sister. You love her. I'm sorry," he answered.

She turned to face him, and he held her while she cried until she was cried out. Then they started cooking.

Soon, the house was full of people. Ruth's family arrived soon after Mike, Kenny, and Pam. Kenny was excited to see the piano. He jumped and clapped. "Are you going to play, Joe? Really?"

"Any song you want, Kenny," Joe promised.

"*War: What is it good for,*" Kenny announced proudly.

Joe burst out laughing. "How long have you been holding onto that request?"

"Eight years," Kenny replied.

They both laughed so hard that Bethany thought they might pass out. Then Joe sat at the piano and played it. They both sang it with gusto.

Mr. Morgan arrived in the middle of the rendition.

Bethany started to feel happier, even with Penelope's cold gaze on her.

After a few songs, she and Joe escaped to the kitchen to finish cooking.

CHAPTER 25

Penelope came into the kitchen with a twelve-pack of Shirley Temple 7-Up cans. Bethany stared at them in horror, remembering her long nightmare began with a spiked Shirley Temple. Penelope smiled wickedly. Feigning innocence, she said, "We had these in the car. We thought we'd share them since we're staying. Can I just put them in the fridge?"

Joe stared, stupefied by Penelope's brazen behavior.

"Why would you do that to her?" he asked.

"Do what?" Penelope replied, a triumphant grin on her face. She stepped toward him. "You...you were always a problem, Joe or Jag, whatever you go by now. If it hadn't been you, it would have been some other unsuspecting teenage sap. You don't even remember yourself...do you?"

"Remember what?" he asked.

Bethany grabbed the counter to keep from falling. "What did you do, Pen?"

"Well, I nearly got rid of you in Washington, DC. I thought about just killing you...for a long time, but in the end, ruining you seemed like more fun. So, I signed the permission slip and told you I'd handle Daddy. Then, I went along as a chaperone. I mean, I was an adult...married. I sent you to the bathroom, telling you we'd wait. Then I led my group away."

"You left me? On purpose?" Bethany whispered. Joe carefully watched Penelope. She was clearly unstable and inching toward Bethy. She slowly picked up a carving knife.

"Oh, I did more than that. I saw the group of Marines.

I made sure they were nearby. It was dumb luck that you chose Joe. You could have gone to any of them. But I guess it wasn't really. You had a type. Tall, pretty boys with dark curly hair. All the way out to DC on the bus, I told you if we got separated to look for the helpers, police, soldiers, Marines. I figured you'd latch onto one you thought was pretty."

"Okay. He helped me find you. That's all. I mean, we had fun looking for you, but that's it," Bethany said, backing away.

"Yeah, I know. I had to drug you both. And he was a big guy. I wasn't sure how much to give him. I gave you both too much in the end. And neither of you remembered it. You throwing yourself at him. Him not fighting you off. I wasted it."

"What?" Joe gasped out. "What are you saying?"

"That you fucked her," Penelope cackled. She was clearly psychotic.

But he had a flash of a memory and grabbed his chest. "Oh, God," he exclaimed.

"Anyway, I learned my lesson the next week. I didn't have to dose Greg. That pervert was into it from the start. I bought the dress, and I convinced Daddy to give it to you to wear, telling him you'd learned your lesson. Then I dosed you, Bethany…just enough so you'd remember it this time but be unable to stop it. Greg was perfect. He's as big a psychopath as I am. He gave Daddy that money right in front of you, telling Daddy it was for the dress because he felt guilty that he hadn't stopped the guy from ripping it. But you…you always believed Daddy knew it was for you. And he might have." Penelope laughed manically. "I'm not even sure if Ryan is Joe's or Greg's. In the end, it didn't matter. With Joe, you'd have had a chance at happiness. With Greg…I won."

"What are you say...what...what?" Joe sputtered.

"When you tried to leave five years ago, I told Greg about Dr. Ramayan," Penelope smiled an evil smile again. "Dr. Ramayan and I met in college. I went to him. He helped me understand that all my problems started when you were born. He taught me about how to use the drugs, to begin with. He specialized in...memory therapy, I guess you'd call it. He messed with your memories, Bethany. Unfortunately, he failed to make it permanent. He'll pay for that. I promise you. But you won't care. Because you ruined it, and now all I can do is kill you." She took another step toward Bethany and raised the knife over her head.

Joe roused himself from his stupor and punched her in the jaw. Then he lowered his head and rushed her, tackling her. "Mike!" he yelled as he pinned Penelope to the ground, slamming her hand in which she held the knife against the floor three times before she dropped it.

Silas stood in the dining room with his mouth open. "Dear God," he said. "Who are you, Pen?"

Mike came running. "She's nuts. She's trying to kill Bethy," Joe gasped.

"I...he's telling the truth. I heard her. She's...lost her mind," Silas sobbed. "Nobody eat or drink anything she touched. And I wouldn't drink those 7-ups."

———

"So that was a weird Christmas," Joe said, sitting beside Bethany on the sofa after the house had emptied.

"Yeah, I'd...agree with that assessment," Bethany added.

They stared at each other for a moment. "Ryan looks like my family...like me...and Blake. He doesn't look like Greg at all," Bethany said after a long pause.

"Yeah, I've noticed," Joe said, his heart in his throat.

"But he smiles like you," she continued.

He rubbed his forehead and nodded. "I don't remember it, but it...sounded familiar," he acknowledged. "It's worth doing a DNA test, Bethy. And if I...I'm so sorry."

She laughed and patted his knee. "Don't be silly. I don't remember it either, but I know you. You'd never hurt me. It wasn't like with Greg. It would have been...like Meghan."

He saw a photo album sitting on the coffee table. "What's this?" he asked, leaning forward and picking it up.

"Oh, Granddaddy left it for us. What with everything..." She trailed off.

Joe opened it, and a face not unlike his own stared back at him. "Hey, Alec," he said, caressing the photo of the boy. "There you are."

They sat and looked through the photos in the album. "Hah. That's Granddaddy with him," Bethy said, pointing at the page.

On the last page, there was an envelope addressed to them both. Joe pulled the letter from the envelope and unfolded it.

"Dear Joe and Bethany," he read. "I think the easiest way to tell you about Alec is to just write it down. He was just a kid. But he was such a nice kid. He was a hard worker. I'm proud that his family has joined mine. Really. Welcome to our family, Joe."

Joe paused and took a breath before continuing, "As I said, he was just a kid, like the little brother I never had. He had a great laugh, the kind that drew you in and had you laughing along, even if you didn't know why. And he was brave, probably the bravest man I ever knew. On November 8, 1965, without going into the gory details, I was wounded.

And I would have been killed had not that brave, stupid kid thrown himself on top of me. That's where he died, protecting me because I had a wife and a kid at home who needed me. I'll never forget him. He choked on his own blood and said, 'Think of me kindly, where an unkindness of ravens can roost.' I didn't know what that meant. But seeing the sign out front, now I know he was talking about home. So, I pass my memories on to you. Think of him kindly. Let him know I am eternally grateful for his sacrifice. And I've done my best to live up to it. With Love, Granddaddy Fred, Master Sargeant, US Army, retired."

———

Three months passed. Bethany passed her GED exams and started classes at the community college. Blake had been offered and had accepted a teaching position at Washington District Elementary starting in January, as a teacher was retiring midyear due to health reasons. He and Trudy had rented a house in Placid Bay Estates just a few miles away. Ruth had bought a camper trailer and was living in it at Ravens' Roost. They had returned briefly to Sterling for a funeral and to move Ruth out of the parsonage. The days grew longer and warmer.

One morning in late March, Joe sat at the dining room table as Bethany served breakfast. She leaned across him to reach for the butter. Her expanding belly brushed his arm, and he grabbed her, pulling her into his lap. She laughed and smacked him on the chest. He laid his hand on her abdomen and smiled before he kissed her.

"Yuck," Ryan protested, taking a piece of bacon from the serving platter and placing it on his plate.

"Really," Jessup agreed, rolling his eyes.

"Well, then I'll just keep the good news to myself then,"

Joe smirked.

"What? That it's a girl?" Ryan teased. "We already know. Mom told us."

"No. It's a boy and a girl. The boy just turned 13 last week. The girl will be 5 next month. And neither of them is Sally Rose Benson's grandchild," Joe announced.

"You got the results? You're our dad? For real?" Ryan whooped.

"For real," Joe confirmed. "Rosalea has withdrawn her suit. Jess will be adopted by Bethy in a week, and we've applied for replacement birth certificates for the two of you. We're all one big family."

"Yes!" Ryan yelped.

"And Silas officially petitioned for commitment for Penelope last month. She's been diagnosed with psychopathy and personality disorders. She won't be bothering us anymore," Joe added. "She's really disturbed."

"Hmmm. Dr. Ramayan was arrested, too. His license has been revoked, and Mr. Morgan has filed a class action suit for malpractice against him. I was the first one to sign on. Silas signed for Pen, too," Bethany added.

EPILOGUE

December 25, 2025

Joe heard the cry. He groaned and covered his head with a pillow as Bethany climbed out of bed to answer the cry. They'd only gone to bed less than an hour ago, what with the Santa thing. And in a few short hours, the family would start to arrive. He opened one eye and smiled as his wife lifted the infant from the bassinet by their bed.

"Shhhh, Melanie, Daddy's sleeping," she whispered, as she sat in the rocker and unhooked her nursing bra to feed the baby. She smiled lovingly at Melanie as the infant latched on and hungrily nursed.

"No, I'm not," he said huskily from the bed. He leaned up on one elbow and smiled. "That is beauty…" he pondered. "Bethy, I love you."

"Hmmm. I love you, too, Joe." She looked up at the clock on the wall. "It's 1:12 am. Merry Christmas, my Love."

"Merry Christmas," he whispered. "Bethy, this has been the best year of my life."

She grinned. "Me too."

The room filled with the scents of Rosewater and Old Spice.

Lacynda Mathes is a graduate of Radford University in Radford, VA. She holds a B.A. in English.

She is originally from Oak Grove, VA, in Westmoreland County near Colonial Beach. She graduated from Washington and Lee High School, Montross, VA, in 1986. She attended Randolph-Macon College, studied abroad at Wroxton College in Oxfordshire, England, and ultimately transferred to Radford University, where she completed her degree.

She currently resides in Sterling, IL, with her husband. She is the mother to their teenage sons, the eldest with special needs, who has been diagnosed with Lennox Gestaut Syndrome, a catastrophic childhood epilepsy, and severe autism.